STANDARD HERO BEHAVIOR

Standard Hero Behavior

John David Anderson

CLARION BOOKS
New York

C.2

Clarion Books
a Houghton Mifflin Company imprint
215 Park Avenue South, New York, NY 10003
Copyright © 2007 by John David Anderson

The text was set in 11-point Meridien.

www.clarionbooks.com

Printed in the U.S.A.

Library of Congress Cataloging-in-Publication Data

Anderson, John David, 1975–
Standard hero behavior / John David Anderson.
p. cm.
Summary: When fifteen-year-old Mason Quayle finds out that their
town of Darlington is about to be attacked by orcs, goblins, ogres, and trolls,
he goes in search of some heroes to save the day.
ISBN 0-618-75920-4
[1. Heroes—Fiction. 2. Adventure and adventurers—Fiction. 3. Humorous stories.]
I. Title.

PZ7.A53678St 2007
[Fic]—dc22

2007013059

ISBN-13: 978-0-618-75920-0
ISBN-10: 0-618-75920-4

MP 10 9 8 7 6 5 4 3 2 1

To Alithea, as promised

Contents

Standard Hero Behavior

— 1 —

Birds and Feathers

On the corner of Oak and Smelter sits a box made of wood warped by sun and bowed by rain, and on a splintered post just in front of this shack sits a sign. On the sign, often, sits a bird. It is an unremarkable bird—brown, with patches of white and beige, short a feather or two. The bird seems to have no purpose. It has no family and no nest; it is a mediocre singer, at best. Mostly, it just sits and ruffles its feathers, hoping someone will notice.

Inside this warped wooden shack sits a young bard, an equally average singer. The two have a lot in common, being blessed with keen eyes and cursed with big noses. They share a tendency to only peck at their food and have both had run-ins with ticks and stray cats. Neither has had a bath in a few days. The bard, too, mostly goes unnoticed.

Mason Quayle dipped his feather into the inkwell and held it poised above the parchment. With any luck, he could get this finished before the end of the afternoon. He had skipped lunch—on account of there being nothing to eat—and could hardly think of anything else.

"All right, Mr. Frinkmeyer. Let's take it from the beginning."

"All right. Lessee . . . He was about forty, maybe fifty, stones away. You could see the fiery *glint* in his eyes." Aldous Frinkmeyer was a frail-looking man. His clothes hung off him in ripples, gathering in piles of fabric at his ankles and waist in much the same way as the wrinkles around his neck. He was the least likely customer a bard could imagine.

"Why don't you leave the poetry to me, Mr. Frinkmeyer. Just give me the facts." Mason scrawled "fiery glint" in the margin and leaned back on his stool, the parchment in front of him mostly blank, the ink on the tip of his quill already drying, his stomach protesting the delay. "And it will be better if we go back to the very beginning. How did this all start?"

"Well, I s'pose it was when my wife, Madelane, told me to clean out the roost. Our best hen had had a fuss the day before."

"What's she like?"

"Oh, she's hard to manage, but she lays an egg pretty consistently."

"I meant your wife," Mason said, sighing.

"Oh, Mady? Well. She's old, mostly. A little portly. Got a mole on her left cheek close to her nose that makes her look like a witch—though I'm *almost* certain she's not."

Mason made a note of the mole and then scrawled the first line.

Her name was Madelane, a buxom princess, marked by beauty fair.

"What color's her hair?" Mason asked, going for the obvious rhyme.

Mr. Frinkmeyer scratched his beard. "Gray now. Used to be brown till she started dyeing it, then it was all sortsa colors. Yella, green, pink. Apothecary said she was going through a 'phase.'"

"Eyes?"

"Hmm?"

"What color are her eyes?"

"Blue . . . I think."

With eyes like dragon's sapphires and streaks of silver in her hair.

"Please continue."

Mr. Frinkmeyer nodded. "Right. So she said it was my turn and I oughta go clean out the coop. Though I'm not quite sure it was my turn. We've both sorta been forgetting stuff lately."

She bid the dreamy knight to do her bidding true.

"What were you carrying?" Mason prodded.

"What's that?"

"Did you have anything in your hands? Tools? An ax? Do you carry a knife of any kind?"

"A knife? Nope. No knife. I had a broom. And a bucket for eggs."

Armed with club in left hand, his helmet held in right.

He strode forth to glean the treasure that had been laid there in the night.

"And then what happened?"

"Well, I turned the corner, and *there it was.*"

"In front of the chicken coop?" It was important to establish the setting in a narrative.

"Yes! Right there! Almost as if it was *guarding* it."

When, lo, his eyes beheld it, standing nigh ten stones away,

The monster—

"I tell you," Mr. Frinkmeyer said, "it was a little . . . surprising."

"That's fine, Mr. Frinkmeyer, just let me get this down."

"I mean, I'm no coward or anything."

"I understand, sir."

"I mean, I had seen 'em before, maybe a hundred times. Just chased 'em off. But this one was *huge!* It wasn't normal, that's for sure."

The monster so enormous out hunting for its prey.

"It had these two front fangs . . . do you call them fangs?"

"We can call them fangs if you like."

"They were like razors."

"Let me handle the metaphors, Mr. Frinkmeyer."

Its eyes a-glint with fire, and fangs like daggers fixed.

Mr. Frinkmeyer was hypnotized now, lost in his own memory. He was staring at a painting directly above Mason's head that showed a musclebound hero, shield raised before him, deflecting the flames coughed up by a three-headed dragon. Mason knew that no hero, no matter how great, could take on a real dragon—even the one-headed variety—alone, not even the magnificent Duke Darlinger. But the painting taught Mason a valuable lesson: If you want to make something sound scarier, give it three heads. Or fire-breath. Or fangs.

"And he turned and stared *straight at me.*" Mr. Frinkmeyer's voice was a crackling whisper. He made a motion with his hand, meant to indicate that Mason should speak in a whisper as well, lest they scare the memory away. "And I swear on my father's soul, the thing *hissed.*"

Mason stopped writing and whispered back in a voice filled with pretend awe, "They can *hiss?*"

"This one did."

The creature stared dead at him, belching fire as it hissed.

Mr. Frinkmeyer craned his neck, lifting himself half out of his chair, watching as Mason's hand scurried along the page.

"*Fixed* and *hissed* don't rhyme," he said. He sounded offended.

"It's *near* rhyme. All the best bards are using it nowadays. Trust me."

"If you say so." Aldous Frinkmeyer shook his head. "But it didn't breathe fire, either."

"That's all right, Mr. Frinkmeyer—we are allowed to embellish a little."

"I don't want people to think this didn't really happen, though."

Who was this guy kidding? "It is the nature of such songs to capture the *emotion* of the moment through descriptive language," Mason said.

"But it didn't breathe fire."

"I promise I will take that part out."

"But it looked like maybe it *could* have," Mr. Frinkmeyer conceded.

"No doubt," Mason said, then looked at the hourglass sitting on the corner of his desk. He wanted to wrap this up, get home, and forget about the day . . . and the day before . . . and maybe the one to come. He wanted to be somewhere else, anywhere else. The chair made his butt sore.

"So he hissed?"

"Or maybe it was more of a squeak."

"Let's just go with 'hissed.' Then what happened?"

"And then it rose up on its hind legs—I swear, it must have been at least two feet high."

It towered high above him and let out a piercing screech

"And then, I'll be darned if the thing didn't come right at me."

And leapt toward our brave hero,

"To be honest, I was a little scared."

Mason went to write something.

"Well, not *scared*, exactly—more like *surprised*," Mr. Frinkmeyer said, watching Mason's hand carefully.

Again Mason touched the point of his quill to parchment.

"But mostly I was stalwart. Yes. That's what *I* would say. *Stalwart*."

"Got it."

But the stalwart warrior held his ground, his courage gathered tight.

"And then I dropped my broom."

And dropped his sword and peed his pants and turned and ran in fright.

Mr. Frinkmeyer craned again, so much that the folds in his neck finally disappeared, but Mason scratched out the line nearly as soon as he had scribbled it. "You dropped the broom?" he said, getting Mr. Frinkmeyer's attention.

"But I swung the bucket."

"The bucket?"

"And caught the beast right across the head," Mr. Frinkmeyer said proudly.

And smashed the evil demon with a swing of armored fist.

Aldous Frinkmeyer's face suddenly fell, his cheek pouches, once pulled taut, now sagging below his chin.

"Or . . . at least I came close."

"Came close?"

"I mean, I kind of *threw* the bucket at it."

"But you hit it, right?"

"No, not exactly. But I *scared* it."

"You *scared* it."

"It turned around and took off."

"So you didn't actually *hit* it?"

"No."

"And it just ran away?"

"But it had every intention of killing me. You could tell by the look in its eyes."

"'Fiery glint.' Yes, I know."

"And it really was large. I mean, for what it was."

"And you are *sure* it wasn't a squirrel?" Mason asked.

"It had these vicious-looking stripes. And these teeth."

"Fangs."

"Right. It just took me by surprise."

"I'm sure."

"It's just . . ." Mr. Frinkmeyer said, no longer whispering but talking through sighs. "I guess I had never seen a chipmunk *act* that way before. I guess I thought that it was . . . something."

The tone in the old man's voice was a warning. Mason could feel this sale slipping away. In three minutes Mr. Frinkmeyer would change his mind, realizing that there was nothing really heroic or adventurous about his story—certainly nothing worth putting down in ink.

It was time to massage the old man's ego. "I would've run," Mason said, shaking his head and leaning back on his stool.

Mr. Frinkmeyer looked up hopefully.

"For certain," Mason continued. "You're a very brave man. Those chipmunks are dangerous. They aren't really native to this area. Not the one you're describing. I'm almost certain they're bewitched."

"You think so, too?"

"No doubt it was going for the chickens. Don't believe anyone who tells you chipmunks eat nuts. They're bloodthirsty carnivores. You're lucky to be alive."

"I am?"

"It was truly courageous of you to confront it. An act worthy of the annals of herodom. I've written *hundreds* of these. I should know."

Actually, he had written fewer than thirty, but Mr. Frinkmeyer smiled nonetheless.

Mason blew on the lines he had finished. It was ridiculous. There were no good stories to tell anymore, and *man,* did his butt hurt.

"There *were* eggs, right?" Mason asked.

Mr. Frinkmeyer smiled. *"Two,"* he said, holding up the same number of fingers. Mason noticed for the first time the gaps in his back teeth. It was hell finding a good tooth-man in Darlington nowadays.

"Excellent. Why confront a dragon if it isn't guarding treasure, after all?"

"It was a chipmunk, not a dragon."

"I know, Mr. Frinkmeyer." Mason put down his quill and screwed the top back on his inkwell. "I will finish your song this evening, and you can pick it up tomorrow at your convenience." Mason helped the old man out of his chair and escorted him across the room. They stood in front of the placard on the wall that listed the various services provided by Darlington's only *public* bardery—the only one that wasn't one hundred percent dependent on the duke's donations. "Now, you agreed you wanted the standard iambic format with rhyming couplets, correct?" Mason pointed to the top line. "With the refrain we discussed, that's going to run you about twelve pence."

"Is that with the coupon?"

"Yes, that's with the coupon. The balance can be paid tomorrow, but there's a four-pence nonrefundable deposit."

Mr. Frinkmeyer fished in his purse for the required coins and gave them to Mason. Holding them in his hand, Mason felt they carried hardly any weight at all.

"So will it be framed or what?"

"All our bard's songs are hand-rolled and elegantly tied with ribbon. We also stamp our seal of authenticity in the corner."

Mason flipped over the OPEN sign on the door with his free hand as he showed Mr. Frinkmeyer out.

"It was my wife's idea," the old man said. "She really wants to believe I'm a hero."

"We all do," Mason said, staring intently at one neck wrinkle in particular, not wanting to look the man in the eye.

Mr. Frinkmeyer nodded once, glanced down at his feet, then nodded again, as if agreeing to something in his own mind, before shuffling off down the street.

Mason Quayle leaned against the door frame, heard it creak against his weight, and half hoped the whole thing would just collapse and give him an excuse not to come back tomorrow, not to bother finishing "The Ballad of Aldous Frinkmeyer," not to pretend anymore that he would ever make something of Mr. Frinkmeyer—or anyone, for that matter.

This wasn't what the job was supposed to be like. Mason had read about bards in all of the histories. He knew about the Anonymous Warrior Poet of Highsmith—the famed scribe who used to record the tales of triumph of the town's former heroes but kept his real name from gracing the pages, preferring an obscure infamy. Real bards rode alongside the heroes whose stories they told; they weren't holed away in a shack on a dead-end street.

Mason was a bard for heroes without victories, old men looking for immortality, young ones looking for self-esteem, wives hoping to get their husbands something different for the holidays. *Yes, Mrs. Boling,* Mason would say, *I think a bard's song about how your husband broke his leg trying to get your cat out of a tree would make a great present.* They came to him with accidents, and he turned them into acts of courage, prettied up to mask the fact that nothing exciting ever happened anymore, all for a meager sum that was barely enough to pay the duke's stupid protection tax, a fee Mason happened to be short on this month.

He went back inside the shop, gathered a few sheets of parchment off the desk, and blew out the lamp. A thick layer of dust sat peacefully on the stacks of books lining the shelves. The books were part of his father's collection, scribed by skalds and troubadours who did it the old-fashioned way: trailing behind *real* heroes, quill in one hand and sword in the other, ready to take a swipe with either, depending on what the occasion called for. On the top shelf sat a lyre, a gift from his mother on Mason's tenth birthday. One string was busted, but it didn't matter. Mason didn't actually sing the songs he wrote; there weren't enough people who cared to listen. If they wanted to hear a story of heroic conquest, they would wait for the duke to return from one of his adventures and buy tickets for the Tribute Concert in Darlington Square.

Mason closed and locked the door out of habit—there was nothing to steal, all the money he made fitting too easily in his pocket. He looked around for Cowel, his best and only friend—the one, no doubt, by virtue of the other. But Cowel was probably still knocking on doors, looking for someone to take pity on him with her purse. The streets of Darlington were nearly empty, as usual. Mason nodded to Ryle Britterbon, the elderly man standing behind his fish cart, three of the five morning catches still unpurchased, baking in the sun.

Mason got half a block down Smelter and was passing by Flax's tavern when he was tapped on the shoulder. He turned to see a gaunt figure, flimsy like wet paper, with granite eyes and pepper hair hanging down in matted flaps beneath a feathered cap. One hand dragged a weather-beaten trunk on two rusty back wheels, and the other pointed directly at Mason's chest with a finger that had too many broken blisters for someone barely sixteen.

"You, sir. You look like a man who can appreciate the pomp and circumstance provided only by a genuine, one hundred percent *authentic,* high-crested coral bobbylink–feathered plume. That's right, a *plume*—that thing that sits on top of your helmet and makes you look *dashing.* Every feather in our plumes is hand-plucked, then carefully preserved using the finest waxes and elixirs known to alchemy." As he spoke, the salesman made flourishing gestures with his hands, as if shaping them into these plucked creatures and flying them in front of Mason's face. "Yes, sir, my plumes come in a variety of styles, from Mohawk to dainty wisp, and easily attach to any helmet, hat, or skullcap. So, what do you say? Own ye a helmet in need of such a fine article?"

Mason chewed on his lower lip a moment and gave the young man a penetrating stare. He wondered how anyone could have clothes with more holes than his own. "How much would I have to pay to see you swallow one of those fine, hand-plucked coral bobbylink feathers?" he asked finally.

The young salesman didn't miss a breath. "How much you got?"

"Believe me," Mason said, rolling his eyes, "not enough." He turned and continued down the street.

The plume salesman picked up the handle of his trunk and followed right beside. "Bad day, sweetie?" Cowel asked with mock sympathy.

"Just the same. You?"

"I had a door slammed in my face six times today. *Six times.* Well, maybe it was only three," he backtracked, "but once I was leaning forward." Cowel pointed to a spot on his nose where the skin looked raw and red. "Headed home?"

"I have a song to finish tonight," Mason said.

"So you *did* make a sale?"

"Old Man Frinkmeyer dueled a chipmunk in his backyard and barely escaped with his life."

"At least he escaped."

Mason laughed. Cowel believed almost anything. He would have made a good bard if his uncle hadn't convinced him to sell plumes instead. Mason wondered what had made *that* sound like a good idea.

"Better than me," Cowel continued. "I spent eight hours on my feet and don't even have enough money to buy the crumbs off a fat man's shirt." He looked up despairingly at the clouds and sighed as he spoke. Mason took the hint.

"You could come over for dinner."

"Really?" the plume salesman asked, with a sincerity that made it sound as if this was the first time Mason had ever offered to share his mother's cooking and not the hundredth.

"I'm sure your uncle won't mind."

Unlike Mason, who still had one parent, whose adoration and suffocating love counted for three, Cowel Salendor had been sent to live with his uncle at the age of four after his own parents died. Cowel's uncle Perlin had been a weapons maker then, known across the five lands. He had been prosperous until all the heroes trickled out of town and took most of his business with them. His wife left, too, having grown less enamored of the beefy, sweaty blacksmith once he could no longer shower her with jewelry and silk dresses. Now, Perlin Salendor spent most of his time at Flax's trying to forget who he used to be and what he used to have, leaving his nephew to fend for himself, which he usually did by mooching off Mason.

"Come on, let's cut through the Alley." Mason veered right, with Cowel in tow, the latter still banging one end of his trunk against his already-bruised legs.

Hero's Alley was actually the second widest street in the city, next to Main, which had been renamed Darlinger Boulevard. The city of Darlington had once been called Highsmith and under that name could boast of every modern convenience: gold depositories, spas, parks, and theaters, and snooty taverns that served undercooked cuisine in tiny portions. In short, Highsmith had been a bustling burg.

Most important, though, it had once had heroes—a hundred of them, more or less. Situated as it was at the edge of the Blackcloud Mountains, which housed countless orcs and goblins, Highsmith offered an ideal destination for a "thrash and bash" or a weekend treasure hunt. Rogue trolls rampaging the countryside, werewolf packs harassing sheepherders, orc raiding parties capturing cows for summer cookouts—there was always work for someone who carried a sword and knew how to use it, and Hero's Alley had been the center of it all.

As Mason and Cowel walked down the street paved in blue stone, lined on both sides with empty shells of houses, Mason remembered being nearly six years old, walking down the same street, with his father—whose face always came out as a blur but whose hands Mason remembered as heavily callused—introducing him to the legends who lived there. It was no surprise that Edmond Quayle knew all of the heroes in the Alley—he had been one of them, after all. Not the most famous, by far, but an adventurer nonetheless, even if he never was able to afford a place on this street.

Back then, Mason couldn't wait to grow up and own his own house on the Alley's edge. *Mason Quayle: Adventurer, Pirate, Slayer, Scoundrel.* Instead, he ran a half-priced barding service out of a box on a no-name street in a one-hero town.

Not that anyone would want to live here anymore. The Alley was deserted. The remaining copper-colored placards revealed the names of yesterday's heroes.

"I don't know why we always take this shortcut. This place creeps me out," Cowel said, kicking at loose stones. "I don't understand why you like it so much."

Mason didn't bother telling Cowel the reason, that it brought back memories he barely kept hold of. Instead, he offered to take over the dragging of Cowel's trunk, and the plume salesman agreed, rubbing his sweaty hands against his breeches and stretching his arms behind him. They passed underneath the fading signs, one after another, Mason whispering the names under his breath: *Johanus Growlford: Adventurer, Barbarian, Bruiser. Arlena Owltree: Bounty Hunter, Orc Smasher, Gnome Wrangler. Moxy Firaxin: Treasure Hunter, Dragon Tamer, Vampire Slayer.*

"You don't think your mother would make those stuffed meaty, bready things again, do you?" Cowel asked, shoving his empty hands into his empty pockets. "God, those are good." Mason just kept whispering. *Roland Warbringer. Cassius Coldhammer. Falgony Griffon.* They weren't real names, but it didn't matter. Heroes grew out of their real names like boots that no longer fit. They needed names with more syllables, something to give the songs that were sung about them some rhythm. No one wanted to hear "The Ballad of Gus Dobbs." There was no poetry in that. But "The Ballad of Brendlor Bowbreaker"—now *that* would capture an audience's ear.

Walking past Brendlor's deserted home, Mason wondered if any of those songs were sung anymore. Eight years ago, Brendlor Bowbreaker—who had once entered a behemoth's lair armed only with his teeth—simply packed up everything he had, family and all, and left for no-one-knew-where. And he was one of the last to leave.

Long after Mason's father.

Mason looked up and realized they were on his street, only a minute from his house, the ghosts all behind him.

The house on Tallow Street was the only thing Mason and his mother owned of any value—Mason couldn't bring himself to count the shack. The house was a three-chamber affair, with a washtub that wasn't used often enough and a pantry that couldn't hold on to anything for too long, save one jar of peach jam that had grown fuzz. Mason and his mother took one room each. The third—and the largest—was both the library and kitchen, the place where the lady of the house spent most of her time.

"I'm home."

"I'll be right there," came a voice like a creaking stair, soon followed by its source, a slender feather of a woman with hair like a wheat bushel, hazel eyes, and pinkish purple lips. She beamed when she saw her guest. "Oh, hello, Cowel."

"Hello, Mrs. Quayle. You are looking radiant as always this afternoon." Cowel was this cheesy with everyone but Mason, especially if someone was willing to feed him. It was an act, but a good one. It was too bad he didn't sell anything that was actually useful.

"Oh, am I? I hadn't noticed," Dierdra Quayle said, giving Cowel the blush he had earned. "Mason, will Cowel be joining us for dinner?"

"I hate to impose," Cowel said, bowing slightly.

"He lies—he already invited himself over," Mason countered, heading over to the fireplace, where a chicken was just starting to blacken.

"I got it from Mrs. Durden," his mother said of their dinner. "I finished her laundry today. She has the ague or the dengue or the plague or the vertigo—I can't remember which one."

"Is she dying?" Cowel asked.

"No, just dizzy."

"Vertigo," the two young men said simultaneously.

"Well, let me go finish up while Mason sets the table. I hope I made enough to eat." Mrs. Quayle fussed out to her garden through the back door.

It was still another half-hour before they all sat down at the Quayles' modest table, adorned with some wildflowers Mrs. Quayle had insisted Mason pick, a few roasted potatoes skirting an overcooked chicken, and a bottle of dandelion wine. Dierdra soaked up Cowel's compliments on the food and then proceeded to tell them all about her day—how she had darned socks for Mrs. Such-and-Such. How she had helped Mrs. So-and-So finish her baking. How she had done such-and-such for So-and-So and vice versa. Her eyes sparkled every time she looked at Mason.

"Did you not have a good day at work, dear?"

"I made a sale. Enough to get us through," Mason lied. "If I can get another one over the next week or so . . ."

No one bothered to fill in the rest of the sentence. They all knew where the money headed.

"The duke's been gone for a while now," Mason said, speaking of the devil.

"What is it this time?" Dierdra asked.

"Goblin hunting. Apparently, the threat level has reached 'imminent danger.'"

"What color is that, again?"

"Red, orange—who knows anymore?" Cowel said. There was a huge signpost in the center of Darlington that indicated the current threat of various monster attacks, all color-coded, so you knew what was about to attack you and when. Everyone would sigh in relief when the color was changed back to blue after one of the duke's adventures.

"It's nice to be so safe, I suppose," Dierdra said. "Though you wonder why he has to tax so much for it. Back when there were a ton of heroes, we never had any 'threat-level indicators' and we didn't pay a protection tax. We just offered up what we had, and that was enough."

"Well," Cowel said, "Darlinger *does* have a reputation to live up to."

"But *goblin hunting?* Mason's father used to go out with goblin hunters every other Friday. There were *hordes* of goblins. We used to send out groups of five or six to fight them off. How can one man possibly do all that work?"

"I'm sure you'll hear all about it when the duke gets back," Mason said through his last mouthful of potato.

"I suppose," Dierdra replied, starting to clear the plates. "Can't wait for your father to come home, though, and see what he has to say about the protection tax."

The room suddenly fell silent, Cowel instantly fascinated by something on his hands and Mason staring at the wall opposite him.

She still said it often. Every other day, at least. She couldn't say it while looking anyone in the face anymore—that was something—but she had never stopped dreaming. Sometimes, she'd whisper it. Most of the time, she'd just watch out the window.

"If you two boys don't mind, I'm going to go read for a bit."

"Thank you for dinner, Mrs. Quayle." Cowel cautiously looked up from his hands.

Dierdra Quayle nodded to herself, managed to relocate the smile that had disappeared only for a second, stole a furtive glance at her son, then retreated.

"You okay?" Cowel asked.

Mason nodded. Shrugged. Nodded again. He worried about her. Nothing could get her to admit the truth—that his father had abandoned them and was never coming back.

"We're quite a pair, aren't we?" Cowel said. "One good mother and one drunk uncle between us. You still think we shouldn't try to hook them up?"

Mason smiled and poured another half-cup of dandelion wine for each of them. They went and sat outside the house underneath the clouds, which had turned orangish purple, as if being bruised by the setting sun. Mason was sometimes surprised that there were still such beautiful things in the world.

Not long after they finished their wine, they heard the faint ringing of the bells from the city center. It wasn't long before Abby Caven, the official crier for Mason's street, shouted that "the hero" had returned.

For a heartbreaking second, Mason thought they might be talking about somebody other than the duke.

The gold pillars at the entrance to Darlington loomed high over the neighboring dwellings. Originally, they had been only half as tall and made of the same gray stone as the rest of the wall surrounding the city. But six years ago, about the same time he officially changed the name of the town, the duke commissioned a more resplendent portal. Bridging the two pillars was a golden archway, engraved with scenes from the duke's own adventures, depicting acts of such bravery and prowess as to make fathers of wussy sons weep. Standing on either side of the arch were twelve-foot ivory statues of the duke, paid for, no doubt, by the people's protection tax.

At that moment, some three hundred townsfolk were gathered near the golden arch. Toward the back of the crowd, Mason and Cowel feigned disinterest and picked at a bag of roasted pumpkin seeds they had agreed to split while waiting for the show to begin.

"I wonder what kind of plume he has on today," Cowel spat, a pumpkin seed slipping out of the corner of his lips before being sucked back in. It was his biggest gripe, one that Mason couldn't go a day without hearing: that the *only* hero in the town—the only person actually in *need* of plumes for his helmets—had his plumes *imported* from a distributor in Yorkville. Mason couldn't blame Cowel for being bitter—he shared a similar complaint.

Cowel was in full rant by the time someone near the front of the crowd pointed to the top of a hill, to a man jauntily straddling his horse. It was the duke, all right. There was no mistaking the advertising. Even from this distance, Mason could see the emblems hanging from the duke's saddle—Darlinger's sponsors, the various town businesses that paid him an extra sum at the end of each month for sporting their names on his equipment. Heroism, brought to you by the good folks at Caley's Pub.

The duke was about one minute's hard gallop from the city gate, but as much as a thunderous charge might liven up the crowd, it would pale in comparison to the regality of plodding ponderously over the hill, the sun nearly finishing its spectrum behind him, his glorious suit of gold armor *still* polished and gleaming despite his having hunted goblins for nearly three days. Come to think of it, Mason had never seen the duke *gallop* anywhere. Near the front of the gate, a twelve-piece orchestra broke into a victory march.

Dirk Darlinger waved to the crowd—a weighty gesture that looked as if he were giving the masses his blessing; his horse, rather repetitively named Steed, lumbered along. The crowd could see the collection of shields, helmets, and swords in a bag heaped on poor Steed's back. They were Darlinger's trophies, proof of yet another successful adventure, of harrowing encounters with blood-lusting denizens of darkness. Otherwise, there was no sign that the town's greatest hero had even had to move a muscle. If anything, he looked more refreshed now than when he had left to hunt goblins three days ago. "Looks like a successful trip," the man standing next to Cowel murmured.

The duke halted just in front of the city gates. A gentleman dressed in colorful servant's robes made his way to the front of the crowd and produced a stack of placards that he held up for the duke to see. Darlinger squinted a bit, made a motion for the servant to come a little closer, a little more to the right, then turned to address the townsfolk who had come to welcome him home.

"Commoners of Darlington," he began, constantly casting his eyes sideways for his next line, "and fine supporters of Verdal's Tavern on the Hill, where every night is dames' night."

"Way to slip that in there," Mason whispered. Cowel nodded. They never went to the Tavern on the Hill—it was drastically overpriced—but being businessmen of sorts, they could appreciate the power of promotion.

"You are safe once again," the duke continued. "The imminent goblin threat has been squelched. Their supposed magiks of mass devastation have been rooted out and destroyed, and your hero has returned to you." Nearly half the crowd, recognizing the space for it, clapped. Darlinger waited until the applause had petered out fully before continuing. "Though the goblins are many, they are nothing compared to the justice and valor contained in one man who rides forth with no thought other than the protection of his people." More applause. Mason groaned. Cowel scratched an armpit and muttered something again about the man's plume. "So tonight, please sleep soundly, knowing that your children are safe and my sword hovers over us all, waiting to fall . . ."

There was a significant pause as the servant struggled to turn to the next sign. Darlinger smiled nervously. "To fall . . . to fall upon the . . . evil makers who would threaten the freedoms we hold so dear. Return home safely, and remember that tickets to hear the tale of my latest adventure will go on sale in the morning. Buy three, get the fourth one *half price!*"

Then, with a flourish of Darlinger's hand, the crowd parted and Steed sauntered through the throng, many of them reaching out just to touch the bootstrap of their hero as he rode toward his mansion. The members of the orchestra played another short victory march and then bantered back and forth about which pub they were headed to.

"His bards are going to be up all night throwing stuff together for that concert," Mason said, kicking at the dirt with his toe. "It's the same drivel every time. The names and numbers change, but I swear the lines all end the same."

"You're not jealous, are you?"

"Of Darlinger? Of course I am. Aren't you?"

"Absolutely not," Cowel said pointedly.

"You lie."

"Honestly, what does he have that I don't have?" Cowel began counting on his fingers. "Wealth, fame, a mansion, his own horse—who needs it?"

Mason nodded, not sure whether his friend was serious. Cowel had lived life with so little for so long, it was possible he really felt all of it was unnecessary. Or maybe that's just what he told himself.

Cowel might have been right about the mansion, the

wealth, the fawning throngs—maybe they were more trouble than they were worth. But Darlinger did have something that Mason Quayle desperately wanted, something his father had had and he hadn't yet inherited.

He was noticed.

More than anything, Mason was afraid that he would vanish one day, just up and leave without a word, and his name would never be spoken. It was a heavy thought for a fifteen-year-old to have, he knew, but, then, Dirk Darlinger was only in his twenties. Mason watched as Darlinger rode off and disappeared, whispers of his name following him, and something inside of Mason grew brittle enough to finally break.

"Are you all right?" Cowel elbowed him in the side. "Come on, let's go to Flax's." He started off in the opposite direction and had to holler back to the still-frozen Mason, staring off into Darlinger's sunset.

Flax Romano never wanted much out of life, which was helpful considering how little he'd gotten so far. Childless and wifeless, though the latter was not for lack of trying, he had known only a brief and sparkling success. At the age of twenty-seven, he opened his own tavern only a block away from Hero's Alley and featured the "Hack and Slash Special": Come in and show Flax your most recent wound—still bleeding, preferably—and your first tankard was on the house. This didn't last long, as people began stabbing themselves just to get a free beer, but it established Flax as a friend to adventurers—not the pompous, Dirk Darlinger types but the hard-working grunts who came home stinking of putrid bogs, missing fingers and toes, and wearing faces scorched or covered in witches' boils.

That was twenty-five years ago, when the town was teeming and Flax's coin purse refused to jingle because it was so full. The rarest treasure for an adventurer in the Hero's District was actually finding a table at Flax's. The tavern had been the favorite of Mason's father and still was the favorite of Cowel's uncle. Though Mason had never once seen his father walk into the place—he would have been put to bed long before his father went out—it was unusual to see Cowel's uncle walk out of it. So when they entered that evening, the first thing Cowel did was go over to his uncle, who was sitting at the far end of the bar. "I'll catch up to you in a minute."

"Okay." Mason liked Perlin Salendor well enough, at least when he had the chance to talk to him, but those occasions were few. Most of the time, Cowel kept his conversations with his uncle private.

"Everything all right?" Mason asked as Cowel shuffled back to the table, his face shriveled like dried fruit.

"Same as always. Don't suppose you want to order anything?"

"I spent my last bit of change on those seeds," Mason said, then stared at a knot in the table while Cowel talked at him, chattering on about what it must be like to hunt goblins, how you couldn't really get a good pair of pantaloons anymore, and how he thought Flax used to put bowls of walnuts on the tables. "The whole damn town is falling apart."

The door to Flax's started to swing freely as more people trickled in. It happened on nights when Darlinger returned from an adventure. The older folk, remembering how life used to be, would head toward this side of town, itching for a story. Mason watched all of their mouths moving, saying nothing, and tried to rub away the lurch in his stomach. Like a drain in the middle of a sloped room, all conversations gravitated toward Darlinger and how magnificent he was. Mason felt his spirits sink even further as he heard the word "savior" repeated over and over.

And it came to him again, that itch beneath the skin, the one he had no idea how to scratch. The more he heard the name Dirk Darlinger, the more he felt as if nothing he would do with his life would be worth anything. He hadn't accomplished one thing he was proud of. To hear his mother tell it, his father was hunting werewolves by the age of fourteen. Here Mason was, older than that already and barely able to feed himself. He pictured a piece of rotting parchment, a title scrawled across the top in faded gold letters: "The Tale of Mason Quayle." Written beneath it was only one word.

Um.

That's it, Mason thought. If someone were to write a song about his life, that's what it would say. *Um,* like the pause as you try to think of something nice to say to an ugly woman who asked you about her hair. He wanted to *do* something. But in this town, there apparently was nothing to do except sit in a tavern and talk about Dirk Darlinger. He grew antsy and started to rub his feet together, a nervous habit. He had done nothing but keep his head afloat, and his legs were getting tired from working so hard to go nowhere. He was still young, he told himself. There was still plenty of time, provided he could figure out where he was going.

He needed a way into that world, the world of adventure and acknowledgment. And with his father gone, his mother lost in some past life, and all the heroes of Highsmith vanished, there was only one person who could give Mason what he wanted.

"I've been thinking," Mason began hesitantly, interrupting Cowel in the middle of a commentary on the difference between soup and stew. Mason knew that what he was about to say wouldn't go over well. The subject had been brought up before but always as a joke. But Mason was tired of telling jokes to feel better about himself.

"Should I applaud or just hold my breath expectantly?"

"I'm not sure I can continue to live, doing what I'm doing."

"Tell me about it."

"I mean, I think it's time I tried something else."

That got Cowel's attention—Cowel, who tried to sell feathers to people who had no caps to stick them in. "Something besides barding, you mean?"

"Not exactly."

"What, then?"

"I was thinking," Mason said, then stopped himself, summoned a breath, and continued, "that I would go work for the duke."

"What?" Cowel's face turned red, just as Mason anticipated. "You pulling my strings?"

"I'm not."

"Work for that pompous peacock? Doing what? Darning his socks?"

"An apprentice, a scribe . . . something."

"You *are* kidding."

"I'm serious." He was. He thought he was.

"I can't believe I'm hearing this. You know what that guy is. What he represents. At best, you'll end up peeling his grapes while he talks about himself. It would be worse than being friends with *me*." Cowel said this in all earnestness.

"It's better than what I'm doing now. I can't keep turning accidents into adventures."

"But *him?* Have you forgotten how much we don't *like* that guy? The taxes? The arrogance? The fact that he kicked all the other heroes out of town? *All* of them?" Cowel didn't need to say any more. Mason understood perfectly.

"I know. But what do you expect me to do?" Mason raised his voice, an open invitation for Cowel to do the same.

"I don't know—leave. Go somewhere else. I'll go with you."

"And leave my mother behind like *he* did?"

Cowel's face flushed. "Well, no. Of course not. I didn't mean that. But there's got to be something else."

"Look around you. You've lived in this town most of your life. There's no chance of me writing anything decent unless I can write about Darlinger. He's all we've got."

"Your mother would kill you," Cowel said. "That's what you said just last year. You said, 'I could never go work for Darlinger because my mother would impale me with one of her sewing needles.'"

"Well, a lot has changed in a year," Mason snapped.

"What? What has changed? I'm still poor. You're still poor."

"Exactly. Nothing's changed, and I'm starting to feel differently about it."

"So *you've* changed, that's all."

"You don't get it, do you?" Mason said, leaning over the table. "I don't want to be forgettable. That might be fine for you, but some of us need more out of life than going door to door peddling feathers for pennies."

And with that, for the first time that evening, he managed to shut Cowel up. The plume salesman turned sideways, his cheeks burning bright red.

"Cowel." Mason angled for eye contact, regretting he had said anything. "Listen. I'm sorry. I just need the money."

"So go, then. Toddle off to his majesty's royal chambers and throw yourself at his feet. Maybe he needs to hire someone to clip his toenails. Maybe you can help give him his bath."

Mason gave up. "Fine."

"Fine."

"Fine. I'll go."

"Fine. Who's stopping you?"

"Fine."

"Fine."

"I'm going."

"Good."

"Fine."

"Go."

"I am."

"Good."

"Good."

Mason nearly pushed his chair over getting out of it, and stormed through the tavern's door, leaving Cowel scowling and gritting his teeth. He struggled for something crippling to say at Mason's back, but the best he could come up with was "traitor." Mason pretended not to hear.

Walking in the night, the wind pricking him beneath his shirt, Mason couldn't keep his head from spinning. Fathers, uncles, mothers, heroes, friends—for some reason, they all felt like enemies. He passed by the shortcut through Hero's Alley but didn't bother to take it.

What the hell is wrong with all these people, he wondered. Don't they see what's going on? He wasn't going to end up like Cowel's uncle, sitting at the edge of the bar. He wasn't going to end up like his mother, waiting by the window, or like Cowel, pretending there wasn't anything better out there. For three years, Mason had sat in that shack pretending, and the thought of it sickened his stomach. If the duke wouldn't have him, there really was nothing left for Mason to do but take off—to find his future elsewhere. He would do the very thing he promised never to do: Follow in his father's steps.

Mason wondered how his father must have felt that day, the day the duke signed the contract with the town's council, promising to protect the townsfolk, making the other heroes obsolete. Whether his father kissed his mother on the cheek or the lips before he left. Whether he kissed Mason at all. Whether he even said goodbye.

He wondered why his father had never come back. If there had been something about the leaving that made returning impossible. Wondered if he had *known* he wasn't coming back when he walked out the door. It must have taken extraordinary courage to leave like that. To set off into the unknown and leave so much behind. A hero's courage.

Mason opened the front door gently. His mother was asleep in the library's only chair, an open book on her lap.

— 2 —

How to Become a Hero
in One Scary Step

Mason was awake most of the night. He sweated through his only sheet, which was wrapped tightly around his neck like a noose, though the rest of his body was cold. What dreams he could remember he wished he hadn't. He dreamt of Cowel being eaten alive by a horde of peacocks, of his mother being swallowed through her window, and of himself walking down a dark passage. At the end of the passage was a door, perfectly smooth, with no latch or knob, not a thing to hold on to. Painted on the door was a sign.

The sign said PULL TO OPEN.

Mason got up and dressed more carefully than usual, putting on the clothes he wore only on holidays or his mother's birthday. The pants seemed too big around the waist, and he wondered if he had lost weight since he last wore them. The cherry-colored cape—the only piece of finery he owned—barely reached his knees. He washed his face in a basin of water and was careful, for once, to brush his hair up and out of his eyes. He still smelled like stale sweat, but there wasn't time for a proper bath. He took another look at himself in his shard of mirror—his mother had broken one and divided the two biggest pieces between them so they would each have a bedroom mirror. He tried to blink away the desperation in his eyes, then opened his bedroom door, trying to think of something to say to his mother when she asked him why he had bothered to dress up.

But she didn't.

She did say, "You look nice, dear," but she said that every day.

He couldn't tell her where he was going this morning. Cowel had been right about that (it was a minor annoyance that Cowel seemed to be right so much of the time). She wouldn't *kill* him if she knew he was going to beg the duke for a job. She didn't have it in her. But she would want an explanation, and Mason wasn't sure he could explain himself—no better than he had to Cowel last night, anyway. So he ate his breakfast in silence and simply nodded at all her questions. Dierdra Quayle blew him a kiss out the door, making him feel even worse for not telling her what he was up to.

The Darlinger estate—a mansion of four stories—lay in the exact center of town where the duke's father had built it. No one knew much about Dirk Darlinger's father other than that when he passed away, the young duke found himself in possession of a great deal more wealth than all the heroes in the city combined. The elder Darlinger was a private man who kept out of the town's affairs—unlike his son, who wrapped the town's affairs around him like a coat and then demanded its pockets be filled.

Mason went over his pitch as he walked. The duke was a busy man. Mason figured he'd have five minutes, at most, to convince Darlinger that he needed another bard—a true bard, one who would literally follow in his footsteps and record everything he saw. Mason would stress his unique traits—his creative rhyme, his sense of stanzification. He would show the duke his samples, the two songs with which he was marginally happy: one about a hunter who had actually confronted a wolf, and the other about his father, written only three months ago and based on a story his mother had told him. And when all that failed, he would beg. He would get on his knees and put his forehead on the floor; he would grab the duke by the ankles and kiss the man's shins all the way up to his knees and back down again. Mason looked at his boots, which had holes in three different places.

The rows of houses in the city center were dwarfed by Darlinger Manor. Of the twenty-plus rooms of Darlinger's abode, Mason had already been in six—the six that were on the Duke Darlinger Tour he and his mother took four years ago, which ended in the Darlinger Gift Shop, where you could buy little statuettes of the duke, necklaces made of vampire fangs, and jars of Darlinger Jam. Now, as he reluctantly approached the front gates, Mason had the impression that the building had lost some of its luster. The trees and bushes were overgrown and wild. The pond was skimmed over with a layer of greenish brown scum that looked solid enough to walk on, while the steppingstones looked as if they might disintegrate underfoot. Clearly, the duke had been too busy bashing goblins or ousting orcs to review the work of his groundskeepers.

The bell you were supposed to ring by pulling on its string was broken. It took four knocks before somebody opened the door. Mason straightened himself.

The familiar-looking man standing in the doorway wore a frayed cloak and a put-out expression. He gave Mason a quick once-over, then moved to shut the door, saying, "Duke Darlinger is not available for autographs at this time," with an air of detached exasperation.

Mason quickly stuffed his foot in the doorway.

"I'm Mason Quayle. I'm here to see about a position."

The man looked back through the open crack, still pressing the door firmly against Mason's foot, hoping, perhaps, to sever it at the ankle.

"There are no positions, unless, of course, you want mine."

"Fine," Mason said, desperate. "I'll take yours."

The servant looked at him slyly. "Believe me," the man with the thinning hair replied, "you don't want mine."

"You don't know how far I'm willing to go," Mason fired back.

"You don't know how far you would have to" was the doorman's ready response, but he didn't elaborate. He did, however, concede. "Come inside. I will go see if His Dukeship is occupied."

He said the word "Dukeship" the way most people say "mother-in-law" and then disappeared into another room, leaving Mason on what was undoubtedly an antique wooden bench, judging by how terribly uncomfortable it was.

The room was much more sparsely decorated than Mason remembered from the tour. He thought there had been expensive paintings on the walls and fancy urns sitting by the door. Finding the bench not worth sitting on, Mason stood up and began walking around the foyer, eventually wandering into the greeting room, a large chamber with a cold fireplace at the far end and various trophies lining the walls. Everywhere he looked he saw dust. He wandered past a mounted basilisk's head with obsidian eyes that seemed to follow him wherever he went and past the many awards—the plaques and medals, the commemorative swords and shields—that the town had offered Darlinger early on, at the start of his career, when the protection tax hadn't been so high.

Mason's amblings took him into the library, which was enormous. Mason didn't know that this many books had been written. He thought of his father's library and its measly one hundred volumes and instantly became hot with jealousy. Most likely, Darlinger never even had time to read, yet he had a room full of books stacked fifteen shelves high. Mason went to the first shelf and pulled out *A Historie of the Wytches of Stygmos*.

Then he realized it wasn't a book at all.

None of them were books. They were all just blocks of wood, the spines and tops carved and painted to look like leather bindings and cut pages. Mason flipped the one book over and over in his hands.

"Enjoying the literature?"

Mason spun, dropped the book on his toe, and yelped. The man who had greeted him earlier at the front door now stood in the archway amused, watching Mason do his bruised-toe little dance.

"It makes for pretty dense reading," the servant said.

Mason started to ask why all the books were made of wood, but the doorman interrupted him with a "The duke will see you now." Mason slid the block of wood smoothly back in its place, massaged one foot briefly with the other, and followed the servant up the stairs and into a sitting room that was as sparsely decorated as all the rest—just a fireplace, a few chairs, and a mirror on the wall. Mason noticed there were mirrors in every room.

Duke Darlinger was sitting with his back to the entryway, staring out the window at his garden as if waiting for something or someone.

"Mr. Quayle to see you, sir," the servant said.

Mason stood as tall as he ever had in his life and held his breath.

"Thank you, Percy." Duke Darlinger swiveled his chair around to face his guest. This was the closest Mason had ever been to the town's only hero. Unlike the face in the DUKE DARLINGER IS WATCHING posters lining the city walls, the man sitting before Mason had crow's-feet. He wore a haggard expression, and his luminous blond hair, which always seemed to hold the light of the world captive, now appeared to be receding on each side—it even looked as though it might be dyed. Granted, the duke was still well manicured and impeccably dressed. His blue eyes sparkled and he held a mouth full of polished pearls, but something—maybe it was the mole Mason had never noticed on his chin—gave the impression that this man was just that, after all.

"Quayle. Where have I heard that name before?"

"My father. He was a hero. Back, you know, when we needed them."

"No, that's not it," the duke said.

"You might just be thinking of the bird, then," Percy commented.

"Perhaps. What can I do for you, Mr. Quayle?"

"Actually," Mason began, his voice cracking, ". . . actually, I was hoping, wondering, curious . . . that is . . . if you were in need of a, you know, a bard . . . or anything, really."

Mason coughed into his hand and looked down at the floor. How do you look into the eyes of a man who has supposedly slain a giant snake with one of its own fangs?

"Actually, I *have* a bard," Darlinger said, without so much as a pause to consider the offer. But this time it was Percy who coughed, or rather snorted, and then also cast his eyes to the floor.

"I understand," said Mason. "You probably have several. But I thought, with how busy you are, with all of the adventures you are always on, that you might want a fresh voice. Someone who could follow you around and take notes, someone you could teach, you know, how to be . . . a hero." He stumbled a bit over the last part. It sounded even more ridiculous out loud than it had in his head. He could hear Cowel saying *I told you so* already.

"That won't be necessary," Darlinger said, this time dismissively, brushing imaginary dust from his knees—the only place in the house where the dust was imaginary.

"But I brought these samples," Mason said, undeterred, clumsily dropping his papers on the floor. "I mean, I'm sure they're not about anything as heroic as what you've accomplished, but I'm ready for that challenge. I've got a keen ear for alliteration. The duke so daring never dallied from the daunting . . ."

But Darlinger shushed him with a wave of his hand and then raised one eyebrow clear up into his too-blond and thinning hair. "Mr. Quayle, as wonderful as your work no doubt is, I simply don't have room on my staff to add another bard, and there certainly isn't room for another hero."

Again from the corner came a snort.

"A house servant, then?"

"Got one."

"A stable boy? Surely you own lots of horses that need looking after."

"Taken care of," was Darlinger's reply.

"Armor mender?"

"Got one."

"Sword sharpener?"

"He's got one," Percy said, finally giving up on standing and slouching into one of the chairs.

"Correct," Darlinger added, directing his words at his servant rather than at Mason. "I have one already."

"Not that it needs it," Percy whispered, just loud enough for both of them to hear.

Mason took a step forward. "Believe me, sir. I'm willing to do anything. I just need a job."

"I'm afraid I can't help you," Darlinger said, then rose from his chair, pointing to the door with an open hand.

And then Mason did it. He dropped to his knees. It felt as if his entire body would melt into a puddle on the floor, waiting for Percy to come mop him up. "Then could I at least get you to waive our protection tax, if only for this month? My mother. We're just a little short. I can make up for it next month . . ."

Darlinger gestured again toward the door.

Mason was doubled over now. "You don't understand—my father . . ." he began, but he couldn't choke out the rest of that sentence, wasn't even quite sure how it ended.

"Percy, would you please show the young man out? And make sure he gets an autographed sketch—free of charge."

"Yes, sir."

Duke Darlinger bowed slightly to Mason. Mason noticed the bare spot emerging on the top of his head. Then the town's only hero disappeared through the door without another word.

It took a moment for Mason to get to his feet, aided by a hand from Percy. On the way down the stairs, Percy apologized, explaining that, unfortunately, there were no more autographed sketches of the duke.

And with that, it should have been over. But it wasn't.

"I don't know what I expected," Mason said as Percy opened the door.

"There is only so much you can ask of a man," Percy said reflectively. "Speaking of which, you said you were a bard. As it turns out, I . . . I mean, Darlinger's bard . . . I and the *other* bards have a concert coming up and we're awfully busy. I have here a few pieces of silver. I can offer you more if you meet me this evening, just around back. I could use the help."

Mason looked at the three silver pieces suddenly thrust into his hand.

Then he looked at the man standing in the doorway and realized where he had seen him before. He was Darlinger's speechwriter—the man who had been carrying the signs yesterday, feeding the duke his lines.

"What exactly is it you do here?" Mason asked.

"More than my share, Mr. Quayle, more than my share."

Mason nodded, confused, wondering how he was leaving the duke's with an outright rejection *and* the promise of more money, the coins still sitting in his sweaty palm. And with that, the door to Darlinger's estate was slammed shut, leaving Mason three coins richer but somehow feeling terrible about it.

By the time the sun nestled into the ground and the moon took up residence, Mason was already where he needed to be. He had had no customers, as usual, and had spent most of the morning muddling his way through "The Ballad of Aldous Frinkmeyer," though the old man never showed to pick it up. But it didn't matter now. The three silver pieces he had been given by Darlinger's butler were enough to pay this month's tax and then some.

But he felt uneasy about the whole affair. There was something unusual about the servant and his request. About Darlinger, the estate, how *quiet* the house was.

The man named Percy stood outside the back entrance of

Darlinger's mansion, several sheets of parchment, some already inked, in hand. Two chairs were at a table nearby. The table held an oil lamp, an inkwell, and a handful of quills.

Mason looked around him. They were nearly blanketed by the bushes and the dipping branches of numerous trees. The effect was claustrophobic. "The duke prefers his back entrance somewhat secretive. The hedges make an ideal spot for clandestine encounters."

"Is this such a meeting?"

"Understand, it's not in my nature to go behind Duke Darlinger's back. And it wouldn't be necessary if . . ." But Percy stopped himself, put a finger to his own lips. "There's plenty of work to go around."

Mason looked at the two chairs. "There are no other bards, are there."

"Let's just say the duke is having financial difficulties."

Mason wondered how a man who collected a monthly tax from every household and also had access to a ton of treasure could suffer from financial difficulties. He must have wondered it out loud.

"The duke has many different expenses."

Mason stuffed his hands into his pockets, feeling the silver in one. The duke at least had enough to pay Percy, who had enough to pay him—and that was all that mattered.

"Shall we begin?" Percy ushered Mason toward the table.

"Don't we need the duke here?"

Percy stopped midstep. "What in heaven's name for?"

"You know, to tell us what happened . . . on his adventure . . . with the goblins."

"You mean, to tell you what *really* happened?" Percy asked, giving Mason a flinty stare.

"Well, yeah," Mason said. "That's how it works, right? You weren't there, were you?"

"Me? Of course not."

"So shouldn't *he* be here to fill us in?"

"Right." Percy let out a deep breath.

"You want it to be true, don't you? You want the song to be realistic."

"Of course. Of course it will be true. It's all true. If you say it, the duke has done it."

"But . . ."

"Really. You are making this more complicated than it has to be. Let me show you."

Percy sat down in one of the chairs, took up a quill, and began scribbling on a blank sheet. "Let's see. Cast of characters. Good guy: Duke. Bad guys: Goblins. Basic outline: Duke gets warning—doesn't really matter from where—straps on his armor, describe armor, mounts horse, describe horse—you're welcome to copy some of my earlier material on that," Percy said, pointing to some sheets of already-scribed parchment on the table. He continued, "Duke rides off, some treacherous weather, ominous clouds, add a vulture or two, tracks the goblins to their lair, is *woefully* outnumbered, makes stirring speech, presumably to horse, who is the only one there to listen—use the word *smite* a few times—draws sword, makes sound like this: *schwiiiinkkk*." Percy went through the motions; he looked to be straddling an invisible saddle as he sat in the chair and swished his arm back and forth. "He rides through the den of goblins like this, slash slash here, slash slash there, here a thrust, there a thrust, so on and so on, probably there is a showdown with the biggest, frothiest, bloodiest goblin—perhaps in a ring of fire, Duke kills him with his dagger or his bare hands or even his toes, stands in victory pose like so"—Percy stood up and raised his arms above his head—"with bodies strewn about, treasure to be had and distributed amongst the poor."

"He didn't bring back any treasure," Mason said, interrupting Percy in midtwirl in his dance around the table.

"Use your imagination." Percy collapsed onto his chair. Mason thought for a second he might be waiting for applause.

"And you're saying that's what happened?" Mason asked.

"More or less. Your job is to make it *sound* pretty. Don't waver too much from the formula. Now sit down and I'll help you get started." Mason sat and dipped one of the quills into the ink. Percy hovered by him, leaning over and pointing to the opening lines of the last goblin crusade the duke had been on. "You see here, last time I actually started with a woman's baby being abducted by the goblins—for emotional appeal, see. To get the audience's sympath—" Suddenly, Percy stopped. "Did you hear something?"

Mason sat hunched over the parchment, quill at the ready, so close to the edge of his seat that he was about to fall off. Then it came to him, two deep voices in the distance, sounding almost as though they were talking through mouthfuls of unshelled walnuts.

"Are you expecting someone else?" Mason asked, just as the glow of torchlight appeared above the hedge walls that concealed the duke's backyard. As an answer, Percy clasped one hand over Mason's mouth and dragged him off the chair with the other.

"Quick—into the bushes!" he hissed.

Mason pressed his belly to the cold earth just as the duke's back gate creaked open.

In the flickering halo of the torch, Mason made out two

hulking figures, clothed in hooded cloaks that concealed their faces and fell to the tops of their feet.

Feet that, Mason noticed in the dancing torchlight, were green. Not just green. But green and huge. And gnarled. And covered in warts. They were the ugliest feet Mason had ever seen, and he had seen Cowel's grandmother's feet once.

"Who are—" Mason started to ask, but Percy, lying next to him, covered his mouth again before he could get the whole sentence out. The two figures approached the back door and stood there a moment. Mason, with Percy's hand still cupped over his mouth, raised his head a little to get a better view.

"So I say to him, I say, 'I don't know who you think you are, but this is my cannibal feast, and if you don't stop chewing on that finger and pass the blood gravy like a *gentleman,* I will per-sonally tear your intestines out with my teeth.'"

"What'd he have to say to that?"

"He says to get my own bloody gravy."

The bigger one grunted. "So then what did you do?"

"What do you think I did? I made him refill the gravy bowl, *if you know what I mean.*"

There was a pause.

"No, not really," said the taller hulking mass.

"It was *blood* gravy. I made him *refill* it."

"I still don't get it."

"I *killed* him and *drained his blood into* . . . Forget about it. Lis-ten, are we going to do this or what?"

"All right," the larger one said. "Let's do it." He removed a battle-ax that he had somehow concealed beneath his cloak and with two blows rent the door to splinters. The sound of the ax's first strike caused Mason to jump and would have given him away if Percy hadn't held him down. The cloaked intruders disappeared into Darlinger's mansion.

Mason rolled over onto his side, glancing quickly back and forth between Percy and the remains of the door. The quill he had been holding in his hand was broken in three places and he had ink all over the front of his shirt. "What was *that?*"

Percy was perched hesitantly on his knees, scanning the area around them, making sure they were safe. "Orcs," he whispered.

"Orcs?" Mason felt as if he had just discovered quicksand the wrong way.

"Keep it down. They aren't here for us, but if they see us, there's no doubt we'll be tomorrow's breakfast. We should get out of here." Percy struggled to his feet, but Mason frantically dragged him back down.

"What are orcs doing *here?* How did they get here? What do they want?"

"I don't really care. I've had as much of this job as I can stomach, anyway."

Again he tried to rise; again Mason pulled him back down. "But the duke is inside the house, right? He'll find them. Everything will be all right, right?"

As if on cue, there was the sound of another door being smashed in, followed by a girlish scream.

"We should leave," Percy said again, trying to pry Mason's fingers from his pant leg.

"But the duke?"

Mason could hear the sound of something being dragged down the stairs. Someone was talking too quickly, the words thrown together into reckless sentences crashing heedlessly into one another. Mason could make out the two looming figures through a window. Their hoods had been drawn back. Their heads were abnormally huge, sloping at odd angles, with bridgeless noses and flaring nostrils that could fit three of Mason's fingers if he were interested in spelunking for orc boogers. Their teeth were a rotten yellow, their ears shaped like raindrops. They each had patches of rust-colored hair on their cheeks but none on their heads.

"You're right," Mason said, jumping to his feet. "We should go."

"It's too late," Percy hissed, pulling on Mason's legs so hard his chin shoveled the ground just as the two orcs appeared at the door. The shorter one put his hand up and looked around the back garden, sniffing the air. Percy and Mason both lay incredibly still, careful not to breathe. The two orcs stood in the light from the house, a body bent over double between them.

"Vincent, go grab that chair." The smaller orc pointed to the overturned chair Mason had been sitting on only five minutes ago.

"We can talk about this," the doubled-over figure groveled, grabbing onto the taller orc's leg. Mason was certain he recognized the voice, but it made so little sense that he doubted himself.

Vincent got the chair, set it in front of his partner, and lifted the limp body onto it. The now-seated man's back was to Mason, but even in this poor light, there was no mistaking who it was. You could tell by the bald spot.

What the heck is going on here? Mason wondered.

"Please. Listen. I don't know what the problem is. I've done everything Grav wanted."

"This isn't about Grav," the short one said.

"Then what is it about? What do you want? Who are you?"

"My name is Tino, and this is Vincent."

"Vinnie," Vincent said.

"We don't work for Grav. In fact, no one works for Grav anymore."

Don't these orcs know who they are talking to? Why isn't anything happening? Aren't I finally going to witness something worth writing about?

"But that's not possible. Grav is the one I meet with. He's—"

Tino snapped two gnarled fingers in front of the man's face. The duke started to rise out of the chair. *Now,* Mason thought, *now they are going to get it. He was just waiting for the right moment.*

Vincent pushed Dirk Darlinger back into the chair.

"We don't work for Grav. We work for Bennie now. Everyone does. The goblins. The ogres. The harpies, the . . . Help me out here, Vincent."

"The ogres," Vincent said.

"Right, the ogres. The vampires. You name it."

"The dragons," Vincent added.

Tino shook his head. "No, not really the dragons."

"But you said everybody," Vincent countered, sounding hurt.

"Yeah, but not the dragons. You can't count the dragons. They don't work for nobody."

"But I thought you said—"

"Listen, just forget about it. The point is," Tino said, turning back to the duke, "your man Grav is out—his head is currently on a pike—and Bennie the Orc is in control now."

"B-but Grav and I had an agreement," the duke stammered.

"Yeah. Bennie found out the kinds of deals you've made, and now he wants *his* share. He figures that since he now controls all the territory surrounding the town, he should be the prime benefactorary."

"Beneficiary," Vincent corrected.

"Thank you. He figures he should be the prime *beneficiary* of your town's generosity, including back pay."

"Back pay?" the duke sputtered.

"Yeah, he figures you owe him whatever you've paid out to all the other goblins, ghouls, trolls, and such."

"But you have to understand, you have to tell him—I can't give him that much. I don't have it. I'm almost broke."

Vincent put a hand on Darlinger's shoulder and the duke practically leapt out of his chair. "He understands you have means of raising money," Tino continued. "He is sympathizory . . ."

"Sympathetic," Vincent piped in.

"That is correct. Bennie says he is sympathetic to your needs. That's why he wanted us to tell you that he is giving you a full five days to raise the money."

"How much money?"

"Twenty thousand gold."

Beside Mason, Percy couldn't stop himself from gasping. Thankfully, it was drowned out by the duke's own protests. *"Twenty thousand . . ."*

"He calculates that's what he's due, more or less. Fork over the twenty thousand in five days and Bennie will consider you square and will leave the town alone for good."

"But it's too much. In five days, it's impossible."

"He says if you can't come up with the gold by the dawn of the fifth day, he won't be able to keep his people—the werewolves and the goblins and the blood trolls—"

"And the ogres."

"*And* the ogres, not to mention all of us orcs—from coming into town and doing whatever we like."

Mason kept blinking, kept waiting, but he didn't know what

for anymore. More than anything, he wanted Cowel to be there beside him, to share in his disbelief. Next to him, Percy was shaking his head.

Tino slapped Darlinger playfully on the cheek. Mason's eyes grew even wider. The duke shook his head. "I can't possibly raise that kind of money, even if I sold the estate, my father's house."

"Bennie thought you might be a little reluctant at first, so he gave Vincent and me permission to motivate you. Vincent." Tino snapped his fingers and Vincent unsheathed a long, wicked-looking dagger from his belt. Mason's pounding heart finally succeeded in leaping into his throat. Dirk Darlinger, the greatest hero the town and perhaps even all the five lands had ever known, looked at the dagger coming toward him and let out a scream.

Then he fainted, slumped over, and fell out of the chair. The two orcs simply stared at him for a minute.

"What was that all about?" Tino asked.

"I don't know. I didn't even touch him."

"Whatever. Just pick him back up and put him in the chair."

"But how are we supposed to scare him if he's blacked out?"

"Here," Tino said, "I'll just leave him a note."

"You want to use his blood as ink?"

Tino looked at Dirk Darlinger and then over at the table conveniently stocked with parchment, quills, and a spilled inkwell.

"Nah. Too sticky." The shorter orc went over to the table and, standing only five feet from the bushes where Mason and Percy were hidden, scribbled something quickly, holding the quill the way he would have held a knife, then folded the parchment and stuffed it down the duke's shirt.

"All right. Let's go. And put your hood up. You remember what this place was like ten years ago. I don't want to take any chances."

And as casually as they came, the two henchmen of Bennie the Orc left through the gate, covered almost completely by their cloaks. Not that they had anything to worry about, with the town's only hero having fainted.

Mason couldn't find his legs. All he could think about was the eight years of taxes he and his mother had paid so that their home would be protected by this man. Next to him, Percy counted to twenty and then stood up.

"This can't be happening," Mason said. Percy brushed the dirt from his clothes, looked up at the sky as if it could provide an answer, and then finally helped Mason to his feet. They both looked at Duke Darlinger curled up on the ground like a worm in the rain.

"Help me get him inside," Percy said, "and then I'll tell you everything."

"First, you must promise not to reveal any of this to anyone."

Percy had lit the fire in the fake library and settled the duke into the chair next to it. There was a glass of wine on the shelf beside him, for when he regained consciousness. Percy offered Mason some, but the young man preferred to stay clearheaded. Percy shrugged and finished a glass himself in three swallows.

"It's a little late to keep secrets, don't you think?" Mason's eyes darted back and forth between Percy and the duke. There was no mistaking what Mason had seen—the town's only hero crumpling at the sight of an orc's dagger—and what it meant.

"You must understand the gravity of the situation. If what I tell you should get out, well, not only would the duke hang, but we would lose whatever hope we have of defending this city."

"How is *he* supposed to defend the city?"

"I know what you are thinking, but believe it or not, the duke *has* protected us for several years. Just in his own way."

"His own way?" Mason was almost shouting—in part hoping the duke would wake up so he could confront him directly. To think, just this morning he had been *begging* the man for help.

"You see, ten years ago, the duke's father, Darby Darlinger, passed away, as I'm sure you well know, leaving a rather outrageous fortune to his son. It was the only kindness Dirk had ever known from his father, and it was more wealth than the young duke knew what to do with. Darby Darlinger had taken up residence in Highsmith because he considered it the safest place to be. From this estate in the center of town, he could run his businesses, ignore his wife—who was just as self-centered as he was—and treat himself to fine balcony views of a city guarded by a hundred heroes."

"That doesn't explain anything," Mason said, "or excuse it."

"I'm getting there. Darby Darlinger was a busy man, too busy to pay much attention when his wife left him, taking as much gold and jewelry as would fit in her pockets, and too busy to be involved in the affairs of his own son." Percy walked over to the chair, felt the duke's forehead with the back of his hand, and sighed.

"You're trying to defend him."

"I'm only trying to explain. When his father died, Dirk was granted land, title, and riches that you or I can only dream of. But he had never done anything worthwhile. And he was *surrounded* by people with reputations forged on deeds of valor, listening to songs sung about his own neighbors in every tavern in town. Naturally, then, the duke succumbed to the same impulse that every young person growing up in this city at the time did: he decided to become a hero himself.

"Which would have been fine had he not been so particularly *awful* at it. His father was no fighter. He had barely trained his son to carry a change purse, let alone a sword. Dirk could ride a horse, fire a wobbly arrow in a generally forward direction, and cut his own meat, but he wasn't really *hero* material. For one, he was deathly afraid of the sight of blood— especially his own. He also suffered from asthma, didn't hold up well in adverse weather, and was too uncoordinated to use a sword and shield simultaneously. Plus, the armor chafed his buttocks."

Chafed his buttocks? "You can only be making this up," Mason said, shaking his head.

"I'm afraid not. But the duke was determined not to simply walk in his father's footsteps, accomplishing nothing worth singing about in his lifetime. He wanted fame—fortune, I suppose, having been handed to him—and so, nine years ago, the duke set out on his first expedition: hunting a pack of goblins, no less, accompanied by three lesser-known heroes from the Alley.

"They tracked the goblins to a cave and smoked them out. The goblins let out a war cry. Their howl startled the duke, who dropped his sword, turned, tripped, knocked his chin on the ground, bit his lip, saw his own blood as he spit up on his hand, and fainted. The three heroes dispatched the six or seven goblins easily, escorted the embarrassed duke back to his estate, and were promptly paid huge sums of money not only to keep it quiet but, in fact, to seek adventure elsewhere. On their way out, they were *kind* enough to tell the story of how the duke had saved *them* from a marauding pack of thirty goblins."

"They *lied* for him?"

"Money can be very persuasive. Unfortunately, the next few adventures went much the same way. Those the duke hired did the work, and the duke himself took the credit. No one got hurt. The heroes were paid handsomely for their bravery and their silence, and the duke garnered the accolades, growing more and more famous. He acquired a taste, I suppose, for hearing his name in songs when he visited local taverns. And it was then, only a year after his father's death, that the duke came up with his master plan. Instead of offering the money to heroes who actually had to do the work, he thought, *Why not give it to the monsters instead?*"

Before Mason could speak, Percy continued, "I know what you're thinking. It would never work. Ogres and goblins and orcs aren't in it for the money. But in that you would be mistaken. It all depended on whom you talked to. And here the duke discovered his true talent—kissing up. It wasn't long before he was meeting with the heads of every goblin clan, every marauding horde, every tribe of orcs. Anyone can be bought for a price—in your case, three silver coins." Mason blushed. "In exchange for a piece of the duke's fortune, the evils of these lands vowed not only to keep the peace but to offer the duke 'proof' of his 'conquests' as well."

"The stuff he brings back with him? The stuff they used to sell in the gift shops?" As impossible as the story was, it was starting to make sense to Mason. He remembered how the duke always returned from an adventure without a scratch on his face or a dent in his armor. The man had never fought a battle in his life.

Percy nodded. "He was quite successful. He had all that money, after all, and he knew how to bargain. The duke was informed about any impending threat on the town long before any other heroes. By the time word reached the Alley that a giant was threatening to stomp across Highsmith, Darlinger was riding back through the gates, a lock of the giant's hair— painfully pulled for the right price—as a token of his victory. The giant had some gold, the town had a hero, and Darlinger got the credit. Before long, the other heroes started trickling out of Highsmith.

"The rest was just business," Percy continued. "Once all the other heroes left town, it became merely a matter of finances. Tax the people a small fee to help keep the coffers full. Acquire sponsors. Give concerts. Gift shops, mail-order tunics, song deals—all designed to bring in extra money to keep the business going."

"The business," Mason whispered.

"Of bribing the bad guys."

"But for ten years?"

"Well, not quite," Percy answered. "I don't remember exactly when it started to go wrong. Three years ago, perhaps. Maybe four. The duke would be gone for days at a time, dishing out bags of gold to greedy goblins at cannibal feasts held in his honor. Word spread of a man—a 'hero'—who simply handed out riches for doing nothing. No plundering. No pillaging. No wars. No violence. The evils of the world are not as blood-thirsty as you might think. If they can grow fat in pocket and belly without lifting a finger, they will. After all, they were used to a hundred heroes picking them off. The duke's deal was too good to pass up.

"We should have seen it coming, of course, but didn't. He should have known that more and more creatures would flock to the mountains and hills outside of Darlington, all looking for their fair share. Worse still, they began to fight with one another about who got more for doing nothing. They reorganized themselves into new clans, all trying to earn the duke's biggest payoff.

"The duke's fortune started to slip away. Taxes were steadily increased, as you no doubt know. The paintings on the walls steadily decreased. We pawned whatever we could to the merchants who came through here. The number of servants slipped from fifty to twenty to five. Now I'm all that's left."

"Why the wooden books?"

"He liked to keep up appearances. But he knew he was running out of time. Last month, the duke made a deal with an orc named Grav—a one-time, lump-sum payment. The number was astronomical—you wouldn't believe it if I told you. We saved for months—all to give to the most powerful of the orcs, who promised never to attack the town of Darlington for as long as he lived. The duke gathered every last scrap of gold he could and delivered the last payment three days ago."

"But it didn't work," Mason said.

"Apparently not. Grav is done and Bennie's in control. And now we are in a much bigger bind."

"He gave away everything he had?"

"Short of his reputation—which is somehow still intact, though how long it will remain so is up to you."

Mason stood up, his lower lip trembling. "And why shouldn't I tell? That's our money—most of it, anyway. Everyone should know what really happened."

"They should, I agree. But not yet. If the orcs find out that the duke has been exposed, they will know there is no hope of his meeting their demands. They will forget their deal, forget the deadline, and simply sack the town without a second thought."

"Then make the duke give himself up. Offer himself as a sacrifice."

"They don't care about the duke as a person. They care about only what he has to offer. And if he has nothing, they will take whatever's left over. They will take our houses. They will take us and use us as slaves. They aren't terribly picky."

"Then it's over!" Mason shouted. "There's nothing we can do but convince everyone to leave now." He started to go, but Percy stood next to the door and grabbed his arm. Percy was stronger than he looked.

"Wait! Mr. Quayle, just wait. There is another alternative, but we would need your help."

"*My* help?" Mason tried to free himself. "Oh, no, I don't think so." This was too much already. To think that this man who had conned the city out of its heroes, its money, its pride—this man who had caused Mason's father to leave his wife and child for good—to think that this man expected Mason to do anything for *him*.

But Percy kept hold of Mason's arm. "Not everyone will go. People are stubborn. Some won't believe you. Others will insist on protecting the city."

Mason wanted to disagree, but Percy was probably right. Some crazy fools would continue to believe in Darlinger. Others would try to defend their homes. "But what could you possibly expect me to do?"

"The very thing you insist that you are good at: tell a story to anyone who will listen. Leave town immediately. Head east, wherever you think you can find heroes to save us. Persuade whomever you can to make it back in four days' time—sooner, if possible—to fight for our city. I can't give you much money to pay them, of course, but I can give you a horse, the fastest one the duke has, and my own personal promise that I will do everything I can to help save this town."

Mason was frozen in place. "This is absolutely insane."

"Our options are limited, Mr. Quayle."

"Trust me. I'm nobody. I'm not anything. Where am I supposed to go to find heroes? I don't know anything about this. *I've never even been out of the city.*"

"Neither had the duke."

"And look what he got himself into! We have to tell everyone—at least give them the choice."

"And I will. If the fourth day dawns and I have not heard from you, I will have the duke alert the town. But until then, there is a chance we can save it. *You* can bring heroes back to the Alley."

Though he had never imagined them said before, they were the exact words Mason had always wanted to hear. At least, until he actually heard them. "Not me. I can't. You have to believe me on this one."

Percy gestured toward the still-unconscious form of Dirk Darlinger. "There is no one else."

Twenty minutes later, Mason found himself straddling a horse and wearing a suit of armor, with a sword dangling from his waist and a shield hanging from one arm, looking nothing like himself.

Ten minutes ago, he had been standing outside the duke's stables with Percy, still insisting this wasn't a good idea. But the servant had disappeared into the shadows and reappeared leading a gorgeous but droopy-eyed beast by the reins.

"This is the duke's fastest horse?" Mason asked.

"This is the duke's *only* horse."

Mason squinted through the darkness and recognized the silver stripe that ran down the horse's nose, the patches of white along his flanks. This was the closest he had ever come to Steed, the most written-about horse of the past ten years—at least in Darlington.

"The horse is almost as recognizable in this town as its owner. You'll have to wear this." Percy again ducked into a corner and reappeared with the same armor Darlinger had worn only yesterday. Nothing Beats a Brantlinger claimed the sticker on the back of the duke's helmet. "It's better to be a famous hero than a horse thief. Once you get far enough out of town, you can ditch the disguise. The armor's mostly for show, but the sword's for real, though I don't think it's ever been used."

"I'm supposed to ride through the streets pretending I'm the duke?"

"Don't act so shocked—the duke's been riding through the streets pretending he's someone else for years. You have to do it only long enough to get out of town. Here, let me give you a hand with that."

Percy helped strap Darlinger's grieves onto Mason's shins, helped him with the chain-mail shirt, and helped pull on the gauntlets. He slipped a tunic over Mason's head. It all reminded Mason of when his mother used to get him dressed. "Not a bad match, except your hair is darker. Hopefully, the helmet will hide most of that." Mason, meanwhile, was testing his mobility with his new metal coating, wondering how anyone could fight wearing all of this, then remembering that the man who wore it had never had to fight at all.

Percy held out a small coin purse. "Here's a hundred gold pieces—most of what's left. It's barely enough for one or two heroes, so you'll need to convince them to come out of their own sense of chivalry." Percy lifted Mason onto Steed. The horse accepted him without so much as a snort.

"You must understand, Steed's been around goblins and demons and witches. Nothing spooks him. He has been trained not to attack anything, so don't expect him to do *any* of the things he does in the songs about him."

"None of them?"

"Darlinger desperately tried to train him to do that rear-back-on-the-hind-legs thing, but he won't do even that. You stick with the duke long enough, you learn to keep your expectations low."

Mason scratched the top of Steed's head, and the horse stretched his neck in appreciation. Percy continued with his advice, checking the straps of the saddle. "The world is full of people who claim to be more than they are. We are pressed for time, of course, but you need to be somewhat selective. We need real heroes. No drunkards or thieves. No one over the age of sixty and no one younger than you. No one who can't supply his own sword—real heroes don't have to borrow weapons." Mason looked at the sword by his side. "Don't bring back any royalty. We don't need another rich kid. Just self-equipped, idealistic, honest-to-god, one hundred percent heroes. Three or four of them, though seven would be magnificent and a dozen would be ideal. And don't bring back any pirates. They're good only if they can swing from something."

"And where am I supposed to go to find them?"

"I don't know for sure, but I have a guess who might."

And Percy gave Mason a description of that person and directions to a tavern near Hero's Alley, and Mason was still too stunned by everything happening to realize whom he was talking about. His head spun and he was afraid he would slip off the horse. "And you promise that in four days, regardless, you will tell everyone the truth."

"You have my word on it," Percy said. "Hurry on, now. Go!"

With a slap on Steed's gray rear, the horse and his new rider were on their way.

And to think, just this morning, all Mason was hoping for was a job. Now he found himself riding a hero's horse and wearing a hero's armor, saddled with a task he hadn't the slightest clue how to accomplish.

He also found as he rode out of the stable that the armor did, in fact, chafe his butt.

The current Salendor residence—a modest one-room shack anchored by two furnaces and with an anvil that acted as a dinner table, complete with a crusty tablecloth—was much smaller than the former one. When she left him, Patricia Salendor insisted that Perlin sell their house, their only mutual possession, so that she could take half the money with her. Perlin found a buyer who thankfully wasn't interested in the attached smithy and didn't at all mind if Perlin and his nephew moved into it. Thus, the new Salendor residence stood on the property of a man named Ferd Forkle, who was often gracious enough to give both Perlin and the young Cowel food when they looked notably desperate—which was almost always.

Cowel Salendor was pitching stones into one of the furnaces—the one that had been cold for six years now—his trunk upended and plumes spilled across the floor. He was muttering to himself about dukes and best friends and betrayals.

He hadn't been able to figure out why he was so angry. At least he was at least certain with whom he was angry, and he knew that the reason had something to do with the decision to go begging for a job. Was it a matter of pride? It couldn't be that. Nothing in Cowel's experience told him that pride and work had anything to do with each other. He briefly considered envy but realized how likely that was and immediately stopped considering it. Instead, he had begun thinking up as many reasons as he could *not* to be jealous of Mason Quayle.

Reason number forty-three: that big honking beak of a nose he had.

Reason number forty-four: he got nervous whenever he talked to girls.

Reason forty-five: he had zits on his chin.

There was a knock on the door.

No one ever knocked on the door. The tax collector always looked for Perlin at the tavern. It could be Ferd or one of the Forkle children, though Cowel guessed it was much too late for that. Ultimately, he decided just to yell, "Go away!"

"Cowel, open the door. It's me, Mason."

Aha, Cowel thought, *all the more reason not to open it.* Decidedly settling himself more firmly in place where he sat on the floor, Cowel said, "In that case, go away faster." He pitched again. The stone ricocheted off the stove's iron door, then popped in. Reason number forty-six: Cowel had much better aim.

"Cowel, listen. I've got something to tell you."

"Did you bring any food?"

There was a pause. "Not really."

"What is 'not really'? Can I eat that?"

"No."

"Then shoo."

"But it's important."

Cowel dragged himself to his feet, walked over, and pressed his back against the door. What could be so important that Mason would come over here at night to tell him, given how they had left things? Cowel hadn't planned to even *think* about forgiving him until tomorrow.

"Let me guess. Did the peacock give you a job?"

"The duke?" There was another long pause before Mason's voice, muffled by the door, started up again. "Well, I suppose. Sort of."

Excellent. Cowel could feel his anger rising.

"Does it come with all the perks? Personal transportation, signing bonus? Do you have to dress up?"

"You might say all of those," came the hesitant voice from outside.

"And you just needed someone to brag to, I suppose. Especially seeing as how you are afraid to go home and tell your mother."

"Actually," Mason said, "I'm not supposed to tell anyone. But I need help. So I came to you."

There was something in his voice that broke Cowel's resistance—something plaintive, defeated, maybe even apologetic. He swung the bolt and stepped away from the door.

"Fine. It's unlocked. Come in, your greatness," he said with sarcastic flair, bowing low as the door opened.

Cowel looked up, lost his balance, and dropped to his knees instead.

It was the duke at the door.

"I'm sorry, Your Dukedom—I mean, Ship—I mean, Your Dukeness. I didn't know it was—"

"Cowel, it's me," the duke said, reaching up and removing his helmet to reveal Mason's sweaty face. Cowel cocked his head to the side like an inquisitive puppy. Then, suddenly, he scrambled to his feet as Mason started awkwardly peeling off the duke's armor.

"Why are you wearing the duke's . . . and dressed in his . . ." Then it suddenly dawned on Cowel what had happened. He should have seen it coming. The begging. The rejection. The subsequent rage. He had seen it building in his friend for more than a year now, had just ignored the warning signs. "Whoa. Oh. Oh . . . oh, no, Mason. I can't believe it. You did it, didn't you? You *killed* him." Cowel was walking backwards, arms in front of him, his mouth a giant circle. "You up and did it. After all that talk."

"It's not what you think," Mason began, tearing off the duke's grieves, throwing his gauntlets to the floor, and advancing toward Cowel as he did so, a wild look in his eyes.

"No! I can see it in your eyes. You murdered him. This is duke-icide. He's dead, isn't he?"

"Not dead, just unconscious."

Cowel put his hands over his mouth to muffle a scream, as if knocking the duke unconscious was somehow *worse* than murdering him. Murder seemed implausible, anyway—Cowel could never *really* believe his best friend was capable of that—but unconscious was different.

"You knocked him *out?*"

"Not me, the orcs." Mason pulled the chain-mail shirt over his head, catching it on his ears. He was calming down now, which was good because Cowel was starting to come unglued. "I have his horse outside," Mason began.

"Orcs?"

"Listen, Steed's outside. I need to hide him momentarily. We need to get to the tavern and—"

"You stole the duke's horse?"

"Borrowed, actually. With his permission. Or the permission of his servant, rather. The butler or assistant—the speechwriter, the guy who hired me to save the town. It's very complicated."

"Orcs?" Cowel repeated, stuck on the topic he was least equipped to deal with. He had never seen an orc. "What do they look like?"

"They look like us. Only greener, uglier, and hairier, and they come with axes." Mason had finally finished taking off all the duke's armor and walked over to Cowel, who had backed himself into the opposite corner and was mumbling something about dukes, best friends, betrayals, and axes. Mason put his hands on Cowel's shoulders. "We need to go talk to your uncle. Is he at Flax's?"

"The orcs knocked the duke unconscious, so you and the butler made away with his *horse?*"

"Let's go see your uncle. I'll explain everything on the way."

Mason was turning to leave when Cowel caught his arm and pointed down to the sword still hanging from Mason's belt.

"I know. I kind of like it," Mason said, and pulled on the door.

Mason had finished an abbreviated version of the duke's deception and predicament and Cowel had nearly gotten over his stuttering repetition of the word "orcs" by the time they spied the sign for Flax's. At Mason's request, they were speaking in whispers, but Cowel's voice had a tendency to rise steadily regardless, and he had just been warned for the third time to keep it down.

"Sorry. So let me get this straight. You and I have been sent on a mission by the duke's butler to find enough heroes to repel an imminent marauding horde under the banner of an orc named Bennie who feels he is owed money since uncovering a deal between Darlinger and some other orc who is now dead."

Mason gave him a shrug. "I still can't quite believe it, either."

"That's just stupid."

"I saw them. I'm telling you the truth."

"And Darlinger's really the wussy that we always wished he'd turn out to be?"

"Right. And now we are the ones who have to find real heroes."

"What do we know about heroes?"

"Well, you stick feathers in their helmets and I make up stories about them."

"And that's supposed to make us qualified?"

"No, but we're the only ones who know about it, and we're supposed to keep it that way."

"Then why are we going to go talk to my uncle?"

"Because Percy seems to think he might know where to start looking. After all, he was the best blacksmith in town. Every hero knew him, and he knew every one of them."

"Yeah, like four thousand drinks ago," Cowel muttered as Mason pushed open the pub door more forcefully than usual. Something had changed in Mason in the past hour. Maybe it was the sound the duke's scabbard made as it slapped against his thigh when he walked. Or maybe this is just what happens when the world collapses. You stand up straighter as the pieces fall around you. Somehow Mason felt a little more . . . *stalwart* than he had this morning.

But just a very little.

Behind the counter, Flax was busy chatting up a member of the Damsels in Distress Club, a group of middle-aged women still looking for someone to marry. "Hiya, boys," he said absently, and offered to get them a drink.

"Is my uncle here?"

Flax pointed to one of the booths toward the back, where a man was sprawled out across the table. As Mason passed by the bar's patrons, men and women barely breaking even in life, he smiled meekly, hoping that when the time came, if it came, they would be smart—they'd pack up what they could and leave this town without a second thought. He helped Cowel shake his uncle awake.

"Touch me again and I'll bite your ear off" was his first response.

"Uncle, it's me."

"Doesn't mean you don't have ears."

Eventually, and with the help of a glass of water splashed in his face, they managed to get Perlin Salendor alert and reasonable.

"Mr. Salendor, we need your help. We need to know if you can tell us where we might pick up some heroes." It wasn't quite what he meant. Mason made it sound as if they were just running low on flour. "I mean, do you know where we would *go* to find one?"

Perlin Salendor adjusted to his surroundings with a few blinks and seemed taken aback by the taste of his own tongue. "Only one hero, boys. You all know that. No need for others. Just ain't no need." His eyes drooped and his head lolled around, then snapped back. "No need for armor. No need for marriage. No fancy house. One town, one room, one duke, no woman, three mugs of ale . . . well, six mugs, really, and two boys. That's what we got. That's all we need." He put an arm around each of the young men on either side of him. "And another drink—whaddya say?"

"Not now, Uncle."

"Besides the duke," Mason asked, "do you know of any *other* heroes who live in towns close to here?"

"Aren't too many towns close to here. Who would live close to *here?* There are some villages. No heroes there, either. The duke's taken care of it all. Protection tax. YouknowwhatI'm talkin'bout."

"But if we *needed* one," Cowel began.

"Or six," Mason interjected.

"Where would we start looking?"

"Don't bother" was Perlin's curt reply, followed shortly by a song, half slurred, half hummed.

"Forget it," Mason said. "He's smashed. We need to talk to someone else."

"Yeah, but who? Nobody around here wants to remember anything."

"Now, there used to be heroes, of course, fine heroes. All over the place," Perlin said suddenly, staring at no one in particular, interrupting his own singing as if his memory had just goosed him. "Need a lot of armor, heroes. Good for business. Good for ale. More armor. More ale. More ale, happier Perlin."

"Let's go," Mason said, not sure where he thought they would actually go.

Perlin continued. "People you could admire. Cassius Cold-hammer. Falco Freelancer. Roland Warbringer . . ."

As the names from Hero's Alley dribbled from Perlin's lips in slurred syllables, Mason stopped tugging on Cowel's arm and slid back into his seat to listen. "Grendel Grindax. Course, he's not here anymore. Going out for a walk, he said, and just never came back. Amelia Morehacker disappeared. And Stalworth's dead, the last I heard, though no one from Darlington was invited to the funeral. Nope. All rumors. Only person who ever wrote to tell me where he was was old Brendlor."

"Brendlor?" Cowel asked.

"Brendlor Bowbreaker?" Mason clarified.

"Last I heard, the Breaker was settled in Riscine. Wrote to

me for a ceremonial sword to be made as a gift for his son on his wedding day. Last piece I ever made. Last hero I ever saw."

"That had to have been at least four years ago," Cowel said to Mason.

"At *least* four years. Still, Riscine's not too far from here," Mason said, getting hopeful for the first time. "Brendlor Bowbreaker was one of the greatest."

"Yeah, *was*. But there's no telling what he does now. Probably dead."

"It's something. And unless you have any better leads . . . or unless you think *he* does . . ." Mason nodded toward Perlin, who had taken a swallow of air from his empty cup. He looked at it like one who has been betrayed and then settled into humming the second verse of his song, his eyes rolling back into his head.

"I think he's done."

"Deep-fried," Mason said.

"We should get him home. I want to leave him a note."

"No. You can't. We don't want a panic."

"Oh, I'm *way* past panic, Mason. Besides, I won't give any details—I'll just tell him that he should leave town in a few days and stay away a week or so. I'm assuming you've already told your mom the same thing."

But Mason hadn't talked to his mother yet. He had no idea what to tell her.

"All right. You help your uncle. Leave him a note. I'm going to gather a few supplies. Food. Water. What else?"

"A miracle . . . and maybe a crossbow."

"Percy told me to be frugal."

"Just the miracle, then."

"I'll see what I can do. I'll meet you back at your place in an hour. Don't pester the horse."

Cowel shook his uncle by the cheeks, enough to keep him semiconscious, and pulled him from the bench. "Will it really take that long?"

Mason frowned. "I have to at least tell her goodbye."

As it turned out, Flax had all of the provisions they needed—two loaves of bread, a few apples, a hunk of ham, and three flagons full of water—certainly more than enough for a road trip to Riscine.

It was a cold walk home. The wind had picked up and the clouds shrouded the moon. The few burning torches cast Mason's shadow, much bigger than he could ever be, against the walls of empty buildings, mocking his bobbing walk. When he approached his door, he could see through the window his mother stretched out by the fireplace, book in hand as usual. Mason was afraid that the moment he entered he would lose the strength to ever walk out again.

Dierdra Quayle smiled at him from over her book. "It's late." There was no accusation in her voice, only concern, which quickly faded to humor. "You left early in the morning dressed all nice and fancy and now come back looking disheveled and lost—if I had to guess, I'd say there was a girl involved."

"Actually, I went to see about a job."

Dierdra's smile fell. "But you have a job."

"This one's a lot better." He wanted to tell her to sit down, but she was already sitting. "It's an important job," he said. "And it pays well. A bag full of gold up front. Here." He took the coin purse out from underneath his tunic and counted out five gold pieces. He had made up his mind to give her some of it, despite what Percy might have intended.

His mother looked at the coins in Mason's hands as if they were things he had dug up from the yard. "Would you like some soup? I made some earlier this evening."

She started to get up, but he put one hand on her knee and set the gold into the folds of her dress. She looked suddenly very lost; her face flushed white against hazel eyes deep with sadness. She took Mason's hand.

"So when will you be back?" she asked.

"Back?"

"Mason. The last time a man walked through that door with a heavy burlap sack in his hand telling me he had something to do, I knew. He had this look, like a child who suddenly forgets what street he lives on. You have his eyes."

"Ma, you have to understand . . ." But he didn't really know how to finish the thought. He had never told his mother she *had* to do anything.

Dierdra Quayle gathered the coins from her dress and stacked them neatly on the table. "Of course. I knew this was going to happen. That's why I tried not to hang on too tight . . . It's part of your nature."

"It's a one-time-only deal. I just have to go pick something up, bring it back to town, and then I'm done. It will only take me three days—four at the outside. Then everything will be better."

Dierdra Quayle nodded, frowning. "Your father said the same thing. He told me not to worry. Told me that they were going to make things right. Just to keep reading his books. Which reminds me." Before he could stop her, Dierdra Quayle was up and rummaging through a trunk while Mason sat with his chin in his hands, wondering how to convince her that he would be coming back.

"Here," she said, holding out a worn leather-bound journal with thin, brittle pages. "He would want you to have this."

The book was heavy. The cover identified it as *Quayle's Guide to Adventures for the Unadventurous*. The feel of it in his hands made Mason inexplicably sick to his stomach. "He *wrote* this?"

"He never finished it," she said as Mason flipped through the pages, noticing that the last third of them were blank. "Though I don't know what else he intended to put in there. He always called it his work in progress."

"What is it?"

"It's practical, he always said, unlike the stuff that bards write. I admit, *I* never found much use for it, but maybe you will know what to make of it on your trip."

Mason looked at the book, wondering when his hero of a father had found the time to write it, wondering how he could possibly have known that Mason would ever want or need such a thing, wondering if he was even a decent writer—or worse, a better writer than Mason. "It's not an adventure," Mason said, trying to reassure his mother, rubbing his hand along the book's spine, keeping his voice steady. "I won't be gone long."

"Just because we leave with one intention doesn't mean others can't get the better of us." The long pause that followed made Mason itch inside. He didn't know what to say.

"Are you going alone?"

"No. Cowel's coming with me."

"Cowel." She said it with a sigh, as if it were a foregone conclusion. "Well, you do me a favor and give Cowel a message for me."

Mason noticed her hands were shaking, but Dierdra embraced her son and whispered in his ear. "Tell him to come back."

"We're both coming back," Mason said instantly, but Dierdra Quayle just nodded and smiled. "Listen, there's one other thing. And it's really important, so I want you to trust me." He wondered if he wasn't asking too much already. "In three days, if you haven't heard anything from me, I want you to use whatever gold you have left and buy safe passage to the town of Riscine. It's less than a day east of here."

Dierdra shook her head. "Someone needs to stay here, Mason. Everyone can't leave."

"You don't have to stay there long. A few days." Mason walked backwards toward the door. "It's where I will find you," he added finally, hoping that would be enough to convince her.

Mason's mother nodded curtly, then simply nodded again when he asked her to promise.

"All right. Okay. I've got to go. But I'm coming back. I swear."

Standing there at the door, Mason could see his mother struggle for something to say. To be safe. To not go. To find another way. But she had said all of those things once in her life already. So, this time, she just sat down in the doorway and watched him disappear.

"You're late."

"I know." Mason set down his sack and turned to see Cowel admiring himself in the window. He was wearing all of Duke Darlinger's armor. "You look ridiculous."

"So did you."

"Yes, but I wasn't wearing the shirt backwards." Mason

stacked four gold pieces on the anvil-shaped table. "This is for your uncle." He looked toward the rope hammocks the Salendors slept in. "How is he?"

"Passed out. I didn't want to wake him. The only time he ever smiles is when he's sleeping. I left him a note, but don't worry, I was scant on details. I just hope he doesn't blow the gold on bottles before the week is out."

"You should maybe put *that* in the note."

"I did."

"But you didn't know I was going to give you any gold."

"Or maybe I know you well enough to have known."

Mason flushed, a little embarrassed that Cowel was right again. "The grieves are supposed to face forward, not sideways."

"Even when you're riding a horse?"

Mason nodded.

"Makes more sense sideways."

"Doesn't matter. We aren't taking the armor. The poor horse has enough to carry between the two of us."

"But we *are* taking the sword?" Cowel asked, pointing to the glittering hilt and scabbard still attached to Mason's side. He had taken the sword off outside the door of his house—no sense in alarming his mother even more—but had strapped it back on the moment he left.

"I like the sword."

"And I like the armor. Especially the helmet. This is the finest plume I think I've ever seen. The duke has good taste."

Mason noticed Cowel was smiling for the first time in a while. It was a strange sight. "When I left you an hour ago, you looked as though the world was to end. Now, you're playing dress-up and grinning like an idiot."

"Yeah, well, all day, I was thinking I'd be alone, that you

wouldn't need me anymore. Now, I'm on a quest to save the town, riding the horse of a hero—or a pretend one, at least—wearing his helmet, and finally leaving this godforsaken town. It just might be the best day of my life."

"It's a terrible burden. The lives of a thousand innocent people rest on our shoulders."

"No. They rest on *your* shoulders. I'm just here to keep you company. So, can I take the helmet?"

"Sure."

"Thanks, Mason."

"It's okay. It's just a helmet."

"No, really, I mean it. You didn't have to ask me to come with you."

They headed out the door. Cowel paused, took the helmet off, put it back on, took it off, then finally just threw it into the corner with the rest of Darlinger's armor.

"It pinches my ears," he said, picking up his dirty yellow cap instead.

Steed was waiting for them outside.

"He's a beautiful horse."

"Let's hope he doesn't mind having two riders."

It turned out that Percy was right about the horse: he didn't mind much of anything, only jerked a bit when Mason pulled Cowel up behind him.

"So what did your mother say when you told her you were leaving?"

Mason guided Steed out around the smithy, past the former Salendor house, and toward the north gates of Darlington, formerly Highsmith—once the home of a hundred heroes, now home to none.

"She said I have my father's eyes."

— 3 —

If the Boot Fits

hapter two, 'Everything You Ever Wanted to Know About Heroes but Were Too Awed to Ask.'"

"That sounds useful."

"It's mostly about SHB."

"SHB?"

"Standard Hero Behavior."

"At least we'll know what to look for."

Cowel was sitting in back with *Quayle's Guide to Adventures for the Unadventurous*. Mason was at the mane. So far, their adventure had been filled with nothing but conversation, and much of that had been Cowel's doing. "There *are* some hypothetical situations."

"Like your-princess-has-just-been-kidnapped-by-a-fairy kinds of things?"

"Fairies aren't listed under common kidnapping suspects. Probably hard to hide a princess in a fairyland, anyways." Cowel was angling the book toward the moonlight, squinting to read in the darkness.

They had been riding for four hours, but they were still a ways from either sunlight or, it appeared, civilization. Having never left Darlington, Mason didn't realize how far away everything else was. The first grand adventure of his life consisted so far of shifting in Steed's saddle so as to spread the soreness equally to both butt cheeks and listening to Cowel—something he could have done anywhere. They had only his father's book to keep them awake.

"So how should we act, then—you know, in dangerous situations?" Mason asked.

"*We* should hide. But a *hero* should be chivalrous, valiant, honest, stalwart, nimble, stealthy, deadly. . . . The list goes on for, like, two pages." Mason could hear Cowel flipping through the book behind him. "Sexy, svelte, generous, suave, dashing, daring, dexterous . . ."

Cowel plodded through the list. Steed plodded along the deserted road, apparently used to taking his time. Mason had done most everything he could to encourage the gray striped horse to go faster, short of thwacking him with a stick. He supposed he could poke him with the hilt of Darlinger's sword, but that seemed cruel. The horse, like the sword, was only on loan, after all.

"Is that all there is—just a list of adjectives?"

"There's also a quiz."

"A quiz?"

"'Is Your Hero a Dud or a Stud? Take This Easy Quiz and Find Out.' I have to admit, your father had a great sense of humor. I never knew that about him."

"Yeah. Mom always said that." At least, she often laughed at her memories of him. Mason would come home and find her in tears from laughing so hard. She never told him what was so funny, and he never asked. They were her memories, and he never felt entitled to share them. "I'm surprised he actually had the time to write the book," Mason said.

"I suppose you have to find something to do while sitting on a horse."

Mason figured that made sense. After all, you never got to read about what the heroes did when they weren't slaying monsters or saving royalty. There were no great poems about heroes taking a leak or enjoying a long nap or brushing their teeth and washing out their underwear. "So take the quiz," Mason said, perhaps a little impatiently. Talking about his father made him even more uncomfortable now that he himself was on a horse headed to who-only-knows-where. Now that he also had told his mother that he'd be back.

"'Question one. It's a steamy Friday night and there's a sense of adventure in the air. You are A) out at the pub polishing off a tankard with some friends. B) at home in front of the fire playing footsie-ticklies with your spouse. Or C) deep underneath the earth in the cavernous lair of a giant man-eating spider, having just sucked the venom out of your own butt where it stung you.'"

"Disgusting."

"I'm just reading what it says."

"How do you suck venom out of your own butt?"

"It certainly *sounds* heroic."

"And impossible."

"So at the pub, then?"

"At the pub," Mason confirmed. Footsie-ticklies didn't sound all that bad, either, but he couldn't begin to imagine himself married.

"How about this one: 'You are battling a horde of marauders who have overrun your castle, killed all of your guards, cut off one of your arms, and outnumber you ten to one. Do you A) plead for mercy, hoping in your pitiful state the marauders will simply take all of your gold and leave? B) dive out of the near-est window, hoping to land in the moat and swim to safety before you bleed to death? Or C) brandish your own severed arm as a weapon, say, "You'll have to do better than that, you scummy ragabouts," and charge your enemy, fighting to the death?'"

Mason thought about it for a moment. He could picture himself saying the phrase "scummy ragabouts," but that was about it. Steed bobbed his head as Mason answered honestly. "Definitely A."

"Me, too."

"I mean, with only one arm, we'd end up drowning in that moat."

"Agreed."

"Ask another."

"All right. 'You are working your way through a dungeon, searching for a reputed DID who has been captured by an evil wizard—'"

"DID?"

"Damsel in distress. Didn't you pay any attention to the list of key terms I read you an hour ago?"

"Sorry."

"All right. So, you are working your way through this dun-geon 'when you come across a drop-dead gorgeous witch beg-ging for a kiss. Do you A) just kiss her already—life is short, damsels are meant to be in distress, and there's no way you were tackling an evil wizard, anyway? B) go running back in the opposite direction like a screaming ninny? Or C) decapi-tate the foul temptress, knowing that she was looking only to turn you into a frog and chew on your legs?'"

Mason said C at first, but he couldn't hold to it when Cowel pressed him further—though he didn't much like the phrase "screaming ninny." After three more questions, Cowel flipped to the scoring table to see where they ranked.

"'Whatever you do, do not go hunting dragons,'" Cowel read. "'You prefer to spend your time dreaming and listening to others' adventures, and though you may long for the hero's life, you simply aren't cut out for it. Your friendly attitude and desire to do what's right probably means people buy you mugs at the local watering holes, but that won't do you any good against a rampaging troll.'" Suddenly, Cowel snorted out a half-choked-off laugh. "Get this—it says you should consider becoming a bard."

Mason turned around in the saddle. "Does it really say that?"

Cowel laughed as he read. "'If the pull of adventure is too great, consider becoming a bard. The pay's not as good, and some heroes may not respect you, but you still get to ride along.' Your father had you pegged, and he wrote this when you were only a little kid."

"My father had no idea who I would turn out to be," Mason said sourly. "Maybe that's enough reading for now."

Cowel didn't respond—he just closed the book. They passed by a few patches of trees—nothing dense, barely enough to qualify as woods. Some adventure. Mason's eyes hurt from straining to see in the dark.

"I think we're lost," Cowel said.

"We are not lost."

"Your saying so doesn't make us any less lost."

"How can we be lost? There was only one road. We are still on it. Flax said to go east until we run into a town. How hard can it be?"

"We've been riding for half a day, at least."

"The sun hasn't even risen yet."

"You know, we're probably going to die out here." Cowel's sudden and morbid attempt at prophesy had the desired effect of getting Mason's full attention. "I'm just saying, if it's only Darlinger's gold that's protecting us out here, and Darlinger's out of gold . . ."

"Thanks for pointing that out."

"I'm sure you thought about it, too."

Actually, Mason hadn't. He had had a hard enough time just puzzling through how he had gotten here to begin with.

"What happens if this Bowbreaker guy turns us down?"

"Then we ask him if he knows someone who won't turn us down."

"And if he doesn't?"

"He will. He'll have to. He was a hero. Heroes know other heroes. They mingle. Everyone mixes with his own kind."

"Oh, yeah?" Cowel said, leaning backwards and stretching out his arms. "How many other bards do you know?"

This trapped Mason. "There have to be some heroes around here somewhere."

Cowel shook his head. "According to your father's guide, only one of every hundred people gets to be a hero. And only one of every hundred of *them* becomes famous for it."

"That could make it pretty tough to find a dozen."

"Could make it tough to find *one*," Cowel said as the road started to curve northward. "Though your dad does offer some suggestions." He opened the book again. "'If you are looking to groom a hero yourself, look for orphans or pig-sloppers. Usually boys, but girls with a rugged beauty and a sense of entitlement work just as well. The best bet is a boy orphan pig-slopper with a mysterious past, a birthmark of some kind, and a sense of entitlement.' That doesn't sound too hard, you know? I mean,

I could slop pigs," Cowel commented. "And I'm an orphan. No birthmark, though."

"I thought you weren't going to read any more."

Cowel ignored him. "How about this: 'Top Ten Most Heroic Acts, or How Best to Win the Hearts of Thousands. Number ten: Single-Handedly Defend a Keep from a Clan of Club-Brandishing Barbarians. Number nine: Jump Off a Cliff into a Seething Vortex, All the While Firing Arrows at a Posse of Circling Harpies. Number eight . . .'"

Listening to his father's words made Mason feel as if he had never known anything about the man.

By the time the village revealed itself, Cowel had read all of chapters two and three and most of chapter four: "Know Thy Enemy—The Difference Between an Orc and an Ogre," including a section on identification by smell that was awfully detailed. The sun had risen, and Mason was exhausted, hungry, and ready to be off the horse. The sighs of relief from him and Cowel as they looked down upon a cluster of houses that made up the village of Riscine were echoed by a grunt from Steed, who was used to only one rider and frequent stops.

"Let's just hope he still lives here," Mason said.

"And that he's as bored as I am," Cowel added.

They could be found everywhere, these tiny towns where people eked out lives that mattered only to them. The folk who lived in Riscine prided themselves on being content and humble, fashioning lives free from the rigors of adventure and the burden of excitement. Any battles the town bore witness to were usually among children armed with sticks, or between husbands and wives armed with accusations, along with the occasional challenge to see who could eat the most sausages before throwing up. Protected from any outside danger more because they had nothing to offer than because some duke had made a few deals, their imaginations were well trimmed, which led to their lack of interest in the rest of the world and vice versa.

In short, it was the most unlikely place you would go to find a hero, especially one like Brendlor Bowbreaker. Brendlor was one of the greats—or so the songs that were sung about him claimed. Of course, if he *had* moved to this small village cut off from all adventure, odds were he wasn't interested in orc bashing anymore.

"If he's here, it shouldn't be too hard to find him. It looks like the town's made up of six or seven people," Cowel said as they passed Riscine's welcome sign. In a town of this size, there was no way someone of Brendlor Bowbreaker's stature could stay hidden. It was just a matter of asking the first person they saw.

"Brendlor who?"

"Bow-Break-Er. He's about six foot two. *Very* muscular. Shaggy red beard. Gruff voice. Carries an ax? You must know him."

"He might not carry an ax anymore," Mason offered.

The old woman stared up at the two young men leaning down from their horse.

"Brendlor Bowlegger?"

"Breaker. As in bones—you know, breaky-breaky." Cowel snapped imaginary bones in the air with his hands. "Forget it. Do you know where the local tavern is?"

But the old woman just shook her head. "You boys are too young to be drinking," she muttered, and then turned her back on them.

"Let me choose who we ask next time," Cowel said, and pointed to a fruit stand. The fruit seller had no idea whom they were talking about, either, but he did convince them to buy a couple of pears. The town was just stirring, and its only street was starting to hum. Mason led Steed to a clearing where the horse could find his own breakfast. The two friends sat in the grass as the sun climbed a ladder of clouds, Mason carving slices of pear with Cowel's knife.

"I think your uncle was out of his mind."

"I don't doubt it."

"I mean, if you were Brendlor Bowbreaker—I mean, *the* Brendlor Bowbreaker, the guy who strangled a gorgon with one of her own snakes—then is this really the kind of place where you'd go to look for work?"

"Did he really do that? The snake thing?"

"That's what they say," Mason answered. But he also knew "they" said a lot of things. He looked around the town square, which was starting to fill as people gathered at the community wells, probably having the same conversations they had every morning. It looked peaceful. Cared for. Maybe *just* the place someone like Brendlor Bowbreaker would want to escape to.

When they had pared their pears down to stems and seeds, they resumed their hunt. A few people had heard the name, but no one could even so much as remember him visiting their town. "I think we'd know it if someone like that lived here, don't you?" said one young man.

Cowel said that was his point exactly.

"Does this town have *any* heroes?" Mason asked.

"The mayor was in a war once," an elderly farmer told them.

"Excellent."

"Fifty years ago."

When they had milked the town square of information, they were left with the names of a seventy-year-old mayor, an insane woman who lived five miles outside of town and claimed she was the reincarnation of a famous general, a thirteen-year-old boy who was the town's archery champion two years running, and a shoe salesman who wasn't any kind of hero but supposedly knew something about them and would occasionally spend his evenings at the tavern making up stories that sounded daring enough.

Mason didn't like their prospects. Percy had been clear about the qualifications. No one too old or too young. He hadn't said anything about insane or reincarnated, but Mason felt he could safely rule out the woman.

That left the shoe salesman. Maybe Brendlor Bowbreaker had bought himself a new pair when he rode through long ago—if he *ever* rode through.

Breckenridge's Boot Outlet and Apparel stood far down the road, linked by a garden to a two-story house. The shop was framed with lilac trees, and the smell reminded Mason of his mother. A large field lay behind the house, and Mason thought he could hear the sound of kids screaming and laughing.

"Successful boot salesman," Cowel said as they walked up to the door. A sign read LORN BRECKENRIDGE, PROPRIETOR, and another read THE BEST BOOTS IN ALL OF RISCINE BECAUSE THEY'RE THE ONLY BOOTS IN ALL OF RISCINE. "Another monopoly," he added, thinking of the duke.

A bell rang when they opened the door, but there was no one inside to hear it. The shop was lined with shelves, the shelves lined with boots—different styles and sizes, but all boots. In the middle of the store, a couple of squat tables were topped with folded tunics, mostly cloth and some leather, IN A VARIETY OF FALL FASHIONS, as the sign above them claimed.

"I guess they don't worry too much about stealing around here," Mason said, hands in pockets.

"No point," Cowel said excitedly. "Do you see how cheap these boots are? Seven coppers *a pair*. Plus, it says buy one, get the second half off. They're a steal already." Mason went to the counter, hoping that the owner was sleeping behind it, while Cowel started taking the frayed strips of leather he called shoes off the puffy pink hams he called feet.

"We aren't buying anything," Mason warned, glaring at Cowel over his shoulder.

"That's a shame," came a third voice. Mason turned around, startled. Cowel dropped the boots he was admiring. The man who had come through the door behind the counter stood a little over six feet tall, skinny and clean-shaven. In one hand was a wooden box, in the other a half-eaten apple, which he promptly set down on the counter so he could shake Mason's hand. His hair was blond, Mason noticed with disappointment. Brendlor Bowbreaker had fiery red hair—the color of a volcano's howl, as the Anonymous Warrior Poet of Highsmith had once called it.

"Welcome to Lorn's Boots," the man said, mashing Mason's fingers. "Can't say as I've seen you around here before, but if you need some footwear—and it looks like you do—this is definitely the place to be."

"Actually," Mason said, "we were hoping for some information."

"*And* some boots," Cowel interjected.

Lorn Breckenridge gave Mason a suspicious stare mismatched with a smile. "Not sure what information I can give you." Then he spoke over Mason's shoulder to Cowel, who had just slid his foot into a Breckenridge Series Seven and was groaning with pleasure. "That's a one hundred percent deerskin upper with a fur-lined insole. The padding you feel is synthetic, but it's basically derived from pigs' fat. They're rain-proof, too."

"They're incredible," Cowel said, succumbing instantly to the salesman's spiel even though he gave his own version of it at least twenty times a day to no effect.

"Buy a pair, get a second pair half off," Lorn Breckenridge said, winking.

Cowel winked back.

"We wanted to know," Mason interrupted, "if you've ever heard of a man named Brendlor Bowbreaker."

The salesman stopped looking at Cowel and turned instead to stare directly at Mason.

"I knew a man once by that name," Lorn Breckenridge said, taking a bite of his apple and talking through the chunks, "but this was a while back."

"Was he a friend of yours?" Cowel asked.

"Something like that."

Mason smiled. They had a lead. "Do you know where we could find him?" Mason asked. "It's very important."

Lorn Breckenridge took a few steps and then sat on the edge of one of his tables, twisting his apple by its stem. "I couldn't tell you where he is—only that you won't find him. He's gone."

"Gone?" Mason repeated.

"Dead, in fact."

"Dead?" Cowel repeated.

"Sure enough. Dead. Been dead a while. Why do you want to find him so bad, anyway?"

"We need his help—or *needed*, I guess. Our town, Darlington, is in danger. The duke, Dirk Darlinger—you might have heard of him—he's put us in kind of a fix."

"We have five days," Cowel added.

As Mason recited the essentials of the story in a speech he had revised a hundred times on the way to Riscine, he looked at his hands and so didn't catch the shop-owner's sneer at every mention of the duke's name. He told the story with only a little embellishment. It was fantastic enough as is.

"We were hoping that you would know where we could find some help."

Lorn Breckenridge looked to Cowel as if to corroborate everything Mason had said. Cowel, new boots still untied on his feet, just nodded. Lorn bowed his head and sighed deeply. "Well, as I told you, Bowbreaker's dead."

"You know this for a fact?" Mason prodded.

"Of course I know it. I'm the one who killed him."

Mason's eyebrows shot skyward. He took two steps back, nearly tripping over a wooden foot measurer on the floor. He forgot he was carrying Darlinger's sword or he might have at least put a hand on it. Cowel started hurriedly kicking off the new boots.

"Well, not *killed* him, really. But I'm the reason he's not around anymore. And I can tell you that he's not coming back." Lorn's voice had deepened to a low rumble, then crumbled into another heavy sigh. "Now, unless you two plan to buy some boots, I have a lot of work to do." He started to walk to the door behind the counter when Mason's hand stopped him.

"Please, Mr. Breckenridge. You have to know someone."

"Heck," Cowel said, coming up behind them barefoot, "if you really did kill him, then maybe *you're* the kind of guy we need."

"Believe me, boys," Lorn said, facing them, "I sympathize. I really do. I know a thing or two about your town, but I can assure you that even if he *were* alive, Brendlor Bowbreaker would be no good to you anymore."

But there was something in his voice, or maybe it was in his eyes. It was enough to betray him, and Mason caught it. "Mr.

Bowbreaker?" he said tentatively, as if he were asking a shy little boy to come out of his closet.

Lorn the boot salesman looked at Mason, and for a moment, Mason was sure his neck was about to be snapped for this discovery—but then the man smiled.

"What are your names?" he asked.

"C-Cowel Salendor," Cowel stammered.

"Mason. Mason Quayle."

Lorn Breckenridge seemed to chew on the name. "Quayle. Yeah. I suppose that makes sense. Let me get you two something to drink." Then the man formerly known as Brendlor Bowbreaker retreated through the back door, leaving the two young men stunned silent.

When he returned with a pot and three mugs, the furious whispering between Mason and Cowel stopped. Lorn Breckenridge looked a lot older than he had only minutes before. His shoulders slouched, and his face was a collage of dark pockets from mouth to eyes. "It's just tea," he said, pouring three steaming cups. "I thought it was still too early in the morning for anything stronger."

"Thank you," Mason said. Cowel tried closing his mouth.

"So Darlinger's a phony. I knew it was impossible to do what he did. He'd accomplish in one day what it'd take a dozen of us a week to do."

"You're really *the* Brendlor Bowbreaker?" Cowel asked.

"I'm actually surprised that you didn't recognize me sooner," he said to Mason. "Your father knew all of us pretty well. I would have thought he'd have said something about me."

"The hair?" Mason asked, pointing to the sandy locks.

Lorn nodded. "Naturally blond. I used to dye it red. I thought it was more in keeping with the character. Someone named Brendlor Bowbreaker couldn't go around with blond hair. That's more of a color for a Perseleus or a Pitt. It's all about the image."

"I've seen drawings of you in some of my books. You've lost weight."

"I don't drink as much. Not as many free mutton chops. But I feel better. This place has been good for me."

"It appears so," Mason said, nodding toward the house.

"When I realized there was no future in being a hero any-more—at least, not in Highsmith—I took what I had saved and bought this house. Eventually, I found that I was pretty good at cobbling, and before you knew it, I had a business. I had most everything I needed already. *Most* of the hundred from the Alley did the same. Took what they had and left—abandoned the whole hero business altogether."

"Why change your name, though? Wouldn't boots by Brendlor Bowbreaker sell better?"

"Yeah. Couldn't you stencil an image of yourself on the side of the boots or something—you know, holding your ax, like this?" Cowel struck a pose of a hero in midstride, imaginary ax held high above him, face set in a serious sneer. He looked idiotic, but Mason didn't say so out loud. "You could call them 'Ax Bowbreakers.' They'd make a fortune."

"You're a salesman, aren't you?" Lorn asked, and got a pleased smile in return. "The truth is, Lorn Breckenridge *is* my name. Brendlor's just what I made up for the bards."

"The alliteration," Mason whispered.

"And no one here knows?" Cowel asked.

"It's a quiet town. It would make them nervous. Besides, they'd treat me differently. I was tired of the hero thing. The long hours. The saddle sores. The scratches, the autographs, the horse manure—waking up cold and wet in the middle of the night, with a lunatic leprechaun sitting on your chest holding a dagger at your throat, demanding that you help him get taller."

"You met a leprechaun? Was there any gold?"

"It's a myth," Lorn said. "They're gold crazy, I'll give you that, but they're mostly just scoundrels. Don't pick one up by the ears, though. They hate that."

"So you gave it all up," Mason said.

"I settled down, raised my kids. It's not so bad."

"But you still know how to swing the old ax, right? I mean . . . if you had to . . ." Mason trailed off hopefully.

But Lorn just snorted, spilling some of his tea down the front of his shirt. "Hardly. Do you hear those screams from out back? Those are *grand*children. I'm fifty years old."

"But you're *the* Brendlor Bowbreaker. You were a hero in Highsmith for twenty years."

Lorn stretched the wrinkles on his forehead. "Yes, but my left knee is practically shot. My right elbow doesn't work when it's raining, and I can't really see without my spectacles— which I don't wear because I think they make me look silly. Does that sound like the kind of person you want defending your town?"

"It was once your town, too."

"I know, but look at me."

"But if you *had* to. I mean, if it was a matter of life or death," Mason prodded. "You could fight."

"If I had to? I don't know . . . Maybe. But I told you boys— Brendlor's gone, and nothing you can say will bring him back. Heroes don't last forever."

"But the town," Mason pleaded. "You can't just abandon it."

Lorn looked pained at the suggestion. "And I don't want to. If it were a situation where a massive shoe shortage threatened to leave the entire town barefoot through the winter, I would work till my fingers bled. But protect the whole city? Me? Not anymore. But you of all people," he said to Mason, "should know someone better able to help than me."

Mason's look indicated he had no idea who the man was talking about.

Lorn seemed almost ashamed to say it. "Your father, I mean."

"My father?" Mason tried not to raise his voice. "No one has heard from my father in nearly ten years. He left town before you did and never came back."

Lorn frowned. "Sorry, son. It was a stupid thing to say. I should have guessed—else *he* would be here talking to me rather than you. You have to understand—word doesn't get around much here. It's a quiet town. Keeps to itself. But there must be some of them still around."

"Some of *them?*" Mason asked.

"I mean, if you could follow the path your father took, you might find what you're looking for."

"But I don't *know* what path he took. I don't know that he took *any* path. For all I know, he leapt off a cliff. To hear my mother tell it, he's off flying on the backs of dragons somewhere." Mason noticed that Lorn was smiling at the last image—as if it fit perfectly with his own idea of Mason's father . . . or didn't fit at all.

"He could actually talk to them, you know. Dragons, that is. At least, he said he could."

This was news to Mason. But it didn't surprise him to be finding out about it now. Like the people here in Riscine, the people in Darlington kept to themselves. They didn't talk much about his father—not to him, anyway. "I don't even remember him saying goodbye."

"Your father was only doing what he thought was best at the time." Lorn picked up his mug. "That's why he had to go."

"But go *where?*"

Lorn set the mug back down again. "You mean your mother never told you where he went?"

"She's told me a hundred different things. The story changes every time I ask her."

There were a lot of stories. Mason was pretty sure his mother got the real stories about his father mixed up with all the ones about other heroes she had read. At some point, Mason had stopped trying to figure out what was true and what was make-believe.

"Maybe he didn't tell her," Lorn suggested. "Had she known, she might have been able to stop him. He was the only one of the ten tied down—that is, the only one with a family."

"The ten?" Cowel asked.

"The ten who left Highsmith together. One last adventure. Had Dierdra known what he was planning, she would have told him how foolish he was. How stupid and selfish. She would have told him the same things my wife told me when I said I was thinking about going with them."

"So you know where my father went?"

"No. I don't know *where* he went—not exactly, anyway— but I do know *what* he went after."

It seemed as if Lorn was waiting for Mason to speak, but Mason didn't know what to say. Instead, he nodded, giving the former hero the permission he needed to tell the story that no one else had bothered to share.

"A dream," Lorn said, and then finally managed to take a sip of his tea without being interrupted. "There was a whole group of them. Some of the Alley's finest: Roland Warbringer and Brax Balenfoe. Devon Bladedancer. Falgony, Cassius,

Morlin. It was their last great quest. They knew that if they could pull it off, they would have enough gold to make even the duke jealous—maybe buy him off and send him packing, not that he needed more money."

Mason snorted. "Oh, he could use it now."

"But it wasn't just the money or the thought of kicking the duke out. Their pride was at stake. And their legacy. Otherwise, they wouldn't have chased after something so . . . impossible."

"Treasure?" Cowel asked.

"Not just treasure. *Fabled* treasure. The best and worst kind imaginable." Then Lorn said the name "Snowbeard," whispering it as if casting a magic spell.

"Snow what?"

Lorn turned to Cowel. "Snowbeard. The pirate. But you could have guessed that by the name, no doubt. All famous pirates are named after their beards. Blackbeard, Bluebeard, Flamebeard, Bushbeard, Trimbeard. It's a tradition."

"I've heard about him before," Mason said, remembering some of the stories his father used to tell him before bed every night.

"He wasn't ruthless the way you think of most pirates as ruthless," Lorn said, "but he wasn't too picky about whom he stole from, either. He wasn't one of your noble, rob-from-the-rich types. He'd steal the chicken leg off his mother's plate. He amassed *lots* of gold, more than his ship could hold. He never lost a battle—and as his reputation grew, it often became easier to simply hand over whatever you had the moment his ship came into sight."

"It's said that he cruised the shores of the five lands until the color of his crew's hair matched the color of his own beard," Mason said, remembering bits and pieces. "Then he did what all pirates did."

"He buried his gold?" Cowel guessed.

"Pirates don't bury treasure unless they have to," Lorn said. "No, he started spending it. Lots of it. On whatever. He was greedy, blowing it all on himself. His men grew mutinous. They made a deal with the authorities to be in a certain cove at a certain hour. They promised that the gunpowder for the ship's cannons would be wet. They promised that their swords would be dull and that most of them would simply jump overboard at the first sign of trouble. They also promised that they would show up later to get some of the gold that would be 'accidentally' unconfiscated when Snowbeard was captured."

"They sold him out," Cowel whispered.

"But he wasn't captured," Mason said, smiling at a memory of his father leaning over the bed with a twinkle in his eyes.

"No. He wasn't captured," Lorn said. "He found out about the revolt. He hired a group of thieves to steal his own treasure from his own ship three days before he himself was supposed to be ambushed. Then he rigged his ship to explode and paid those same thieves to help him carry the rest of his treasure to the center of the Windmourn Mountains—at least, that's how the story goes—where he planned to build himself a modest three-story cottage, hire thirty or forty bodyguards, and live into his old age comfortably."

"So did he get there?" Cowel looked at Mason, who shrugged his shoulders. He must have been asleep by this part of the story.

"Nobody knows. When the authorities came as promised, Snowbeard's ship was gone. A few weeks later, a hunter came across the remains of a caravan in the Windmourn Mountains, including the remains of six men. No gold, no Snowbeard. Maybe the thieves thought their fee was too small compared to the treasure they were carrying and tried to fight the pirate. But how Snowbeard beat them all and managed to escape with his treasure by himself—wagonloads of it—only adds to the mystery. The hunter himself died searching for the treasure, as have the hundreds, maybe even thousands, who have ventured too deep into the Windmourns looking."

"And that's what my father was after?"

"I told you, it was the worst kind of treasure. And that's the *least* fabled part," Lorn said. "Maybe there was no real treasure, or maybe it sank with the ship, or maybe Snowbeard sank with it. Regardless, the story grew, as stories do, and became much too big for any facts to support it. Even more fantastic than the treasure itself were the stories about what guards it. Hobgoblins, demons, witches, and, of course, the most prevalent myth—that it is hoarded by the oldest dragon in the five lands, with wings as large as houses. Make-believe—it's all they had to go on, and it's why I couldn't go with them. A foolish quest." Lorn Breckenridge took another sip of tea, then noticed the look on Mason's face.

"I don't mean to say your father was a fool. I didn't mean it that way."

Mason didn't flinch. "But he was a fool. He left my mother and me behind for something that doesn't even exist."

"He was impetuous, maybe. But your father had the interests of his family at heart. He—how should I put this—he really *thought* it was real. He believed in it more than any of them. I suppose *that* was the real problem."

Mason nodded and then shook his head, unsure what to think. This was the first time anyone other than his mother had spoken to him directly about his father's leaving. The duke's monopoly and the resulting exodus of heroes was a sore subject for most. Of course, when asked where his father went those many years ago, his mother always answered with something she wanted to be true.

Mason had gotten to the point where he thought *everything* his mother had said about his father was a story. Maybe she thought it was easier for him to remember his father only as a hero—a man of honor and courage—rather than the runaway he turned out to be. Maybe it was just easier for her. But now, hearing this man speak of his father as a farsighted adventurer and a nearsighted dreamer, Mason felt sadness for her still to be watching out the window, waiting.

"I wish I could tell you what happened to them, Mason. Even if it was horrible, I wish I knew. When I moved out of Highsmith a year later, no one had heard a word. It's hard to tell how far they got. I can't imagine a beast that could have bested them—not together, which is why I think maybe they gave up and went their separate ways. It's also why I think that if you head south, you might find an answer."

Lorn got up and straightened a pile of clothes on a table. "There's a town or two along the way where you might find someone who can help you. The Windmourns are full of danger, make-believe dragons aside. Anyone willing to live there knows his way around a sword."

Mason felt a twitching dance its way up his legs and along his spine. There were a thousand other questions, but they were all just another way of asking the same thing. There was a possible answer now, and somehow, that made it worse. He didn't know where to go from here.

Cowel was more practical. "No offense, Mr. Breckenbreaker," he began.

"Breckenridge."

"Right. But we really don't have a lot of time. What we need is a bona fide arse-kicking, head-cracking warrior to come bust up on a band of greedy, good-for-nothing green-faces."

Lorn Breckenridge looked from Mason to Cowel and back again. "I'm not sure you know what you need," the boot-maker said, still looking at Mason. "But if it's just some head-busters you're after, there's someplace else you can go. Just head northeast and follow the road. It's several hours' ride. Either of you boys ever been to the sea?" Cowel shook his head; Mason stared at the floor, lost in thought. "You'll smell it before you see it. The town is called Ancherton, but everybody who lives there just calls it the Hive. No doubt you'll find plenty of brawlers there. The first problem is that you'll have to sober them up. The second is that you'll have to pay them off. How much gold do you have with you?"

"About a hundred pieces," Cowel said.

"That's it, eh? You might be able to pick up a mercenary or two if you haggle with them."

"Mercenaries?" Mason asked.

"What did you expect? If you're looking for nobility and honor, the Hive's not the place to go. Then again, I don't know what would be anymore."

Mason contemplated the path before him. Imagine being able to return to his mother with an answer. Almost ten years and no one had heard from them.

Mason had less than five days. Less than four, given how long it had taken to get to this place and how long it would take to get back. Mason looked at Cowel, who stared back at him urgently, expectantly.

"I can't promise that if you head south, you'll find what you're looking for," Lorn Breckenridge said. "I'm only telling you because I think you should know."

"And you're certain that if we go to this place, this Hive, we will find people who can defend our town?"

"You'll find plenty who *can*, but I'm not sure you'll find any who will. To be honest, the Hive is not really the place for two fresh-faced boys from a town coddled under the duke's protective purse."

"You could come with us," Cowel suggested. "Dye your hair red again. Find a hatchet. Break some bows, or whatever."

Lorn snorted. "Just beyond Riscine, the road splits."

Mason glanced at Cowel, who threw his hands up in the air, as if he thought the answer was obvious and just wasn't at all happy about it. And then, there was a moment—albeit a quick one—when Mason saw something else in the former hero's eyes, like the last glow of an ember before it dies, the final orange cough. But then the eyes clouded over again with comfort, and Brendlor Bowbreaker settled even more firmly into Lorn Breckenridge.

"I can't go with you," he said with a sigh. "But I can make certain that your feet barely touch the road when you walk."

They left moments later, both with a pair of Breckenridge boots caressing their callused feet. The boots squeaked with newness, and Cowel rocked back and forth on his heels. Mason stumbled out of the store, trying to find his footing.

"Pirates. Treasure. Dragons. Your father had a big imagination," Cowel said.

"It's the kind of story people always told their kids. No one ever mentioned it to you?"

"There aren't a whole lot of storytellers in my family, Mason," he said.

Mason could tell that he was thinking something over and was reluctant to say it out loud. "You don't believe it, do you?"

"Do you?" Cowel replied.

Mason shook his head. "It seems far-fetched. But at least

going off in search of a legendary treasure is better than what I always thought happened."

"What did you think happened?"

Mason finished checking the saddlebags. He turned around to see Cowel still admiring his new shoes. "I'm not sure. Different things. It would be easier if I could think he was either a hero or a loser—but he seems to be stuck in the middle."

"Like us," Cowel said.

The sun had nestled within its blanket of clouds. From where he was standing, Mason could just make out where the road split in two. "Which way, do you think?"

"I don't really see how there's a choice," Cowel said. "I know what you're thinking, but traveling to those mountains with a horse that likes everybody and only one sword borrowed from a dress-up hero doesn't sound like such a great idea."

"But walking into a den of thieves and pirates *does?*"

Cowel shrugged, "I think Brendlor knew what he was doing. Small town. Short dreams. No problems."

As if he knew they had been talking about him, Lorn Breckenridge appeared at the door with a piece of parchment in his hand. Written on it was the name of an inn in Ancherton. "The owner's name is Sal Beerbalm. He may be able to point you in the right direction, or at the very least, he could give you a place to stay. Here." Lorn fished twenty gold pieces out of his pocket and handed them to Mason. "I can't stand Darlinger any more than you can, and I'd like nothing else than to see the orcs get ahold of him, but I certainly don't want to see anyone else get hurt."

"Thanks, Mr. Breckenridge," Mason said.

"It's Lorn. Just Lorn."

"Well, I hope we get a chance to meet again, Lorn."

"If we're still alive," Cowel added.

And twenty gold pieces and four boots the richer, Mason led Steed toward the fork in the road, his own quest before him but his father's last one on his mind.

Imelda Breckenridge was half-asleep when her husband walked back through the door, the empty pot of tea in a hand that she noticed was trembling. The look on his face told her not to ask questions, just wait for him to get it out. She pretended to doze, secretly watching him wipe out the mugs with an already-dirty cloth.

"It's just . . ." he began, cloth draped over his hands.

She didn't bother to answer—just let him sigh his way through it.

"It's just that they're so *young.*"

"That's how it always is," she said.

She thought over everything he had told her earlier. Two boys from Highsmith-now-Darlington—one was Edmond Quayle's boy—had figured out who he was. Their town was in danger, they were looking for help, and her husband was their only lead. She didn't much care for the town, but she wished the boys well and didn't begrudge them the twenty in gold that Lorn had given them. Just so long as he didn't go back on his promise—the one he had made so many years ago.

"You were no different when you were their age. But you're *not* their age anymore."

"You think I don't know that?" he said defensively. "But they don't know what they're doing. They're going to get themselves in trouble, and from what they've said, no one from the town knows what they're up to." He was avoiding her stare. It wasn't a good sign. "So I don't really have much choice, now, do I?" he said to himself, though Imelda was close enough to hear him. She watched him silently as he started to gather a few things together on the table—including some bread and a flask of water. It wasn't until he opened up the chest in the corner of the room and removed the thing she was hoping he wouldn't that she snapped, bolting out of her chair with her fists on her hips.

"Lorn Breckenridge, you promised me."

"They're going to need some help," he said, closing the trunk.

"Yes, but they don't need yours," she said.

"No. Not mine." Lorn began stuffing what he had gathered into a sack. "But there is somebody I can probably convince."

Making sure there was nothing heavy and throwable within arm's reach, Lorn Breckenridge—the humble, compassionate family man, formerly Brendlor Bowbreaker, an ale-loving, impetuous hero—sat his wife down and told her about one very passionate night he had had just over twenty years ago, not long before he and Imelda had decided to get married.

And the rather surprising consequences.

Passion was not a part of Steed's vocabulary. After all, he knew nothing of the hundreds of stories told about him "racing off at a gallop that could outrun a hawk's dive." So, as they passed the sign saying that Ancherton lay due north, Mason just gave up and let the horse go at his own pace.

There was no sign telling them what they'd find the other way. *That*, Mason thought, *would be too easy*.

Cowel had Mason's father's book open again and had turned to chapter eight: "Quests—Why They Don't Always End HEA." In it was a list of some of the most famous uncompleted adventures in the history of the five lands. It was a collection based on rumor and myth, but it made for exciting reading, nonetheless.

Of course, there was an entire page, scrawled in lovingly looping letters, about the treasure of Snowbeard the pirate, complete with backstory, possible locations, estimated value in gold (Cowel counted eight zeroes), and a list of the most famous heroes who had gone to look for it and failed—either giving up or simply not returning at all.

Edmond Quayle, of course, was not on that list.

Mason hadn't said a word since they became horse-bound. His world had grown much too large in the space of one day. At the fork, he had paused and considered everything Lorn had told him, wondering just how many stories ended happily ever after.

But with a nudge from Mason, Steed turned northward, toward the Hive and the hope that someone there might help them. Away from his father. From treasure. From rumors and lies and a story without an ending. Away from where his heart beat.

"It says here," Cowel said, "that the best thing about an adventure is coming home from it."

Mason didn't respond; he just followed the road north to the sea.

An hour later, a blond-headed man on horseback, an ax dangling from his side, approached the same fork in the road. But he ignored the dirt roads pointing him either north or south and simply went straight.

After all, only people with boring names like Lorn Breckenridge bothered with roads.

—4—

The Queen Bee, the Rusty Nail, and the Narcoleptic Somnantilist

The second warning came that morning, and it didn't smell too good.

Dirk Darlinger woke up and scrunched his nose. The meager sunlight bathing the curtains told him it wasn't even close to noon, so he rolled over, away from the window, hoping to go back to sleep and forget about the disaster his life had become—the money he needed to raise, the people who would love to see him hang, all the wasted years he had spent massaging his reputation—trying to forget that his bed smelled terrible, like dampness and spoiled eggs.

He flopped his arm around something very cold and very slippery.

Percy heard the scream from the kitchen, where he had spent most of the night finishing his farewell note, explaining to the duke why he would have to face the town's wrath alone. By the time Percy made his way up the stairs, he found Darlinger in a corner, huddled up into a knot.

The fish head was half-rotted, with one eye missing and the

other dangling. But the note stuck in the fish's mouth was clear. Percy could read it from where he stood.

4 Days Left

It's definitely time, Percy thought, *to pack my bags.*

When he was six, Mason Quayle worshiped his father the way any son did. But being the son of a hero wasn't easy. A lot to worship meant a lot to live up to. So when he left and never came back, in some ways, Edmond Quayle let his son off the hook.

And in some ways, he just drove it in deeper.

For the past few years, Mason had tried to forget him. Tried to ignore his mother's sighs, tried to ignore the trace of his father left behind on all the books in the library and even on the empty shelves, which were waiting to be filled up, he had told Mason, with books that had yet to be written.

A day had changed all that. Mason felt like a man who had starved himself. Since hearing about his father's last quest, Mason couldn't help but want to know everything. But all he had was a book. It was his only chance to hear his father's voice again, much to Cowel's dismay.

"But I'm tired of reading."

"Just a little more. Just to the end of the chapter."

"Last night, you didn't want me to read."

"Well, now I do."

"Can't we stop for a bit?"

Mason looked up to his left. Judging by the sun, they had been on the road for most of the afternoon. They had passed only five people, all of whom had ignored them save for an ivory salesman, who had just gotten off a boat in Ancherton and was on his way south to Heartwood, where he would switch out his ivory for furs. He had tried to convince them that what they *really* needed was an engraved horn used to summon warriors to battle. "All your problems will be solved," the ivory seller promised. "With just one blow."

"All our problems will be solved," Cowel repeated to Mason.

"So blow on it," Mason dared.

"Well, there have to be heroes around to *hear* it, of course," the ivory salesman said.

"Then it doesn't really help us, does it?"

The ivory seller eventually gave up, but not without earning a sympathetic shrug from Cowel, who was now flipping through chapter five, "Only as Good as Your Tools," which detailed the kinds of equipment required of any hero. He was disappointed to find that battle horns were mentioned only under "accessories," which, as Edmond Quayle put it, were there simply to make you look menacing or fashionable.

"It does say that when searching for missing persons, it's a good idea to have a witch's eye or a diviner's rod. It's a shame Brendlor sold only boots. It also says that a crossbow would have been a great idea. 'There's nothing like killing something from farther away than it could possibly kill you.'" Cowel took on a deeper voice when he quoted Mason's father, a habit Mason found, like most of Cowel's quirks, both endearing and annoying.

"What's the single greatest thing you've ever done? Your greatest accomplishment?"

The question fired in Cowel's direction came from nowhere—it was the most Mason had said since they left Riscine besides "We don't really need one," "We can't afford one," and "Just keep reading." It was so sudden and direct that it nearly knocked Cowel sideways off the horse.

"If I answer, can I stop reading until we get to Ancherton?"

"Sure. But you have to give me a real answer—none of your phoniness."

"Deal. Single greatest accomplishment," Cowel said thoughtfully, rubbing his chin for good measure. "I don't know. I guess becoming friends with you." He patted Mason on the back.

"I'm serious."

"All right, all right," Cowel said. He thought about it for another minute or so, intent this time, and finished with a shrug. "I don't know. I can't think of anything. What's yours?"

"That's just it," Mason said. "I don't have one."

"You've got to have one."

"You said *you* didn't know."

"Yeah, but I didn't ask the question. And it doesn't mean I *don't* have one. I *have* to have one. I mean, if everything I've ever done with my life has been simply mediocre, then I just pick the *least* mediocre thing among those and that's my greatest accomplishment, right?"

"I suppose so."

"So what I'm looking for is the least crappy thing I've done. Well, I sold a plume to a guy with no helmet once."

Mason turned around to check if Cowel was being serious.

"What? He couldn't afford a helmet," Cowel said, his hands in the air.

"Then why did he buy a plume?"

"Because I convinced him that if he bought the *plume,* it would be only a matter of time before he had a helmet. I told him it was destiny."

"And he believed that?"

"He bought it."

Mason turned back with a look of disbelief. "That's terrible. You cheat someone out of money, and that's your greatest accomplishment?"

"No, I guess not" was Cowel's weak reply. "I just thought it was kind of like selling a jug of water to a fish—or something like that." Then with a sly tone: "I kissed Gwyndolyn Broadmore."

"Get off the horse!"

"Seriously. I didn't tell you because I didn't know if you liked her or not."

Gwyndolyn Broadmore was only one of the prettiest girls in Darlington—which wasn't saying much, relatively, but it was sort of a given that anyone their age would like her. "So what was it like?" Mason asked.

"Honestly?"

"Honestly."

"Slippery."

"Slippery?"

"I drooled on myself."

"That's terribly sweet. When was this?"

"Two weeks ago," Cowel said nonchalantly, then added, "At your house."

"What?"

"You were at work. Your mother was out. She left the windows open like she always does."

"But *my* house? You weren't on my bed, were you?"

"Where else would we go? I couldn't take her to my place. Let her sit on the anvil?"

"You should have told me."

"I *am* telling you," Cowel said, a little contritely.

"You didn't drool on any of my stuff, like my sheets or anything, did you?"

"Of course not." But Mason could see by the smile on Cowel's face that he had slept on dried Cowel-and-Gwyndolyn drool at least one night of his life. "So how 'bout you, then? What do you have that tops that? There must be something."

"I've never kissed Gwyn Broadmore." Actually, Mason had never kissed any girl, though he had certainly been close to it once or twice and had thought about it a hundred times in the past year. There wasn't a lot else to do around Darlington.

"It's your stupid question, remember?"

Mason looked around him. Looked back in the direction of Riscine, looked southwest toward Darlington. Looked at the sword that was still hanging from his belt, at the horse he was riding, at his new boots and his old pants and the way his hands already felt rougher from holding on to the reins. He looked at how far away he was from anything he knew.

"This," he said with a sigh. "This is it. You're looking at it. This is the single greatest accomplishment of my life."

"We haven't done much," Cowel said. "Rode into one town, had a conversation, and pitied someone into giving us free shoes. We're basically beggars on a borrowed horse."

"I know it's not much." Mason thought about it and tried to figure out what was so remarkable about what they were doing. "But we didn't say no," he said. "That's the thing. We could have run from it. I don't know. It's the potential of it that makes it so great. I'm starting to understand why my father left now. Kind of . . . Do you get what I'm saying?" Mason turned around and looked at Cowel, whose head was bowed. "Cowel?"

Cowel looked up. "Yeah. Sorry, Mason, mashing lips with Gwyndolyn Broadmore was *way* better than this."

Mason reached down into the saddlebag beside him and pulled out one of the apples, already bruised by the journey. He handed it to Cowel, who cut it in half with his knife. It was the sour kind that made your eyes water with the first bite.

An hour and two more apples later, thanks to the unerring cruise control of Darlinger's horse and a nice, straight road with no detours, they had found their way to the Hive.

Everything the small town of Riscine didn't have—burglary, beggars, bar fights—the town of Ancherton had double of. The taverns never closed, the fires that helped guide ships were never extinguished, and the local authorities were never without something to do. It was this buzz of activity—the merchants along the pier, the sailors and pirates brawling in the taverns, the locals looking to keep their purses in their pockets and their eyes in their sockets—that had earned the town its nickname.

To enter the city from the south—as Steed did, carrying the two unlikely looking young men who had never seen the sea—was to behold something wholly unremarkable. Small weather-beaten hovels with sloped roofs were on the verge of collapse, standing in a lonely line along a dirt road that eventually gave way to sand and then to the sea.

But you didn't *see* it at first—the sea, that is. Lorn Breckenridge was right—you could smell it from a mile away. Cowel said it smelled like the beginning of the world. Following their noses, Mason and Cowel passed by the rows of houses and lonely streets and the occasional person inevitably headed seaward. On the docks, there were people everywhere: rolling barrels, tilting back flasks, pulling ropes, wrangling deals, dealing cards, throwing dice, or throwing someone out of a door. It was too much to take in all at once, and Mason felt his head spin from trying.

The town had its own smell as well, but it didn't hit you until you were right on top of it—a gut-wrenching bouquet of ale, sweat, smoke, and salt. The sounds of the Hive followed the smell—the echo of smashed chairs, broken bottles, and the vibrant language of seafaring types. Beyond the curses and carousing, you could hear the sound of ships being loaded and unloaded. Behind that, if you listened hard enough, you could hear the sea lapping along the edges of the world.

Mason and Cowel passed through a gate in a low wall that separated the pier from the rest of the town. They found themselves staring through a smoky haze at an endless row of buildings to one side, two large frigates, and innumerable smaller boats all moored along the docks. Beyond the boats was the foam-tinged sapphire sea stretching into infinity. A man was either passed out or dead in the street and a little girl was rifling through his pockets, taking anything she could find. She looked at Mason and stuck her tongue out.

Mason pointed to the knife the little girl had tucked into her belt. In fact, there were swords and daggers everywhere. That was one requirement taken care of, at least. Everybody in the Hive was armed: even old women walked around with battle-axes slung over their shoulders. One small boy was pulling the string back on his crossbow. Cowel tucked his kitchen knife into his belt, having wiped the juice from the apples on his pants. He summed up Mason's concerns perfectly when he said, "Maybe we should have turned south, instead."

Mason looked at the piece of parchment Lorn had given them, checked the name of the inn, and then nodded toward a sign—which showed a picture of a bird falling into the ocean—hanging from the porch of a large rust-colored building. It stood right next to one of the Hive's dozen taverns, the Rusty Nail.

"You really think we are going to find someone here?"

"Are you kidding? These people all look like they were born to fight."

"Yeah," Cowel said. "But none of them look *happy* about it."

Mason and Cowel rode up to the inn and slid off the horse, and Mason tied Steed's reins to a post with a chunk of knots— as if, somehow, more knots would stop people from stealing him when, really, they could just as easily cut through the strap. Beside him, Cowel sneezed a few times. He had had a small sneezing fit when they first entered the town, and it hadn't gone away yet.

"I think I'm allergic to something here," he said. "Maybe it's the sea."

But Mason knew it was something else. Cowel had had a similar fit when they were both eight years old and a couple of bullies had pulled his underpants up to his nipples. He'd had another one last year when a man accused him of cheating on a sale and had threatened to bury Cowel alive.

"Come on," Mason said. "The sooner we find a hero, the sooner we get out of here." Mason looked at the sun setting behind the ships' masts, stacking pinks and oranges on the sea's surface. He put a hand on the hilt of Dirk Darlinger's sword, but it didn't ease his nerves any. Then again, it hadn't done anything in Darlinger's hands, either.

The name on the slip of parchment read *Sal Beerbalm*. The name on the gold plate sitting on the front counter of the inn said the same.

The place was cleaner than Mason expected—much cleaner than the streets, which were littered with broken glass and unconscious bodies. There was a crackling fire, a nice fur rug, and a few chairs. The inn was empty, save for the man standing behind the desk, eyeing them warily as they walked in—the only kind of eyeing anyone did in the Hive. The man finished sizing them up and then buried himself back in his ledger. By the look of him, he was well fed and spent quite a lot of time in the sun. The scars on his face and arms were enough to suggest that he had lived in the Hive most of his life.

"Welcome to the Spiraling Albatross, where there's a bucket by every bed."

Cowel started to ask why there was a bucket by every bed when the innkeeper interrupted him.

"It's because I also own the tavern right next door, and my customers find them handy when they wake up. Unfortunately, I have more potentially inebriated customers than I do beds, so if you are looking for a room, I suggest you go to the Stumbling Monkey. Or better yet, you might go to ABH before you lose an eye or a finger."

"ABH?" Mason asked.

"Anywhere but here," Sal Beerbalm said, then went back to his ledger.

"Actually, Mr. Beerbalm," Mason began.

"Call me Sal," Sal said.

"Okay . . . Sal," Mason began again.

Sal's head shot up, his eyes boring holes in Mason's forehead. He slammed a fist on the counter, making Cowel sneeze again. "Don't ever call me Sal!" Sal shouted. "Don't call anyone here by their first name unless you know them. If they tell you to call them by their first name, it's because they are looking for a scuffle. People around here will use any excuse to pick a fight. They will spill ale on themselves and say you did it. They will always assume you've spent the night with their spouse, even if they aren't married." Sal Beerbalm spit as he spoke. Mason found it all very unnerving.

"Mr. Beerbalm," Cowel said, wiping his nose and jumping in almost fearlessly, "we were sent by Lorn Breckenridge."

Mason, noticing the total lack of interest on Sal Beerbalm's face, amended Cowel's comment. "Actually, it was Brendlor Bowbreaker."

As though a key had opened a chest, Sal's face suddenly relaxed. "Bowbreaker sent you, did he?" The beefy innkeeper smiled. "How is that maniac? I haven't seen him in—what has it been?"

"Probably about eight or ten years, sir," Mason suggested.

"Yes. About that. How is old Redbeard?"

"Blond, actually."

"And clean-shaven," Cowel added.

"No. Really?"

"He dyed it," Cowel said with a wink.

"I always knew he was hiding something." Sal closed his ledger and opened his arms. "So, what can I do for two young friends of Brendlor Bowbreaker?" Then, suddenly, his arms dropped to his side, one of them settling on the hilt of a wicked-looking curved sword at his waist. "This isn't about that night in Horsdale, is it?"

"No. Nothing about that," Mason said, though the look on Cowel's face indicated he was ready for the rest of *that* story. "Actually, we're looking for a hero. Or two."

"Or five," Cowel added.

"Whatever we can find. Lor—Bowbreaker thought that there might be quite a few swords for hire up here, and he thought *you* might know where to look."

"Oh, swords. Yeah, we got plenty of swords. And maces

and clubs and daggers and hatchets. If you can kill some-body with it, odds are there's somebody in the Hive that has one and will do it for you. But what do you need them for?"

"Orcs," Cowel said.

"And goblins."

"And trolls."

"Oh, my," Sal said, rubbing the nicely tanned slick spot on his head. "Sounds expensive."

"How expensive?"

"Well, prices have gone up, you see, ever since that doodle-rod in Highsmith took over."

"You mean Darlington," Cowel corrected.

"He means Darling*er*," Mason said, correcting Cowel.

"Doodlerod's fine by me," Sal concluded. "But ever since he's been doing his thing, there hasn't been much need, even all the way here in Ancherton, for that kind of work."

"Actually, Darlinger's the reason we came. Turns out he can't handle his responsibilities anymore. That's why we need help."

"He ain't dead, is he?"

"Not yet," Cowel said.

"Too bad," Sal remarked. Mason detected no sarcasm in the response. "Let's see here." Sal opened up his ledger to a blank page and started scrawling numbers in script too tiny for Mason or Cowel to see from where they were standing. "You say you're looking for how many?"

"Five would be nice," Cowel said.

"But three would do," Mason added.

"Right. Three warriors. Plus travel expenses—horse rental, food, lodgings—plus a finder's fee for me—I'll give you a discount on that, seeing as how you're a friend of a friend—and the total comes to"—Sal stuck out his tongue as he added the figures—"twelve forty."

Mason almost hit the floor.

"Twelve *hundred?*" Cowel spit out.

"About that. Though I could probably get you just one really good one for five hundred and five fairly average bounty hunters for the price of three. But you don't want to skimp on quality."

"That's a problem," Mason said, finally reestablishing his footing. "We have only about a hundred in gold."

"A hundred, eh?" Sal Beerbalm cocked his head. "For a hundred, I could get you a drunk pirate or a witch-burning farmer."

"I'd go with the farmer," Cowel whispered to Mason. "I'm a little afraid of pirates."

Then Mason remembered what Percy had said, that they would have to appeal to the heroes' sense of chivalry rather than their pockets.

"We could pay them in honor," Mason blurted out.

Sal Beerbalm didn't say anything—he just stared at Mason as if he were speaking a strange language. "I haven't the slightest clue what you're talking about, son," the innkeeper finally said.

"Honor. You know. Glory. Gratitude. What heroes used to fight for. Surely there's somebody here who still believes in those things."

"Listen, fellows. Let me tell you something." Sal leaned over his counter and flexed his scars. "People in the Hive aren't interested in solving your problems. They have problems of their own. In fact, I can think of only one man in the whole town who might believe in the kinds of things you're talking about, and I'm pretty certain he's not what you're looking for."

Mason's eyes brightened. "Can you at least tell us where we can find him?"

Sal rubbed his armpit. "Most likely he's next door. That's where he spends a good deal of his time. If you really want to talk to him, just ask the bartender for the somnambulist."

"The what?"

"Just ask him. He'll know. Though I'm telling you again that I don't think you'll be interested."

"But he might help us anyway?" Cowel asked.

"I haven't the foggiest idea. But I've seen him do things for people for no good reason—which seems to be about the only kind of reason you two've got. Just one piece of advice," Sal said. "Be very careful how you wake him up."

"You mean the somnambulist," the bartender said after Cowel mangled the word three times. "He's over there against the wall. The table with the candle burnt out. With the sword in his hand."

Actually, there were about twenty people in the bar with swords in their hands, but only one sitting at a table with an extinguished candle. He was sleeping deeply, which was a little odd, because it didn't seem possible that anyone could sleep, given the din of the Rusty Nail. The place was full of bodies shoving, cursing, drinking, laughing, and leering. Mason thought the guy would have a better chance of sleeping with a rat crawling down his shirt. "Thank you," Mason said to the bartender, who looked a lot like Sal Beerbalm. He dragged Cowel in the direction of the man's table.

The man was dark-haired, with a trim mustache. His clothes were dirty and riddled with holes, patches, and slashes, but they had the kind of flourish that a prince or a ship's captain might have—ruffles around the sleeves, a frill along the collar. Compared with all the gap-toothed, scar-studded men and women around the room, the somnambulist—or whatever he was—looked out of place.

"Be very careful," Mason said as they picked their way through the crowd. "Don't call anybody by their first name."

"I don't know any of these people's first names," Cowel protested.

"And don't touch anyone," Mason said as Cowel almost tripped over an outstretched foot. When the man who owned the foot growled at him, Cowel sneezed and pushed Mason forward.

"Don't talk to anyone," Mason hissed. "And don't say you're sorry. You don't want to show weakness."

"You're not making this any easier," Cowel said, though *It must be nice to be the one with the sword* was what he was thinking.

Laughter pummeled Mason's eardrums and smoke stung his eyes. Something underneath his foot cracked and he hoped it wasn't anybody's anything. He could feel Cowel's hand on his back, grabbing a wad of Mason's shirt and twisting it. To his right, someone was reciting dirty limericks. To his left, two women were arm-wrestling, their tattoos bulging. Mason couldn't help thinking that all these people needed a bath worse than he did.

They were almost to the sleeping man's table when suddenly Mason's shirt got even tighter as Cowel's twisting brought them to a stop.

"Nice boots."

Mason turned to see the man who had tapped Cowel on the shoulder, and choked on whatever it was that had suddenly lodged itself in his throat. He guessed it was his heart or stomach—or maybe his liver. The person speaking had all the features that a man should have but was shaped more like a boulder. He was all muscle; his shaven skull seemed to flex. His two buddies standing obediently beside him—standard accessories for a town bully—looked much more human by comparison, but that wasn't saying much.

What *really* didn't help was the fact that this goliath with fists the size of a child's head was wearing a dress.

A nice dress. Flower print. Spaghetti straps. Cotton blend. Summery, though the air was a little crisp for it. It hung just below the knees, revealing trunks for legs that were covered with a thick bark of black hair and feet that looked way too small for his body—making them about Cowel's size.

Small enough to fit into Cowel's new boots.

And he had earrings. Diamond studs. One in each ear. And a pearl necklace.

It didn't take long for Mason to realize what this was all about. He didn't have a problem with men wearing dresses—whatever raises your drawbridge, as Cowel would say. But he remembered what Sal had told them—about people doing anything to pick a fight—and had a good guess at the motive here, which meant it was time for *him* to grab onto the back of *Cowel's* shirt and start twisting, to try to prevent the very thing the giant in the dress *wanted* to happen.

"I said, nice boots," the man repeated.

The crowd leaned in and Mason twisted harder, putting his other hand on Cowel's shoulder, ready to pinch the moment it started. The giant in the white sundress with blue and yellow flowers didn't move and didn't say anything else—he just stood there as still as a house and almost as large.

"They're yours if you want them," Mason said, hoping the man would simply take the boots *without* Cowel's feet still inside them. But mostly, he hoped Cowel wouldn't do what he was about to do. He could feel Cowel's body start to shake through his shirt. He squeezed his friend's shoulder as hard as he could.

But it was too late.

It didn't come out as laughter, exactly. It came out as a snort. A kind of half-choke, half-giggle that was followed by a yelp for Mason's pinch. But regardless of what it was, it could be interpreted as laughter.

The flowers started to heave as the giant took two steps toward them.

"He didn't mean it, sir. I mean, you know. He has a condition."

Cowel nodded but then snorted again, an incontrollable, half-swallowed laugh that was followed by a huge sneeze that blinded him for a moment.

A sneeze that shot a wad of snot onto the front of the giant man's dress, where it clung in an oozing glob.

With an instinct he didn't know he had, Mason grabbed Cowel and spun him around, pulling him to the floor just as the behemoth came lumbering forth, both of his fists landing on the table that had been behind Mason.

The table occupied by the sleeping man.

The man who didn't wake up, not even as the force of the dress-wearing giant's blow caused one of the table's legs to splinter and another to crack, making the table lean at an awkward angle. The sleeper simply sucked on his lower lip a moment, readjusted his head on the arm that was propped up perilously on the table's edge, and continued to snooze.

Mason, meanwhile, had drawn his sword, which he realized was a mistake the moment the crowd went, "Ooohhhh." The lackeys accompanying the behemoth drew their own swords to an "Aaahhhh" from the crowd and advanced to stand next to their leader. Cowel and Mason huddled on the floor like sacrificial lambs at an orc wedding reception, Mason holding Darlinger's sword in front of him.

The dress stretched as the giant finished his work on the table, tearing the splintered leg from its socket and holding it like a club. The table collapsed. The sleeper's hand fell to one side, though he didn't drop the sword it held. He mumbled something that Mason couldn't make out, and then his head fell backwards and he let out a snore.

The dress bulged. It looked as if wild animals were wrestling underneath it.

Cowel screamed and sneezed at the same time.

And then suddenly, the swing of the table leg that was meant to take off Mason's head was met by a sword only inches from his face in a moment of poetic unity that caused no end of surprised looks on the faces of everyone in the bar, save for the man holding the sword, who remained expressionless.

The crowd dutifully let out an "Ooohhhh."

Mason and Cowel both turned to see the man, the somnambulist, standing upright, his sword arm stretched before him. His head was still flung back. Eyes still closed. A little bit of drool hung from one corner of his mouth.

He was still asleep.

There was a moment of stunned silence, punctuated only by a "What the?" from Cowel.

The mass of muscle reared back for another blow with the table leg, this time aimed at the sleeping swordsman, but the blow was met with equal grace by the man whose body seemed to act independently of his mind, as if he were a puppet with one string broken, head lolling from side to side but limbs flowing in the fluid, graceful dance of an expert fencer. The giant delivered two more swings, but in the same space, the swordsman delivered three, catching the giant's two and then cutting across the giant's neck and severing his string of pearls and one strap of his dress, which now hung flapping at his side, revealing half of his heaving chest.

The pearls clattered to the floor. The man in the dress, spared from having his throat slit by only a quarter of an inch, took two steps backwards, and the swordsman, still snoring, raised the point of his sword up to the giant's nose. All of this Mason saw through his one open eye.

The next minute and a half were blurry. The other two goons advanced as their leader tried to regain his balance, but even being outnumbered two swords to one *and* still out like his candle, the sleeping swordsman quickly disarmed them both, leaving one nursing a bad cut on his arm and the other scrabbling on the floor for part of his thumb.

The crowd said, "Aaahhhh."

The giant let out a roar that eclipsed the sound of the swordsman's snoring and prepared to make a puddle of his opponent, but the swordsman deftly stepped to the side and, with a *snick, snack,* caught the giant across the ear, causing a diamond stud—and much of the lobe it had been attached to—to tumble to the floor.

A string of pearls, half a thumb, and part of an ear in the hole, the three brutes stumbled through the parting crowd and out of the Rusty Nail.

The swordsman stood there for a while, weapon at the ready. Not a soul in the tavern moved as the sword slowly danced back and forth, like a snake still looking to strike. Then, there was a flutter of lids. The head lulled to one side, then snapped upright. After a deep, stuttering breath and a long blink, the swordsman found himself before a crowd of people all staring back at him.

He raised his other hand and coughed once, trying to find his voice, and then finally said, "Sorry. For . . . you know . . . whatever." He turned and looked at the broken table, put a hand against the wall to steady himself, and then gave up and collapsed onto the bench.

After witnessing three more blinks and a yawn, the spectators grew uninterested, turned around, and went back to their own business.

"Better let him wake a bit," the bartender said, handing over the drinks he said they needed. Cowel wiped his nose on his sleeve, leaving a trail, and Mason finally slowed his heart enough to speak.

"What just happened?"

"From here, it looked like the Queen Bee was about to make honey out of you two and the man over there wiping the sleep from his eyes saved your skins." The bartender was busy removing the diamond earring from the fleshy remains of its mooring. The pearls had been scrabbled for by the customers after the goons left.

"The Queen Bee?"

"That's what he calls himself. He wears the dress hoping that some idiot will say something, then he beats the tar out of 'im and takes 'im for all he's worth. We all learned not to laugh a long time ago, though seeing him now . . . it's going to be tough."

"I'm sorry," Cowel said to Mason.

"It's all right. What about *him?*" Mason asked, pointing to the man who held his sword in one hand—still—and a mug of coffee in the other. "What's his story?"

"His name's Corner. Nobody really knows his last name—if he even has one. He's narcoleptic—at least, that's what *he* says. Not sure if he just made the word up, but it means that he sleeps a lot. Either that or he sleeps at odd times. I've had conversations with him and he'll nod off, just like that." The bartender snapped his fingers. "I've seen him fall asleep eating. Almost drowned in his stew once. He doesn't yawn or anything, just *boom*"—he smacked the bar this time—"and he's gone."

"But you called him something else earlier," Cowel said. "A somabullix."

"A somnambulist. That's his word, too. He says it means he walks while sleeping."

"He does a good deal more than walk," Mason said, staring at the man who was now rubbing his eyes with a free hand, still recovering from what must have been an exciting dream.

"Aye. He trained himself to do that. Nobody knows how. Some say he lived for a few years with a blind monk. Others say he's possessed by a demon that has control only when he's asleep, but I don't buy it. Most of the time when he sleeps, he's as peaceful as a lamb. Only when he's provoked does he do his . . . you know." The bartender made some swishing motions. "They say he might be one of the best swordsmen in the five lands if he could only stay awake long enough."

"Is he a noble man, do you think?" Mason asked.

"Don't know about noble, but he saved you two; I suppose that counts for something. He looks 'bout spry enough for a word or two," the bartender said, nodding toward the somnambulist. "But be careful if he nods off again not to poke him or any such thing."

Mason thought this was kind of like telling someone not to sit down on a bed of hot coals, but he said thank you, anyway.

Corner the swordsman, the man who had saved Mason and

Cowel in his sleep, couldn't stop blinking. He had trouble focusing on them as they approached side by side, stepping carefully.

"Good morning, lads." Corner yawned and put a fist into his mouth to stifle it. It was the same hand he offered to shake with. The other hand, Mason noticed, never left his sword. In fact, the man didn't seem to even own a scabbard to keep it in. "Sorry if I interrupted anything back there. Business venture or the like. From the looks of it, there was a misunderstanding. I can only assume I got involved." He sounded charming and sincere. It was clear that if he weren't so dangerous, this town would have made sausage out of him long ago. "If I've done you any disservice or if I owe you anything, please let me know."

By the look he was given, Mason could tell Cowel saw an opportunity. After all, the man *had* been asleep the whole time. But Mason couldn't lie to a man who had just rescued them from a terrible clubbing by a dress-wearing psycho.

"Actually, we owe *you*," Mason said. "Though we don't have much to give."

Corner groaned. "I didn't kill anybody, did I? Please tell me I didn't."

"No, you didn't kill anyone."

"Thank the maidens. Believe me, boys, there's nothing worse than waking up, finding out you've gone and killed somebody, and then having everyone around you try to convince you that the person deserved it. Except maybe waking up and having people tell you the person didn't," he added.

"That's happened to you?" Cowel said, amazed.

"The first version. When I was just starting as a somnantilist."

"A what?"

"A sleep fighter. There are only a few people in all of the five lands who can do it, and it takes years of training and a fair degree of talent. There's also a little bit of magic involved, but I certainly don't want to go into *that*. Besides, it's more of a curse than a blessing. At least, it seems that way." Corner sighed. "They can teach me how to fight with my eyes closed, but they can't keep me from falling asleep in the middle of the afternoon."

"But what you did is impossible," Cowel said. "I mean, there's no way you could have known."

"I woke up once on a raft of logs I had built myself, headed out to sea having fallen asleep in this very bar only hours earlier. Don't talk to me about possible."

"But *how* do you do it? Do you see what's going on?"

Corner the swordsman eyed the young men suspiciously. Most people in the Hive never bothered to walk near his table, let alone take an interest in his problems. "I kind of *half dream* it. In my dream, though, I wasn't fighting. I was dancing. With three lovely women."

"I wouldn't say 'lovely,' exactly," Mason said.

"The dream ended badly," Corner continued. "I blew in one's ear—she got embarrassed, turned, and ran away. Then I woke up to find my usual table in pieces and you two on the floor. I keep thinking that one of these days, I'm going to wake up to find I've burned the place down. That's why they never light the candle at my table. I'm surprised they even let me sit here."

"But you *are* a great swordsman," Cowel said.

"Believe me, it is not something to be envious of. I've slept through the most exciting moments of my life, and I spend most of my waking hours simply trying to put together the pieces." The narcoleptic somnantilist took a sip of his coffee and smiled at a few of the bar's patrons who were giving him strange looks.

"Do you know what causes it—the falling asleep, I mean?" Mason asked.

"I've seen twenty or thirty different alchemists about it, but no one has been able to help. I had a witch cast a spell on me once that kept me awake for seventeen days straight—but it almost killed me. Eventually, I just gave up on finding a cure and studied the art of sleep fighting instead."

"And when you wake up, you don't have any idea where you've been or what you've been doing?"

"Only what people tell me."

"Maybe we could help you," Cowel said. "Maybe we could, you know, follow you around and record everything you do while you are sleeping—that way you'll know. Mason here is a bard. He could make it sound like a fairy tale. And in return, you could maybe do a little something for us."

"A little something?" Corner may have been the kind of man who fell asleep at a moment's notice, but he was smart enough to guess when "a little something" was actually a lot. "I'm afraid I'll need more information than that."

So Mason told the narcoleptic somnantilist about Dirk Darlinger, Bennie the Orc, the town, the money, and the rather limited time frame. Once, it looked as if Corner was about to slip back into sleep, but he insisted it wasn't because the story was uninteresting. Mason finished with his plea, promising that the town would give him whatever it could in return—maybe someone there could even help him with his problem.

"I'd love to help you," Corner said, massaging his sword hand with the other one without letting go of the hilt. "The problem is that awake, I'm not half the swordsman I am when

I'm asleep, and when I am asleep, I don't know *what* I'm going to do. Surely there is someone here who can offer you at least *conscious* assistance?"

"Nobody we can afford."

"Really," Cowel confirmed. "You're the only person, apparently, in this whole town who would be willing to . . . Mr. Corner . . . hello?"

But somewhere during Cowel's sentence, it happened. The head lulled forward. The mouth fell open. The thankfully empty mug was knocked over, and he was gone.

"Great—you put him to sleep," Mason said.

"Why me? You're the one who had to tell the whole story. Like he cares where we got our boots?"

Mason went to snap his fingers in front of the swordsman's face and then thought better of it.

"What do we do now?"

"I don't know. Do we wait for him to wake up?"

"He was awake for only fifteen minutes."

"But how long do you think he sleeps?"

"I don't know."

They sat and stared at Corner for a minute, almost two. Waiting. Finally, it was Cowel who said what both of them were thinking. "Do you really think this is what Percy had in mind?"

"Well, he seems interested. And he *is* a good swordsman."

"Sure. But how do we even get him there? He can't ride his own horse—not like that—and I'm sure as heck not letting him ride with me."

"I don't see why not. He saved your life."

"He saved yours, too. But he thinks dancing with ladies and cutting off ears are the same thing. Imagine what he's like when he has a *bad* dream."

"Are you saying we shouldn't take him back with us?"

"I'm saying I don't know how we can. I mean, when he's awake, he seems like a great guy, but when he's asleep, he's a disaster."

"Keep your voice down."

"I'm just saying," Cowel whispered, "that he won't do us any good on the way back to Darlington if he's asleep, and he won't do us any good there if he's awake, and I have no idea how to keep him one way or the other."

Mason sighed. Cowel was right, of course. Corner the narcoleptic somnantilist was just what they were looking for: courageous, young, skilled, and noble—but he had one too many issues.

"We can't just leave him here, though. We should say something."

"Write him a note."

Mason fished in his pocket for the piece of parchment with Sal Beerbalm's name on it and then went to ask the bartender if he could borrow a quill. After much quibbling over phrasing, Mason and Cowel filled the space not occupied by Beerbalm's name on the front and back.

Dear Corner,

Please know how eternally grateful we are to you for saving our lives. As this is our first time having them saved, we are not sure how to thank you. Unfortunately, our funds are limited, but you should find a small gesture with this note. Although we think you are a fine warrior—one of the finest swordsmen we've ever seen—we are afraid that, given your condition, asking you to come with us would result in our untimely deaths *afford undue risk, and we therefore regret that we cannot hire you at this time.* We do hope to

return to the Hive If we should ever pass this way again,
we promise to visit.

Sincerely,

Mason Quayle and Cowel Salender
of Highsmith / Darlington

Cowel folded the parchment, and Mason plucked three gold pieces from his purse and tucked them into the note. He slipped the folded sheet into one of Corner's sleeves, snatched his hand back, and watched.

The swordsman didn't move.

"Do you think it will be safe there?"

"Would you try to take something from him after what you'd just seen?"

Cowel conceded the point, and the two of them slunk along the inner wall and slipped out of the Rusty Nail.

Once outside, though, Mason felt a warmth rising within him, the same feeling he had had when he was on his knees begging Darlinger for a job. He and Cowel had been confronted with danger, possible death, and they had fallen all over themselves. Mason had drawn his sword and held it in front of him, hoping that it would do his fighting for him and all he would need to do was hang on.

The shame didn't replace the relief, however. That he was still breathing, that his head was still firmly attached to his shoulders, that his limbs were unbroken—these things were still most important. But the fact that he had *had* to be saved— and by someone who was *asleep*, no less—made Mason wonder how he could possibly be expected to defend his town.

And after all of that, they still had nothing to show for it.

Back in the Spiraling Albatross, Sal Beerbalm offered his regrets about Corner when the two told him what happened. "Will you two be stayin' the night, then?"

The innkeeper got two different answers, but Mason prevailed—he didn't want to spend another minute in this town if he didn't have to.

"You don't happen to know somewhere else we might go to find a hero—a *cheap* hero—do you?"

Sal looked at the two boys and shook his head. "If it were me—and thankfully, it's not—I'd go toward the mountains. There are a few towns from here to halfway up 'em, though Heartwood is your best bet. You can stay on the road to get there, though that will take a while, or when you see the sign, you can take the shortcut through the forest."

"Shortcut?" Mason repeated.

"Forest?" Cowel asked.

"It would save you almost a day, provided you didn't get lost. Now, how about one gold piece for old Sal for all the trouble you've caused? Think of it as a keeping-your-horse-from-getting-stolen fee," he added.

Mason fished the gold from his pocket, trying not to look too annoyed for fear that Sal Beerbalm would demand more. Then, with a "Good luck" full of stifled laughter, the proprietor of the Spiraling Albatross bid them a good night.

"We shouldn't travel in the dark," Cowel grumbled as they were untying Mason's many knots.

"I don't like this place."

"We won't be able to see where we're going."

"The moon is out."

"Even worse. Vampires. Witches."

"You're thinking of werewolves. Besides, it's not a full moon. Not even close."

"I'm thinking of myself," Cowel said. "I'm tired."

"And you want to stay here? These people will kill you in your sleep. Some of them may even kill you in *their* sleep."

Cowel nodded. There was no arguing that. "I'm starting to think that maybe a sleeping swordsman is the best we're going to find," he said. "We should just go back and wait for him to wake up."

"There's got to be someone better out there."

"Sure. But there's bound to be a whole lot worse, too."

Mason forced a smile, pulled himself into the saddle, and then turned and offered his hand. "What's to worry about? We've just stared death in the face in the form of a three-hundred-pound, club-swinging, dress-wearing giant named Queen Bee. I don't see what we really have to be afraid of anymore." So all the way out of town, Cowel made Mason a list, just off the top of his head, starting with those werewolves Mason had brought to his attention.

Behind them, the Hive was swarming. Somewhere, a ship's cannon went off—whether it was accidentally or on purpose, the locals didn't care so long as it wasn't aimed at them. Somewhere, Mason thought, the Queen Bee was probably nursing his sting. And in the Rusty Nail, people were getting hammered, filling the room with smoke and laughter, while a lone swordsman without a quest or a cure slept through the whole mess, dreaming of waking up.

— 5 —

Cackles, Pixies, and Cough Syrup

Perlin Salendor had read the note four times already since yesterday, though the first two he had been brain-burstingly hung-over and the last two he had been busy not learning his lesson. Now hung-over again, he made another attempt to decipher why his nephew had given him gold, half of which was already spent.

> Dear Uncle,
> Darlinger's a fraud. Orc problems. Don't tell anyone yet—no panic. Have left with Mason to find heroes, save town, etc. Here's some gold. If you haven't heard from us in three days, GET OUT! Tell everyone to get out! Again: Don't panic. And don't spend the gold at Flax's.
>
> > Cowel

It still didn't make a lot of sense, in part because he didn't quite get the thing about the orcs, but mostly because he had ignored the last bit.

In three days, or however many were left, he might have something to worry about—that much he understood. Until then, Perlin figured he still had two gold pieces and some change. But first he would lie back down. He had been standing for all of seven minutes—his longest span yet—and the weight of his throbbing head was too much for him.

No sooner had he lain down than there was a knock on the door.

No one ever knocked on the door.

His first thought was that it was the orcs from the note come to chop off his head. His second thought was that his wife had come back. Perlin struggled out of his hammock and ambled to the door, hoping for orcs.

Standing there was a woman, but it wasn't his wife. He saw her through a haze, and it took a moment to realize who she was. He could immediately smell the muffins she had brought, though.

"Perlin Salendor. You look like you've been trampled by a wild boar." The woman took a good whiff of him and it made her eyes sting. "It's a shame that Flax's tavern is only two blocks away."

"Terrible shame," Perlin concurred. He tried to straighten himself up as he stepped to the side to let her in. He had met her only a couple of times, but he had heard enough about her from his nephew to consider her one of the few people he'd actually bother to welcome inside.

"What can I do for you?" Perlin said, shutting the door to get the sunlight out of his face.

"Our boys—you know, they've taken off—and . . . well, I just stopped by to see if you knew any more about it than I did."

Perlin squinted at Dierdra Quayle, then went over to the anvil and got Cowel's note. He was torn between the muffins and the pull of his hammock. He hoped he could trade the note for the muffins and then sit down.

Dierdra read it twice. She folded the note and put it into the pocket of her dress.

"It's worse than I thought," she said, and handed the grateful Perlin the basket.

Then she told him to eat quickly, because somehow or another, they were going to get to the bottom of this. And Perlin's headache got considerably worse.

Mason woke with a start, his hand going to the hilt of the sword that wasn't there. His first thought was that he had been taken prisoner—by whom, he didn't know—the Queen Bee and his drones, most likely. They had disarmed him and thrown him into a dungeon where he had to sleep on the floor, which could explain why his back was so sore.

Then he remembered where he was and the agreement he and Cowel had made—that whoever was keeping watch got the sword. A glance over the fire—kept intentionally small so as not to attract attention—revealed Cowel, Darlinger's blade across his lap, reading the *Guide* in the flickering light.

"Bad dream?"

Mason sat up and rubbed his eyes. They were camped in a clearing in the middle of a field. The wildflowers made his eyes watery. "I heard buzzing."

It was Mason's own fault they were in the middle of a field, so he didn't have much right to complain. Heading back south from the Hive, they had passed close to Riscine and the home of Lorn the boot-maker hours ago. Much to Cowel's dismay,

Mason had insisted they ride on, claiming he wasn't the slightest bit sleepy. A few hours later, his head was bobbing up and down, his eyelids anchored to his cheeks. They had no choice but to stop for the night, he said, reluctantly eating his own words.

It wasn't the first time Mason and Cowel had slept outside. They used to camp in the fields across from the granary in Darlington, though the whole area was protected, in a manner of speaking, by the duke.

"How do you feel?" Mason asked.

"Hard ground as my bed, one thin blanket, a rolled-up cloak for a pillow, and bad dreams to haunt me all the way through? I feel great."

"We should keep going, I guess."

"I'll steer for a while," Cowel said.

They were resaddled and back on the road, heading toward the mountains, when Cowel made a request. "Sing me a song."

"What are you talking about?"

"You're a bard. That's what you do. So sing a song. We'll both stay awake until the sun comes up. Then we'll read some more."

Mason snorted. "I don't have any of them memorized," he said, which was pretty much true. He could remember a few lines from various pieces he had written and a few more from the famous bards' songs he had read, but he couldn't recite a complete song from memory.

"Make one up, then," Cowel insisted.

"You can't just *make up* a song off the top of your head," Mason said indignantly, but that, of course, was a lie. The ability to make up a song on the spot—*freebarding*, it was called— was often what separated the true poets from the pretenders.

Mason had heard of places where freebarding competitions were held. He had also heard that although these competitions started out good-naturedly, they inevitably degenerated into satire, full of name-calling and nasty references to other bards' mothers.

"What kind of bard are you? You can't memorize songs. You can't make them up. You don't sing them. What exactly *do* you do?"

"I put my seal of authenticity on them, tie them with a ribbon, and charge money for them."

"And I used to admire you," Cowel said.

"All right, fine. I'll make something up. But I get the last apple."

"No problem." Cowel didn't bother to tell him that he had eaten the last apple while Mason was asleep. "What's the title?"

Mason thought about it for a moment. "It's called 'The Ballad of the Battle with the Bee.'"

"Sounds like a nursery rhyme."

Mason whispered to himself, trying to find just the right start. The first line would set the rhythm for the whole thing, and he would be stuck with it. That's what he didn't like about being spontaneous—the inability to go back and erase. It's pretty much why he never bothered to change anything about his life—he knew where he stood and there were no real surprises. Up until a couple days ago, that is. And he already had quite a bit he wanted to take back.

Finally, Mason got inspired by the buzzing from his dream. With a hum, he began.

"The Hive, it was abuzz that night; the scoundrels all were out—
The finest troupe of vagabonds that any town could tout.
Along the streets the urchins swiped the gold from out your pocket,

And everyone who closed a door was wise enough to lock it.
The thieves and pirates, arm in arm, caroused along the streets,
While little tykes with daggers stole the shoes from off your feets."

"'Off your feets'?"

"Can you do any better?"

"You could have just said 'street.' Then you wouldn't have had to say 'feets.'"

"Fine. If you can do so much better, by all means, go ahead, maestro."

"Absolutely not. Please. I'm sorry. Continue."

"When onto this scene appeared our handsome fresh-faced heroes
Equipped with sword and dagger, but . . ."

There was a long pause. "But what?"

"I don't know. You've got me distracted. I need something that rhymes with *heroes.*"

"How about fearos?"

"What's a fearo?"

"It's the plural of fear."

"The plural of fear is fears."

"Hey, do you want it to rhyme or not?"

"And you had a problem with *feets?*"

"Trust me. It will work."

"Equipped with sword and dagger and lacking any . . . fearos."

Mason couldn't see Cowel's expression, but he was certain that if he could, he'd find a smirk on Cowel's face.

"Into the Rusty Nail they went, a daunting drinking station,
Searching for a warrior with unmatched reputation.
For word had spread that here there dwelled a swordsman kind and fair,
Who made a table for a bed and slept without a care.
A graceful fencer, fighter bold, who never once was dissed—

The man they called the narcoleptic somnambambulist."

"I don't think that's the word."

"What is it, then?"

"I think it's just somnambulmist."

Mason ignored the comment and continued.

"A graceful fencer, fighter bold, with heart so pure and deep,

Who could best the worst there ever was while snoring in his sleep.

"I like the first version better."

"This is the worst audience I've ever had," Mason muttered.

"But as the heroes approached him—"

"What happened to handsome?"

"But as the handsome heroes approached the swordsman still at
rest,

They were rudely interrupted by a giant, daintily dressed.

With flowers for a pattern and a necklace made of pearl,

The behemoth stood above them looking nothing like a girl.

'Nice boots,' the giant bellowed as his summer dress stretched tight.

It was clear the earringed bully was out looking for a fight.

But Cowel simply laughed—"

"Cowel the brave and dashing."

"What?"

"I think it should be 'Cowel the brave and dashing.'"

"Fine."

"But Cowel . . . the brave and dashing . . . just laughed in the
giant's face,

While Mason . . . the more humble . . . drew his sword with quiet
grace.

'I am the Queen Bee of this Hive; my anger will be sated,'

The giant said and launched a blow our heroes just evaded."

"You know that doesn't really—"

"Would you just shut up and let me finish?"

From the front of the horse, Cowel threw his hands into the air in a gesture of defeat. Mason whispered the lines back to himself, trying to pick up the thread.

"The giant's goons drew swords as well and teamed up with their Queen.

It looked as if our heroes would not see the sun again.

When suddenly the sleeping swordsman leapt into the fray—

Though he hadn't yet awoken, his sword was still in play.

He moved with catlike quickness; he struck with viper's speed.

And with two strokes he'd torn the dress and made the giant bleed."

"Exciting."

"Thank you."

"While Mason Quayle the mighty went deftly to attack,

And flipping from a table stabbed one villain in the back.

The skill of these two warriors was something to be feared,

While Cowel the brave and dashing simply stood aside and cheered."

"What?" Cowel's voice was pitched high enough to be heard by wild animals. "'Cheered'? That's hardly fair!"

"Fine. I'll change it."

"But Cowel the intrusive was the one most to be feared,

As he wiped out thirty goblins who had suddenly appeared."

"You didn't have to go overboard. One or two goblins would have been fine."

"Do you want me to change it?"

"No. It's fine. I like it. Just finish the song."

"And the villains then retreated with their pride and honor broken,

Leaving two triumphant heroes and a swordsman finally woken.

And Cowel . . . the brave . . . and Mason sipped some coffee from the tap,

While the narcoleptic swordsman sat back down to take a nap.

And the Hive, it stayed abuzz with talk long after the battle's end,
As the tale of these three heroes could be heard above the din.
It was, perhaps, the greatest sight the Hive had ever seen,
When the sleeping, snoring swordsman took the sting out of their
Queen."

Mason said the last line slowly and with a great deal of pomp. When he was finished, there was a trickle of applause from the front of the horse.

"Thank you, thank you very much. I can see we have a packed horse here today," Mason said in his cheesy entertainer voice.

"Terrible joke, but great story."

"Best I could do off the top."

"I especially liked the part where that guy named Mason somersaulted off the table like an acrobat, without falling on his face. Really, a nice move for someone who used to trip over his own shoelaces."

"Listen, I'm sorry about the cheering line," Mason said.

"It's okay. It's probably better that way. When you add the goblins and the handsome and all of that stuff, all of a sudden, I feel—you know . . . ."

"Kind of stupid."

"Yeah, a little. I mean, not that I'm *not* handsome or anything."

"You are," Mason said, then quickly backtracked. "I mean, I could see where somebody might think so."

"Oh." There was an uncomfortable moment of silence.

"But I know what you mean. That's the way all my customers feel, too," Mason added. "Every time they come to pick up their songs, they realize that what they actually did and what they wanted to *think* they did are so different that they can't pretend any longer. It's kind of sad, really."

"It's terrible."

"It's pathetic."

"Do me a favor, will you?" Cowel said. "Don't sing any more songs."

They rode in silence for another hour, the tips of the Windmourn Mountains starting to break through the clouds far ahead of them. The road had narrowed to be barely wide enough for two horses brushing shoulders, and it was lined on both sides with golden stalks that stretched as high as Steed's ears. Once the sun offered enough light, Mason figured it was his turn to read and cracked open his father's book to chapter seven, "Transportation—Or Why It's Always Better to Be the Lead Horse." Cowel, meanwhile, was humming some tune to himself, making up the words as he went along just to see if he could, but he got stuck on finding a word to rhyme with *pretty* that wasn't vulgar. They had no idea how far they were from where they were going, mostly because they didn't know where that was.

And then the narrow road curved and they saw the sign. The one Sal Beerbalm had told them about. One arrow pointed east, toward the wide, inviting fields, and the other south, toward a horizon dense with trees. The road east beckoned them with a gravel path leading into the rising sun. Mason thought he could hear birds chirping along the way.

The sign pointing south simply said: FOREST SHORTCUT. BEWARE.

"Huh," Cowel said, then turned around, no doubt to confirm that there was really only one path to take. But Mason stared instead at the dirt path headed toward the line of trees.

"You can't be serious," Cowel said, reading Mason's mind.

"We don't have a lot of choice, now, do we?"

"That's exactly what I was thinking," Cowel said.

But Mason had made up his mind. He had started to wonder if he had the whole hero thing mixed up in his head. He always thought of it in terms of action, blades crossing, arrows soaring, heads tumbling off shoulders. But maybe it wasn't necessarily like that. Maybe heroism was simply a matter of taking the road less traveled.

Maybe there were shortcuts to becoming a hero.

Besides, they had already wasted a day. They were running out of time. In more ways than one, Mason said, it seemed like a shortcut was just what they needed.

That, Cowel said, and a serious slap to the head.

But he reluctantly steered Steed southward anyway.

In the bards' songs, everything was pretty clear-cut, almost predestined. The heroes rode out of the gates determined and rode back in victorious. Motives were clear: good and evil, right and wrong. Heroes didn't sell boots. Swordsmen didn't take naps. Bullies didn't wear dresses. There was no such thing as a shortcut. It almost seemed as if there was no such thing as a choice. There was SHB, and everybody stuck to it.

Outside of the songs, however, there were decisions, which were irritatingly always accompanied by consequences.

Mason and Cowel had been riding through the woods for at least an hour—or maybe three. The way the treetops obscured the light and the way the landscape never changed—just more green and brown everywhere he looked—made Mason lose all sense of time. Cowel had insisted Mason take over the reins when the dirt path suddenly disappeared less than a mile into the forest. There was some talk of going back and taking the long way, but Mason reasoned that if they just headed in the same direction, they would have to come out of the forest eventually.

"That's not what your father says," Cowel said from behind. He was flipping his way through chapter nine: "Location, Location, Location." "We could technically be in a Never-Ending Woods."

"How do you know if you're in a Never-Ending Woods?"

"He says if you never get out, it's probably never-ending."

Mason was starting to get a little annoyed with the book.

"According to this, though, there are basically only two kinds of forests: haunted and not haunted."

"That sounds easy enough."

"But within the category of Haunted Forests there are several subtypes: 'Evil Haunted. Wicked Haunted. Spooky Haunted. Mysterious Haunted. Demon Infested. Spider Infested. Demon Spider Infested. Super Evil. Super Wicked. Evil Wicked. Wicked Bad. Wicked Good. Flying Monkey Infested. Sleepy. Hollow. Imaginary. Living.'"

"Living?"

"That means when the trees are alive."

"Aren't all trees alive?"

"It says here: 'alive and kicking.'"

"Trees can kick?"

"The list goes on. Do you want me to keep reading?"

"Does it say what kind of forest we are in right now?"

"Well, do you see any spiders?"

"No."

"Demons?"

"Not yet."

"Witches, warlocks, ghosts, monkeys—flying or nonflying, caged spirits, walking trees, burning bushes, hanging carcasses, giant snakes, toads wearing crowns, goat people staring at themselves in ponds of water, talking plants, or smoking caterpillars?"

"No. None of those."

"But you feel creeped out?"

"Actually, before I was just creeped out. Now I'm seriously *freaked* out."

Cowel ran his finger down a chart on the page in front of him. "Then I'd say we are dealing with either Generic Creepy or Generally Spooky Haunted or Plain Old Unhaunted."

"Let's hope it's just plain."

"And not never-ending," Cowel added. "It says that regardless of what kind of forest you are in, you shouldn't talk to anything with fangs."

"Got it."

"Especially if they are dripping."

"Good." This at least sounded like something they could accomplish.

By the time Cowel had finished reading chapter nine out loud, Mason knew the basics of forest navigation. Avoid houses made of bread or candy—or anything edible, for that matter. Avoid anything that looks as though it may swallow you, including patches of loose dirt. Generally, avoid everything until you get out of the forest—unless, of course, you went into the forest searching for danger, in which case you should have gone at midnight and followed the screams and pounding drums.

They rode in silence for what seemed like another hour, the woods marching on forever on all sides. Steed didn't seem at all nervous to be stuck in the middle of a possibly Generally Spooky Haunted Forest—he probably would have walked right up to a flying monkey and nuzzled it, if they had seen one. Behind Mason, Cowel had fallen asleep, his cheek pressed against Mason's back.

Mason heard a low growling and looked around nervously before realizing it was his own stomach. He reached into the saddlebag for what was left of the bread and chewed it slowly, but it only made him hungrier, his stomach going from a murmuring burble to a full-throated roar.

It was then that Mason noticed the smoke rising through the trees.

A few minutes passed, and then he could see the source of the smoke. A cabin—or more of a cottage, really—made of wood rather than stone was up ahead, the chimney puffing a steady stream.

For hours they had been in this forest and Mason hadn't seen so much as a chipmunk. Now there was this. Mason didn't need to read appendix C of his father's book—"Omens and Portents"—to know that anytime you are lost in a forest and you realize you are hungry and a cottage *suddenly* and *fortuitously* appears from out of nowhere, it is *not* a good sign. Anything that just *happens* to be there when you need it was most likely put there by someone who wants something from you in return, such as a bent-over hag who just happens to have a recipe for young man's kidney soup that she's been *dying* to try and a predictable shortage of donors.

But nothing was that simple. Could be this was the house of an experienced woodsman, a ranger swift of feet and sharp of eye, with a bow hanging over his fireplace—maybe just the person they were looking for.

Then he heard the cackle.

It wasn't a cackle so much as high-pitched laughter followed by choking and coughing, but he heard it three times, more than enough to convince him to give the house a wide berth. Behind him, Cowel mumbled something about a dress. Mason kept one hand on the hilt of his sword for appearance's sake as they veered away from the cottage and its cackling.

The house vanished behind the trees. But Mason still kept

looking over his shoulder, disturbing Cowel, who finally woke up. He tried to wipe the drool from the back of Mason's shirt, but it was already soaked in.

"Still in the forest," he said.

"Still here."

"How long have we been out here?"

"Hard to tell. Feels like hours. I don't think it's evening yet. You missed the witch's hut," Mason said.

"Are you serious? There was a witch's hut and you didn't wake me up?" Cowel all of a sudden sounded really annoyed, though it could have just been after-nap crankies.

"Don't worry. It's not like we stopped by for a visit. I didn't actually see anyone. I just heard her."

"She sounded witchy?"

"Kind of. Actually, it sounded more like gagging than cackling. By the way, before you go rummaging, we're out of food."

"That's not good," said Cowel. "Did you check to see what your father had to say about witches?"

"Sorry, no. I was so busy guiding the horse *and* keeping us out of danger that I didn't have any time to read."

"You don't have to be sarcastic about it."

"Thanks for the advice, said the kettle to the pot."

Cowel rubbed his eyes and took the book from the bag. Mason, meanwhile, was starting to believe they were truly lost. The trees seemed to be getting denser the farther they went. It didn't seem to be much of a shortcut, but this *was* Mason's first trip through potentially haunted woods.

"There's a page and a half here on witches. Do you want history or classifica— Hey!"

The sound of Cowel slapping his skin made Mason jump.

"What happened?"

"Something bit me."

"Bit you?" Mason hadn't even seen a bug yet, but they *were* in the woods.

"Mother pus bucket."

"Did you get it, at least?"

"No. It got me right in the back of the— What the . . . ?"

There was another slap.

"What?" Mason said, twisting around in the saddle to look at Cowel. "Did it get you again?"

"On the bloody ear!" Cowel was rubbing his ear with one hand. With the other, he had closed the book and stuffed it back into the satchel.

"Maybe you should slap a little faster next—" But Mason didn't get to finish his sentence as a sharp sting pierced him just above his ankle, where his pants met his new boots. "Bastard!" Mason bent over to look and almost fell off the horse when Cowel slapped him hard across the back of the head.

"What was that?"

"I saw it! I saw something. It landed in your hair and—" But the next ten words were a string of barely comprehensible curses as Cowel returned to slapping the back of his neck, then his shoulder, then the back of his arm. As Mason examined his heel, he felt a touch on his shoulder followed by another sharp sting. He cried out again and slapped wildly for it. Behind him, Cowel was thrashing around madly, looking over as much of himself as he could, hunting their attackers.

"What the heck is that thing?"

"What? What is it?" Mason asked, starting to get frantic.

It wasn't till one landed right on Mason's nose, perching there as if settling on a branch, that he had the slightest clue what they were dealing with. Mason stared cross-eyed at the little wonder an inch in front of his eyes.

Where he expected two wings, there were, in fact, two.

Where he expected six legs, however, there were also only two.

Where he expected no arms, there were also two. And two hands clutching a miniature spear that looked no thicker than a sewing needle. A spear that was promptly jammed into Mason's nose before he could come to grips with what he was seeing.

Mason cursed and slapped himself across the face, but the tiny person was too swift. Launching itself from the bridge of Mason's nose, it reared back in the air and threw its spear, lodging it in Mason's hand. Mason pulled it out and sucked on the wound just as another creature landed on his leg and started jabbing him with a sword the size of a thistle. The little beast was about half a finger high and slender—but despite its size, Mason could make out that it was wearing clothes made from a leaf. Its hair was blond, and it had barely perceptible pricks for eyes. Even though its face was no bigger than a raisin, Mason could see that it was set in a look of fierce determination. He swung at the little creature, sending it tumbling off his leg. Behind him, Cowel started sneezing.

Mason could see them now, now that he knew what he was looking for—about ten of them buzzing in the air above him. Cowel was barely staying on the back of the horse, his arms flailing about him. Steed seemed unperturbed, even though Mason was digging his heels into the horse's sides. One of the creatures flew in front of Mason's eyes, gesturing as if threatening to poke them out. Mason managed to swat it away.

Cowel grabbed onto the back of Mason's shirt with one hand to keep from falling, swinging the other frantically like a ball and chain. "What are these things?"

Mason had some idea, having read about creatures like

these before. They were either fairies or sprites or pixies, though he couldn't tell one from another. So instead, he just said, "They're annoying," as he smashed one in midair, watching it somersault to the grass.

And that was when they heard it. The pixie war cry.

Because these weren't fairies or sprites. As the *Guide* would later inform them, sprites were loners, not used to hunting in packs and more prone to mischief than assault, and fairies were peaceful, free-loving sorts, often too high on their own dust to get up off a leaf and do anything.

But pixies were vicious and well trained. Highly territorial, they defended their sections of forest from intruders of all sizes. The fearless and minute warriors always sent a scouting party in advance to gauge the toughness of their enemy, get them disoriented, and make them overconfident. Then, they would bellow their war cry and reveal their true numbers.

Mason and Cowel both covered their ears, and then Mason pointed to the dense cluster of trees ahead. A cloud was forming—a thick green and beige cloud that seemed to vibrate as it undulated down out of the tree trunks, a screeching cry emanating from it.

"Oh, pig shit" was Cowel's understated response as the cloud billowed toward them at three times the speed of Steed's trot.

But Steed wasn't trotting anymore. At the sound of the pixies' cry, he had stopped. His ears had perked and he had started to walk backwards, kicking out with one of his front legs and snorting. Something had finally gotten the horse's attention.

Mason could now see the particles of the cloud and make out the hundreds of armed and irate pixies heading their way. He yanked hard on Steed's reins, hoping the horse had finally gotten excited, but Steed didn't respond. That is, not until one of the members of the scouting party flew into his ear.

Steed's eyes went wide, he reared back, and he shook his head.

And then, for the first time in Mason's company—though Mason had *heard* about it a hundred times before—Steed let loose. It took everything Mason had to turn the horse around and head back the way they came. The chase was on.

Mason's butt slammed hard against the saddle, his body slipping one way and then the other, as the horse galloped hard through the trees. Steed careened from side to side with his head down, still shaking, even though the pixie had vacated his ear a while back. Mason started to tell Cowel to hang on, but he soon realized that Cowel didn't need the message. Mason could hardly breathe because of how tightly Cowel had his arms wrapped around him. If either of them fell now, they would both be at the mercy of five hundred miniature swords.

Mason had his face pressed into Steed's mane, but he knew by the sound that the swarm was close. A pixie scout still had a grip on one of Mason's arm hairs and was swinging back and forth. The trees flew by to the right and left. Somewhere up ahead, Mason thought he caught a glimpse of smoke.

The thundering of hooves and the buzzing of a thousand wings echoed throughout the forest, and Mason could feel the war party catching up. Either that or Steed, who was not used to galloping, was already slowing down. Mason felt something in his hair and shook his head as hard as he could, slamming his ear into his own shoulder. Behind him, he could hear Cowel stop sneezing and start to cough instead. Was there a less noble demise than being pricked to death by hundreds of people so small you could fit ten of them in your pocket? Would he bleed to death droplet by tiny droplet? How would this one go down in the books? The coughing over Mason's shoulder grew worse.

Then, suddenly, the buzzing stopped.

Mason looked behind him. The cloud of pixies had halted their pursuit, having driven the interlopers out of their territory. Mason heard what he assumed to be a victory cheer, and then, in the same manner as it had appeared, the mass of pixies drifted back up into the trees and vanished.

Cowel's face was red, his eyes were closed. Mason gave Steed the only command he knew the horse would follow, and the sweaty beast slowed to a canter and then to a stop, circling around to make certain for himself that the swarm of pests had disappeared.

Mason flicked the last pixie from his arm and turned to his friend. Cowel didn't look too good. His face was pink and green, and one hand clutched at his stomach.

"I think I swallowed one," Cowel managed in a raspy whisper.

"What?"

One of the pixies Mason had swatted during the chase had lost control and tumbled backwards, Cowel said. He had started to sneeze, shutting his eyes and opening his mouth. There had been a sharp intake of air, followed by a more surprising intake of pixie.

"I think . . . I think it's inside." Both hands were holding his stomach now. His eyes crossed, then shut again.

Mason checked to make sure that no more pixies had hitched a ride and then quickly took out his father's guide.

"It hurts."

"I know. Hang on."

"What does the book say to do?"

"Hang on, I said. I'm looking. Pixies, pixies, pixies. 'Where they live, different species, kept as pets, infestations and removal . . .' Aha—'remedies.' It says there's a product available from most apothecaries called Pixie-Off. Wait—that's just designed to repel pixies. It says nothing about what to do if you've *swallowed* one."

"I think it's tying me into knots down there, Mason. What do I do?"

"I don't know. Try burping."

"Can't. What if I swallow a lot of water? We could drown it."

Mason checked the bag. "We don't have any more water."

"Oh, god."

"It says here that if a pixie manages to cast an enchantment on you, the only way to have it removed is by a witch or a wizard. Would you call this an enchantment?"

"I swallowed the damned thing!" Cowel made a kind of gurgling sound, then doubled over himself.

"Right. Right. So we need a witch, then."

"A what?"

"That's what it says. 'If all else fails, your best bet for pixie problems is a witch.'"

"Great. And where are we supposed to find one of those?"

Fira Firaxin massaged her throat, which was already quite sore. She wanted to give up but had promised herself to do this for an hour a day until she got it right.

She cleared her throat and looked in the mirror hanging above her fireplace. "Here goes. Yeh-heh-he-he-ha-ha-har-hrch-erch-hck-hck-mph-cmph-hmph."

She whispered a breathless "Crap."

She always started high, as she was supposed to, but as the cackle trickled down into the lower registers, she inevitably ended up coughing. This would be fine if she were sixty, had a cold, or was a smoker, but a seventeen-year-old witch should be able to produce a nice, full-throated cackle.

The best Fira Firaxin could do was screech, cough, and curse.

And unlike her orange hair, which she could at least dye black whenever she had to make an appearance, the cackle wasn't something she could just gloss over. It was the only thing holding her back.

Well, to be honest, there was also her nose—a cute, upturned button that was as far from a crooked witch's stick as you could get. Then there were her fingers, which were short and stubby, and her nails, which she desperately wanted to grow out to the required two inches but couldn't because of her nervous chewing. She had once painted her nails with pepper juice for a week, hoping it would curb the nail biting, but that had only gotten her used to the taste of pepper juice, which she now drizzled on everything she ate.

Some would say the fact that she was pretty—or if not pretty, at least cute in a nymphish sort of way—was a drawback, but there was no rule against a witch being pretty so long as she had either the nose or the cackle going for her. But Fira had neither. Nor did she ever ride her broom, being deathly afraid of heights. She also didn't wear her hat because she liked the feel of the sun on her face.

Which explained why she was so interested in the cackle. If she could get *that* down, at least, she would make a passable witch. If there was any mistaking her identity—if anyone guessed her for a sorceress or an enchantress—she could give them a cackle and prove them otherwise.

"Reh-he-he-he-herng-ungh-ugh-ugh-ugh-ooph ... Crap, crap."

Her mother would be giving her a look right now if she were here. That was the hard part, seeing her mother's looks in her own mind. The pitying "I told you so" look. The condescending "Why couldn't you have gone to apothecary college and simply set up your own shop in town" look. Or the "Why don't you just find a nice businessman like I did and get married rather than live like an outcast in the middle of the forest scaring away any hope you might have of landing a husband" look. That one was the worst, because her mother was right about the scaring-away part. Just today she had heard hoofbeats from outside her window and looked to find two young men on horseback skirting her cottage.

At least her grandmother understood. Fira smiled weakly at the mirror, and the mirror smiled sympathetically back. *It's all right, dear,* it said. *Don't worry about the cackle—they're overrated. Just get the door.*

Seconds later there was a knock on the door.

Fira Firaxin checked herself in her *other* mirror, the normal one beside the cauldron on the mixing table, and tucked some loose hair behind her ears. Most likely, it was her stepfather, sent by her mother with a basket of bread and another plea for her to move back home and forget this witch nonsense. Or maybe it was a couple little kids who had wandered too far into the woods and had run out of bread crumbs. She always gave them candy—Fira made exquisite cream-filled chocolates that didn't turn you into anything but fat. What she didn't expect, though it was what she hoped for most, was that it was someone who actually needed her—someone *looking* for a witch. Fira considered putting on her hat.

From above the fireplace the mirror told her to go on, hurry up, she looked fine.

She opened the door to see two young men, one leaning over trying to gag himself, the other one holding him, breathless and scared. Fira first made a note of the sword hanging from the second one's side, but a glance at his face and a little witch's intuition told her it wasn't much use to him yet. The second thing she noticed was that he had a witch's nose, but short of that, he was handsome enough—the kind of guy her mother would no doubt approve of, though the gagging one might be the cuter of the two if he wasn't . . . well . . . gagging. Finally, she noticed that both were dotted with red welts. Obviously, they were in a bind.

"Sorry to bother you," the one still standing upright said, holding out three pieces of gold as if that explained everything, "and please don't take this the wrong way, but are you a witch?"

The moment she opened the door, Mason knew they were in trouble. No hat. Orange hair. She was wearing a sweater that had "Forest Vixen" glittered across it and a pair of pants that had been cut just below the knees. Her hair looked brushed and was tucked coyly behind her ears, rather than falling in limp, oily strings down the sides of her face. She looked about his age, which made her at least twenty years too young, and he didn't see a wart on her anywhere. She didn't smile deviously when she opened the door but instead seemed to bite her lower lip in concern. Her teeth were too white and her fingers weren't crooked. Her eyes, he noticed, were green, but that was about it.

She was no closer to being a witch than he was to being a hero.

Beside him, Cowel collapsed. Mason had to grab him and pull him up.

The young woman at the door didn't say anything, just stood there for a moment, as if she had never considered the question before, as if Mason had asked her, *Do you ever wonder how they first discovered that chocolate and peanut butter went well together?* rather than *Are you a witch?* Then, finally, she nodded and pressed her back to the door, welcoming them inside and pointing to a bed where Cowel could lie down. Mason stood in front of the door, taking *his* turn at being hesitant, as if her nod could have meant, *Sure, you idiot, walk right into a witch's hut where you could easily be put to sleep by a spell and then turned into a newt,* but another groan from Cowel erased his concerns. Mason dragged him inside and laid him down.

A quick look around confirmed that if this girl was not a witch, she had at least hired one as an interior decorator. A cauldron stood simmering in its stand. The table was lined with at least twenty vials and bottles filled with liquids and smoke of different colors. There were dusty books sitting on a shelf in a corner, skulls used as bookends. The mirror above the fireplace was obviously bewitched, reflecting the image of an old woman who wasn't in the room but seemed to be smiling contentedly nonetheless. There was even a broom propped up next to the door.

The girl closed the door, and Mason spun around, half expecting to be zapped by a wand. But she just stood there, wringing her hands, still chewing on that lower lip, and then biting the ends of her fingers, somehow as nervous as he was.

"Pixies," Mason blurted out, as if that explained why they were there even better than the three gold pieces he still held in his sweaty palm.

"Pixie *bastards*," Cowel amended through his moaning.

"Yes. They've a nest not far from here. You must have walked into it." The girl went over to the bed and looked over the small, red bumps on Cowel's face and arms. "How many times were you stabbed?" she asked.

"No, that's not it. We think he swallowed one," Mason said.

"Bloody lunatic jumped down my throat!" Cowel's eyes were clenched shut. He looked as bad as Mason had ever seen him, worse than he did when he thought he was going to be smashed by the Queen Bee.

"Oh. Oh, dear. Was he armed?"

"They all were. Swords. Spears. Daggers."

"I think he had a dagger," Cowel said.

"That's not *as* bad," the young witch said.

"Not *as* bad?" Mason asked.

"He's probably trying to cut his way out. But if it's only a dagger, it would take a while."

"What does she mean, *cut his way out?*"

"We need to get him out as fast as possible." The girl pointed to an iron pail sitting next to the door. "We'll need that," she said, pushing Mason toward it. Then, she turned to the mirror above the fireplace and made a face. The old woman in the mirror shrugged her shoulders, and Mason heard the young witch huff as she settled at her worktable, uncorking one bottle after another, taking a good whiff of each.

"Are you going to poison it?" Mason asked.

"We can't poison it without poisoning your friend as well." She wrinkled her nose at one vial, recorked it, and put it back down. Mason brought the bucket to the bed and Cowel squeezed the hand he offered. Then he turned to see the witch uncap a small flask full of brownish purple liquid and grimace the moment she brought it to her nose. She quickly restopped it, looked the label over, and then held it up to the mirror. The old woman in the mirror nodded.

"This should do it," she said, coming over and kneeling beside Mason. "Hold his head back. Tilt it. Yes, like that. Good. You have to drink this," she said, speaking louder to Cowel, as if he were farther away. "All right. Don't hold his nose. It's better if he smells it, but you might want to hold *your* breath."

Mason took a deep breath and looked back and forth from Cowel to the witch, hoping that nobody this beautiful could be evil enough to transform his best friend into a toad. The girl covered her mouth with one hand and popped the cork again with her thumb. Cowel's eyes watered and he shook his head, but before he could seal his lips, she plugged his mouth with the bottle's opening and held it there until empty.

Cowel's body trembled for a moment as the witch threw the empty vial in the fireplace, where it shattered and gave off a faint green smoke.

"Give him the bucket," she said to Mason, "and go outside."

Mason didn't move, though. Cowel's face was turning different colors, no longer red but now a kind of rotten yellow. Mason saw his friend's fingers twitch and his cheeks bulge. The young woman put a hand on Mason's shoulder. "Trust me. It won't be pleasant." Mason could smell the remains of the potion, a combination of vinegar and sulfur and onions. He watched Cowel's stomach bounce, the muscles contracting forcefully. Mason realized the girl's suggestion had been a good one. He got up and moved toward the door, the witch right behind him.

It sounded bad.

Mason had many memories of being sick. It happened quite a lot when he was a child. He remembered his mother kneeling beside him, wiping his forehead. His father wasn't around then.

A long, heaving retch came from inside the cottage, followed by some coughing. Two seconds later, Mason heard the shattering of glass.

"That was it," the witch said, and started to get up. When

Mason tried to follow, she put out a hand. "Don't worry. I'll take care of him. Stay here."

So he sat and waited, inspecting the welts that were growing more inflamed on his arms and legs, wondering if the one on his nose made it look even uglier. When the witch reappeared, everything in the cottage was quiet. She brushed her hands on the front of her sweater.

"He's fine. Resting. I gave him something for the pain."

"Did he break something?"

"That was the pixie. Went straight through the window."

"Through the window?"

"They are remarkably resilient. I think it was happy to be out of there."

"We'll pay for the window," Mason said. Then he just had to ask: "What did you give him?"

The witch sighed. "It was supposed to be cough medicine. It had all the right ingredients, but it was the foulest-tasting stuff I've ever concocted. I didn't think I would ever find a good use for it."

"He's going to be okay, right?"

"Oh, he'll be feeling it for a while," she said with raised eyebrows. "You shouldn't piss off a pixie."

"We didn't know."

"That's the problem. They look all innocent, with those sparkling wings and the glitter and everything. Find one in your shoe and it's no problem. But get around a swarm of them and you're done for. Is that your horse?" The girl pointed to Steed, who was resting after his gallop through the trees.

"More or less. We're borrowing him from a friend."

"You must have a lot of friends."

He wondered how she came to that conclusion, wondered when having two friends, especially when he really had only one, qualified as a lot. "So, how long before Cowel can travel?"

"That's his name, Cowel?"

Mason blushed. "I'm so sorry. I'm Mason."

"Fira."

Mason couldn't believe he was shaking hands with a witch. He also couldn't believe she didn't have any boils. He wondered if that meant she was a really great witch or a terrible one. He didn't want to ask.

"He'll be okay by the time he wakes up, though he won't feel like eating for at least a day. Maybe two," Fira cautioned.

"We're very lucky you were here."

"It's not as much coincidence as you think," Fira said. "Every haunted forest has at least one witch. This one has three, though the other two are notoriously antisocial. You were bound to run into one of us."

So it *was* a haunted forest. "If there's anything we can do to thank you," Mason began, but Fira just waved him off.

"Don't worry about it. It wasn't even a very witchy thing to do. It made me feel useful for a change." She noticed Mason was staring at her hair, which made her self-consciously run a hand through it. She also noticed his knees were knocking together and he didn't smell too good.

"So what's it like being a witch?"

"It's about what you'd expect. I study. I read. Mix potions. Practice spells. Go searching for frogs with identity complexes. Lately, I've been trying to cackle."

"I heard. To be honest, we passed by here earlier."

"I know. I saw you."

"You mean, like through a crystal ball or something?"

"No. I just looked out the window." She picked at the letters on her sweater.

"We should have stopped and asked for directions," Mason said, shrugging. "It wasn't personal. I mean, I didn't know. You're very nice . . . and pretty." Mason held his breath. He hadn't actually meant to say the last part.

But Fira hadn't heard, or at least she didn't say anything, though Mason did catch her biting her lip again. "So tell me, Mason, how do two lads such as yourselves get mixed up with a nest of pixies to begin with? Aren't you a little young to be adventurers?"

Mason wanted to ask if she wasn't a little young to be a witch. "Believe it or not, we're on a mission." Then Mason told her everything, starting with the town and its hero and going through the boots, the Bee, and the shortcut. She listened intently, rising only once to check on Cowel, who she said was sleeping soundly.

"I've heard of Darlinger, of course, though I never would have guessed that what you said about him was true. I suppose reputations are really only as good as the words they rest on. I've heard of Highsmith, too. I had an auntie who once lived there—Moxy Firaxin."

"Moxy Firaxin, the hero?"

"Well, that's not what my *mother* calls her. But my grandmother says she was the best treasure hunter in the five lands."

"Your grandmother? The woman in the mirror?" Mason had noticed streaks of orange mixed in with silver in the old woman's hair.

Fira nodded. "She was a witch, too. She had two daughters, one a little more adventurous than the other. Moxy left home when she was only fifteen. Meanwhile, *my* mother got herself caught up in one night of passion, found herself abandoned and alone *and* expecting, and sought out the first wealthy man she could and seduced him—my stepfather, though I probably would have grown to accept him as my father if my mother hadn't always been in the way."

"Sounds terrible," Mason said.

"It gets worse. Mom thought Grandma has been too free with them and couldn't bear the thought of raising her daughter the same way. So instead she choked me to death. She never let me do anything, I mean, so I decided to follow in my grandma's footsteps and moved out here. I changed my name from Fira Delacorte to Fira Firaxin—Delacorte wasn't my real name anyway—and I've been living here ever since."

Mason drew lines in the dirt with his heel. "I never really knew my father, either. Only that he was a hero—a really good one. At least, according to my mother."

"What was his name?"

"Edmond Quayle."

Fira nodded and bit one of her nails.

Mason guessed she hadn't heard of him. "He left almost ten years ago with a bunch of other heroes and never came back."

The young witch's eyes brightened. "Auntie disappeared a long time ago, too—maybe they left together. That seems odd, doesn't it?"

"I suppose it does," Mason said, then added, "What does?"

"That your father and my aunt might have known each other and that the two of us should meet now."

"I guess. My father knew all the heroes in town. But it's still strange."

"Maybe it's destiny."

"Yeah. Maybe," Mason said, but he didn't believe it.

"My stepfather has a business in Heartwood, and he knows lots of people, too. Maybe he could help you. It's not far from here—a couple of hours' walking. We should wait until your friend feels well enough to ride, though. Grandma told me we should let him sleep as long as he wants."

"That could be a while," Mason said.

They chatted some more, until Mason couldn't think of anything else to say. He stared at her, at this witch with a witch for a grandmother, a different kind of witch for a mother, and a hero for an aunt. A witch who couldn't cackle or make cough syrup, who made his heart beat in his ears whenever she wiggled her toes, which she did often. This witch about whom he desperately wanted to write a song in the hopes that she would laugh with him and let her hair fall in her face. He didn't have these kinds of thoughts often.

Finally, the silence got overwhelming. "I'm going to go around back and pick some mint leaves," Fira said. "When your friend wakes up, he's going to have a terrible taste in his mouth."

She was right, though when Cowel *first* woke up, he started slapping himself and scratching his head. Pixies on the brain, Mason figured.

"Who is she?" Cowel said, staring dreamily at Fira. His voice was raspy, as if it was painful to talk. Mason thought that might not be such a tragedy.

"This is the talented Fira Firaxin. The nicest witch of the Winding Woods and niece to Moxy Firaxin of Highsmith."

"How are you feeling?" Fira asked.

"Like I swallowed a hornets' nest."

Cowel sneezed. Fira wiped his nose with a cloth, and he looked at her in shock. Mason figured Cowel wasn't used to people being nice to him, either.

"My tongue tastes like cows' hooves."

"Here. Chew on this." Fira offered him spearmint leaves and then started applying some salve to the stings on his face and arms. She had put the same on Mason an hour earlier, and each time she had touched him, he had felt little electric jolts. That's when Fira had told him she thought his nose was adorable, as if he needed any more reason to like her.

"Fira's aunt was a hero. We think she may have been one of the ten who left town with my father, believe it or not."

"It's a small world," Cowel commented.

"She says," Mason continued, talking to Cowel as if Fira weren't kneeling right beside him, "that we aren't far from Heartwood. There might be someone there that her stepfather knows."

"Good. You take her and the two of you come pick me up later. I'm not going back into that forest until it has been thoroughly sprayed with Pix-Off or whatever that stuff is."

"You don't have to worry anymore about pixies," Fira said. "They're easy to take care of."

"Easy," Cowel retorted. "*Easy.* They chased us halfway through the forest. They made a pincushion out of my face. They practically—" But before he could finish his tirade, a pain in his stomach shut him up.

"Witches don't have to worry about pixies," Fira said, dabbing the last bit of salve on a splotch on Cowel's chin, "because pixies are deathly afraid of brooms. It's hard to hit a pixie with a sword, but with a broom you can take out scores of them. They think brooms are evil."

Mason looked at the witch's broom propped next to the door. "But how do you fly it and swing it at the same time?"

"I don't. I walk everywhere. It's the only way a witch has of keeping in shape. After all, we spend most of our time huddled over our cauldrons, and we are notoriously addicted to chocolate. At least I am."

Mason wanted nothing more at this moment than to have a piece of chocolate to give her.

"In fact, as soon as you feel up to it, we can go. On the way you can tell me more about this quest of yours. I'll even let you," she said to Cowel, "hold the broom."

Mason felt a pang in his chest as the orange-haired witch slipped Cowel a sweet smile.

Before they left for Heartwood, they had to say goodbye to Grandmother.

This took a lot longer than Mason expected.

"Now, remember, don't tip your hat to another witch unless she tips hers first—you're still an apprentice. And if you should come across some fellweed, be sure to pick it, but only if it's the four-leaf variety. The five-leaf kind will rot your fingers."

"Yes, Grandma."

Mason made a mental note not to touch anything with five leaves.

Cowel made a mental note not to touch anything.

"And don't listen to anything that your mother says about me, but tell her I hope she wallows in her own regrets."

"I'll tell her you said hi."

"Tell her whatever, but don't say anything to that husband of hers. He's suspect."

"He's a nice man, Grandma."

"I think he's a block of wood that's been bewitched to look like a man. I've seen it happen. He can't be too smart—he married your mother."

Cowel sneezed, though Mason didn't know why. Perhaps he was starting to feel nervous around Fira's grandmother.

"And you might have your friend there save some of his snot. Young men's snot is good for lots of potions. Mix it with a little snail slime and wart crust and you have the makings of a glue that can stick to anything."

"You don't have to save your snot," Fira whispered to Cowel, who smiled and wiped it on his pants.

"And if people throw stuff at you, remember to duck. And if they hit you, do not be afraid to zap 'em one, okay? Just use that osteosis curse I taught you."

"Osteosis curse?" Mason whispered.

"It causes bones to shrink," Fira said. "It's actually quite dangerous. Mostly, if I have problems, I just give people the tickles. You feel like there are a thousand little bugs crawling over your skin."

Cowel shuddered. Mason scratched his head subconsciously.

"You are taking your broom, aren't you?" The woman in the mirror wasn't done.

"Yes, Grandma."

"And your hat?"

"No, Grandma."

"Well, at least paint a wart on your nose."

"I'll be fine, Grandma. We have to go now, really. We'll be back soon."

"And don't flirt too much with these boys."

"Grandma!"

"It's just that you don't want them getting jealous. Boys are stupid and petty and would probably kill one another just to get attention from a witch like yourself."

Mason and Cowel looked at each other. They were, *Who, me?* looks, but Mason was really thinking, I would never *kill* him.

"I have to apologize for her. She's been in that mirror for

years. She doesn't get out . . . *ever,* so she has this kind of screwed-up little version of the world."

"Don't talk about me as if I can't hear everything you are saying, Firamina Firaxin."

"Sorry, Grandma."

"Now, come over here and give your granny a kiss."

Fira walked over, stepped up onto the hearth, and pressed her lips against the mirror, leaving a smudge. *Great,* Mason thought. *Now I'm jealous of the stupid mirror.*

Grandma was still talking as Fira pushed them out the door. Cowel, who still wasn't feeling that well, got the privilege of riding Steed, which was fine with Mason, who walked beside Fira and held the bridle. Mason made a point to bump into her on occasion, pretending that he was never really able to walk straight on account of one leg being longer than the other. Fira said the osteosis curse could help with that, up to a point, but then all of his bones would break and he wouldn't be walking anywhere.

On the horse, Cowel was holding the broom with its straw head upright as if it were some kind of spiritual symbol, looking around wildly for the first flutter of wings.

— 6 —

Family Matters

The orc whose reputation and cutthroat practices had driven him to the top of the minions of darkness sat behind a desk of polished bone, his head bent over a piece of parchment, his trademark sable Mohawk arcing forward like a cresting wave. His skin was seaweed green and sandpaper smooth, with only one scar that extended from his right ear to within a half-inch of his flared nostril. His office was decorated with the most fashionable skulls and animal hides, imported from the surrounding mountains. A goblet of goat's blood sat untouched on his desk. In three days, he figured, he could drink all the goats he wanted.

A knock on his door was followed by the entrance of four armed guards escorting a bearded human looking a little roughed up. This was the first prisoner the orc had seen in a while. The duke's coffers had kept the dungeons empty for years.

"I assume this is important," Bennie the Orc said.

"Scouts outside Darlington picked up this man on horseback," one of the guards said. "His saddlebags were full of gold—all with the duke's seal on it."

Bennie shrugged his shoulders. He knew he wasn't the only

one with his hand in the duke's pockets, though he did feel he had first dibs, given their recent agreement.

"One of the scouts identified him as the duke's personal assistant."

Bennie stroked his Mohawk. "Does he have anything to say?"

"He says there is no way the duke can raise the money you are asking for."

Bennie shrugged. "Then we will just take whatever the duke can get and whatever else we can find afterward."

"He also says he wants to make a deal. He says he has some information that you might find interesting."

"Information?"

"A potential problem, he says."

"That's fine. Just leave him here. I'll take care of it."

The guards left their prisoner on the wolf-skin rug and retreated. The door to Bennie's office was left open just a hair. Through the crack, the guards watched Bennie get up and say something into the man's ear. Just a few words. Suddenly, the man's tongue was tripping over itself as if it couldn't move fast enough.

When he had apparently heard enough, Bennie spoke again into the man's ear, shutting him up instantly. The guards admired their boss's efficiency. Most of the orcs around there had gone soft. They had love handles and flabby arms. They didn't remember what it meant to be a nostril-flaring, ax-swinging terror anymore.

Less than three minutes later, Bennie called the guards back into his office. The captive was sobbing so hard it seemed he might cough up his lungs on the floor. Bennie sat at his desk and started scrawling something on a blank piece of parchment. "Take the gold he came with, make sure he has nothing else of value, and deposit him somewhere in the mountains. Anywhere is fine, just so long as he's breathing when you leave him."

"Yes, sir."

"The duke is not cooperating as fully as I had hoped. Apparently, he dispatched a messenger. He's using his gold to buy mercenaries rather than giving it to us."

"We can deal with mercenaries," the head guard said.

Bennie shook his head. "That won't be necessary. This messenger couldn't have gotten far. But if he does get far, it could be a problem."

"Do you want to round up a hunting party?"

"No. Just send the Wolf."

"The Wolf?" the guard asked. They rarely used the Wolf for anything anymore. He was too demanding and unstable. Not to mention that he refused to take anyone alive.

"Let's just take care of it."

"Yes, sir."

"And have that sneaky goblin come here, if you can find him—the one with the pant leg on his head. I want to be sure that the duke and I are absolutely clear about our agreement."

Bennie the Orc slumped back into his chair, tapping gnarled fingers along the edge of his desk. If Darlinger was spending some of his gold on swords for hire and having the rest of it stolen by his servants with only three days left, there was no way he would fulfill his end of the deal.

Which meant it was probably time for Bennie to start sharpening his sword.

Cowel managed to stay awake through the last of the forest, chewing on the stash of mint leaves Fira had given him as if it were a recently acquired addiction and swinging the broom back and forth once in a while in a menacing manner. Once the trees parted, he drifted off again, smothering his face in Steed's mane and snoring fitfully.

Mason, meanwhile, was content to pass the time in conversation, for once forgetting about who he was and what he was doing. He still couldn't believe he was walking with a witch.

"I'm not really a witch yet. I still haven't managed to transmogrify anybody. Until I do, I can't be a witch."

"Transmogrify?"

"Turn someone into something. A toad. A squirrel. A weed. Or I could do it the other way around. Turn a weed into a human. But it can't be just any weed. It must have once been human. Otherwise it will look like a human but think and act like a weed—just standing in one place and annoying everything around it."

"Sounds like Cowel some days."

"Oh, I think he's sweet," Fira said, turning to look at the slumbering pixie swallower with the broom precariously balanced across his lap.

Mason quickly steered the conversation away from Cowel. "But you like being a witch otherwise—minus the toad-turning part?"

"It's better than being my mother," Fira said.

Mason nodded as if he had met the woman, when really, given her daughter, he couldn't imagine how she could be anything but charming.

"How about you?" Fira asked. "Have you always been an adventurer?"

Mason snorted. Cowel would have laughed if he had been awake. Steed just plodded on. "Adventurer? No. I'm a writer," he said.

"Oh, how *terrible.*" Fira covered her mouth as soon as she

said it, flushed with embarrassment. "I didn't mean that. I just can't imagine sitting in front of a piece of parchment all day."

"It's okay. It's not terribly glamorous."

"Do you sing?"

"Poorly."

"Play an instrument?"

"Not well. Even worse now that one string on my lyre is broken."

"But you enjoy it. You must, I mean, if you are as bad at it as you say you are." She laughed, and the sound of it, like swimming through wind chimes, made Mason laugh with her even though they were laughing about him.

"Do you know any songs? I mean, could you recite one?"

Mason shuffled his feet. He felt the reins slip in his sweaty hands. "I know one. Just made it up yesterday."

"Would you mind?" Fira said, and Mason couldn't tell for sure, but he thought that maybe, just maybe, she had winked at him.

Mason cleared his throat and, as best as he could remember, recited "The Queen Bee's Defeat," offering it up under its new title. When he finished, Fira applauded, causing him to turn pink in embarrassment. He admitted that most of it was fiction—or at least highly embellished. He wasn't half as heroic as the poem made him out to be.

"You shouldn't be so hard on yourself," she said. "Knocking on my door was a courageous thing to do. I might have given you the pox."

"What's the pox?"

"Oh, it's terrible and it spreads all over. And you don't even *want* to know how much it oozes," she said, and then gestured toward a hub of points and boxes in the distance. "There's Heartwood. That's the lord's castle. He's a pansy, just so you know, so I wouldn't bother asking *him* for help. But my stepfather will certainly know someone. He's a horse dealer and knows just about everyone in the town."

"Your stepfather raises horses?"

"Just sells them. He'd probably give you a good deal if you were looking to trade up. Your horse looks a little . . . plodding."

Until something flies into his ear, Mason thought to himself. "Do you think your folks will be happy to see you?"

Fira smirked and rolled her eyes in a way that, Mason found, made his right knee buckle. "Oh, they'll be ecstatic for the first five minutes. After that, you might want to stand to one side."

"Why's that?"

Fira narrowed her eyes, staring at the nearing town.

"You don't want to get hit by anything," she said.

On the way through town, Fira told Mason everything she knew about Heartwood, though there wasn't much to tell. The town relied mostly on the exportation of the furs and skins it collected from smaller villages in the mountains, she said. That trade relied heavily on caravans, and caravans relied on horses, which was why her stepfather was so successful. "Honestly," she said, "the whole town is downright snotty, if you ask me. And superstitious. They don't like witches, that's for sure."

"You've had trouble?" Mason asked.

"I've had my share of rocks thrown at me. Of course, my mother tells everyone it's not me. She says *her* daughter is off at boarding school learning to sew."

Mason thought about his mother, sitting in her chair, reading a book, and looking sideways at the door. He wished he could tell her he was all right.

Unlike their experience in Ancherton, where they stuck out like pimples about to pop, in Heartwood nobody bothered to give Mason and Cowel a second glance. Mason was a little worried about traveling with a witch—mostly for her sake—but without her hat and with her hair not dyed, she didn't attract much attention, though a couple of people did look suspiciously at the broom that was looped through Steed's saddle. "We'll probably have to venture into the center of town to find what you are looking for," Fira said, "but we can first at least see if Frank is home. Besides, I could stand some more clothes."

When they finally stopped, Mason had to drag Cowel off the horse to wake him. "Where are we?" he said, spitting out chewed-up leaf bits and scraping his tongue with his teeth.

"We're here."

"Where's here?"

"Fira's house. And stop spitting."

The Delacorte residence was large—three stories, with nine rooms and two washrooms. Despite Fira Firaxin's warning that it was all just for show, Mason couldn't help but be impressed by the marble tile, the ivory columns, and the gold-trimmed vases that sat on fancy three-legged tables by the door. They were greeted at the entrance by a butler dressed in sweeping blue robes. He stood almost a foot taller than the young men and had a curled mustache that looked as if it might wrap twice around his head if you stretched it.

"Aha. Young Miss Delacorte has returned. I assume these two are here for a ransom." The butler looked down at the three of them standing by the door. Mason wanted to say something in response, but Fira beat him to it.

"Blue robes this month, is it?"

"Your mother's idea, entirely," the butler said. "She also has been making me speak in a ridiculous accent when there's company. I swear, if you don't banish her to another dimension soon, I'm going to smother myself with one of her gold embroidered pillows."

"You can always find another job, Famadore," Fira chided, giving the butler a hug.

"And leave behind all of Mr. Delacorte's money? I figure, with you disowned and no other children, I stand to inherit the house."

"You can have it," Fira said. "Is Frank home?"

"He's at the lot. But your mother is taking her second nap. Shall I fetch her for you?" The look on Fira's face was answer enough. Mason and Cowel exchanged uncomfortable glances.

"Actually, sandwiches would be better. Do you have any real food in the house or is Mina on one of her diets again?"

"I keep some stuff hidden away for your stepfather's midnight snacks."

"Thank you, Famadore."

"Certainly, my dear." The servant beckoned to Mason and Cowel. "If you two gentlemen would like to follow me."

Mason looked at Fira. She nodded. "It's all right. Grab something to eat, and then we'll go track down Frank. I'm just going to sneak up to my room and get some things." Fira kissed Famadore on the cheek and then smiled at Mason and Cowel before tiptoeing up the bearskin-lined stairway.

"Please, come in," Famadore said, suddenly much warmer, and led Mason and Cowel into the kitchen, where a modest wooden table—the only unassuming piece of furniture in the entire house—was quickly accessorized with two mugs of ginger beer and a couple of mutton sandwiches.

"Do you take lettuce and tomato?" he asked, shutting the kitchen door.

Mason shook his head while Cowel nodded and sucked

down his own saliva. How he had already managed to find his appetite after having puked up a pixie earlier that day was far beyond Mason.

"You must understand, lettuce and tomato are all Madam Mina eats anymore—that and rice-cakes. We are never without the fixings for a lettuce, tomato, and rice-cake sandwich." Famadore grimaced. Mason smiled self-consciously. He hoped Fira would hurry up so they could take their grub and eat on the road. The house made him uncomfortable.

"And how do two young men such as yourselves happen upon our fiery-headed little witch, anyway?" Famadore asked.

"Pixies," Mason said, causing Cowel to choke on only the second bite of his sandwich. It wasn't long after that he pushed his plate toward Mason, telling him he was welcome to the remains.

"How long have you known Fir—Miss Firaxin?" Mason asked back.

"I've known Miss Delacorte all of her life. She's a remarkable young woman." Famadore then launched into a series of anecdotes from Fira's childhood that Mason swallowed voraciously, ignoring Cowel's half-sandwich, which Cowel eyed with both longing and disgust. The servant was in the middle of telling about the first potion Fira had mixed, using him as her guinea pig—and how long it took him to grow all of his hair back—when they heard squeals from the stairs.

"Fira, *darling*. What a surprise. I had no *idea* you were stopping by."

"What in the five lands was that?" Cowel asked. Mason thought maybe a small animal was being slaughtered at the top of the stairs. But those squeals were followed by the sound of Fira's voice, her words indistinguishable but her tone all points and edges. They could just make out the sound of bickering through the closed door. Mason wanted to get up and go see what was happening—do something, offer support—but Famadore shook his head.

Then, Fira must have said something particularly salty, because the bickering turned to shouting.

"You ungrateful little witch" came the mother's squeal.

"I'm getting taller" came Fira's retort.

"You should not speak about your father that way. He has given us this house. He paid for your education—"

"*My* father did only one thing, which he probably regretted in the morning, which is why he left. And yes, *your* husband has given you a nice house, and a fancy carriage, and pretty little vases, and I think you've done a marvelous job of hiring people to take care of them."

"Don't use that tone with me, young lady. You are the one who . . ."

"And if you didn't always chastise me every time I came . . ."

". . . off in the woods eating children and . . ."

". . . sit on your butt all day thinking up new ways to make my life miserable . . ."

". . . talking to that conniving witch of a woman who got herself stuck in a mirror . . ."

". . . making Famadore, or, better yet, *Frank,* do *everything* for you, showing off your expensive jewelry when you go slumming in the markets with your girlfriends . . ."

". . . just like your grandmother, head in her dirty pots, talking to imaginary creatures who . . ."

". . . was a wonderful woman—unlike you—and who wants me to tell you, by the way, that she hopes you are still breathing, though I'm sure she wouldn't really care if you . . ."

". . . throw away your life just like she did, just like your aunt did, for nothing."

And then, there was the sound of something very brittle smashing into something very unforgiving. Mason's guess was vase/floor. Cowel suggested wall. As if that was his cue, Famadore stood up and went to the door, stopping to pick up a small brush and a flat scoop to sweep up the pieces of what was left out there—vases, egos, whatever. Mason and Cowel looked at each other, then hurriedly followed.

It was vase/wall as Cowel had predicted, judging by how far the pieces had scattered, littered across the first five stairs. Fira was standing at the bottom, her mother at the top. Clearly, Fira hadn't been aiming to hit her, just to shut her up.

It didn't work.

"That's just like you, breaking a vase that is probably worth more than everything you own just to spite—"

But as soon as Mason and Cowel appeared in the doorway, Mina Delacorte stopped and smiled at them. Mason was a little shocked. He had expected to see a snake-headed gorgon. Instead, Mrs. Delacorte was a relatively attractive woman, obviously the source of Fira's sunburst hair, though she looked much more plump than her daughter around the thighs and hips. She smiled again, weakly, then turned back to Fira.

"You didn't tell me we had guests, dear. Nor did you, Famadore."

"Mah soncere apologes," Famadore said, affecting the accent Mrs. Delacorte insisted he use that month. "May ah presaunt Monsieurs Mason and Cowel."

They just stood there, both of them, wondering if they should bow, wave, or offer one of the dirty hand gestures they had learned from their very short time in the Hive. Instead, Cowel smiled and Mason frowned.

Fira didn't need reinforcements, anyway. "And just so you know, Mother, these are just *two* of the *hundreds* of young men who come to my door. But see, unlike you, I don't need to leech off someone else just to feel better about myself. In fact, I don't even need this crap." Fira threw down the pile of clothes she had been carrying, pilfered only minutes before from her dresser. "I don't need anything else from you or your husband or this stupid house."

"You shouldn't get so angry, dear," Mina Delacorte told her, her voice soft and even, tinged with that artificial niceness that turned her words into icicles. "Every time you yell, it screws up your face and makes you so ugly."

"*Arrrgghhhh!*"

Fira Firaxin tore the front door open as hard as she could, but it hit the stopper and rebounded closed again, which made her even more frustrated. With another scream, she threw it open again, this time throwing her shoulder into it so it stayed.

Then, she turned and stuck her tongue out at her mother.

"Firamina Delacorte!" Her mother's voice had changed, sapped of its artificial sweetener and now just bitter. Mason thought he could see the snakes starting to sprout from her head. "You walk out the door without apologizing and it will be the last time you ever step foot in this house."

Fira turned back around to face her mother. "In that case," she said, much calmer now, "let me break one more vase—just to tide me over." Fira kicked the stand holding a vase on the other side of the hall, sending it smashing to the floor. She turned to Mason and Cowel, who were still standing dumbstruck and lamblike in the hallway. "We're leaving," she said as a mother would to two children. Mason expected Mina Delacorte to say something, to stop her. But Fira's mother just glared, standing proudly at the top of the stairs.

Instead, it was the servant Famadore who spoke up, though

in the heat of the argument, he had forgotten his fake accent. "Shouldn't you at least give her the letter?" He spoke to Mrs. Delacorte, but Fira, with one foot already out the door, heard him and stopped.

"Letter?" she said, turning and staring at Famadore.

"What letter?" Mrs. Delacorte demanded from the top of the stairs.

"The letter. The last letter from Miss Moxina. The one she wrote to Miss Fira specifically. The letter you were supposed to give her when she turned fifteen."

"You have a letter from Aunt Moxy and you never gave it to me?" Fira glared at her mother, eyes like embers.

"As if you deserve for me to give you anything," Fira's mother retorted. "Besides, I lost it years ago."

"I saw you reading it three days ago," Famadore said. "You keep it in the silver box under your bed."

Mina Delacorte's own eyes sparked and then went dead as she turned to stare at her butler. Her ears were glowing red. "You've been *spying* on me?"

"The letter *is* hers," Famadore said. "Miss Moxina even addressed it to her."

"You mean you've *read* it?" Mina glared at the butler with a look that should have turned him to stone. "Should I be afraid to ask what else you've been snooping through?"

There was a moment of silence, one Mason knew would be perfect for a gesture, either him touching Fira's shoulder in sympathy or Cowel playing comic relief, but neither of them moved.

It was Mina who spoke first. "Fine. Treat it as your farewell present. Famadore, you may go get it since you know where it is. Please consider that your last duty in the Delacorte household. And given that the only sorts my daughter would associate with are thieves and murderers," she said, looking at Mason and Cowel, "I suggest you two turn yourselves in at the earliest opportunity in the hopes of avoiding a hanging. Good afternoon to you all."

And with that, Mina Delacorte, wife of a horse salesman, sister to a vanished hero, and both daughter and mother to witches strode mock-triumphantly down the hall and out of sight, slamming a door behind her.

Fira steadied the angry tremble of her lower lip and put a hand on Famadore's arm. "I'm sorry. I really didn't mean for you to get involved."

The servant shrugged. "Honestly, I was going to quit anyway. The last two years without you have been torture. She is a hard woman to live with. Too bad Mr. Delacorte isn't home enough to notice."

"Maybe that's *why* he's never home," Cowel offered.

"I'll go get that letter," Famadore said. "I would have told you sooner, but I just found out about it myself."

"No, I'll get it. If you would, pack up some food and fresh water for the road. I'll meet you all outside."

Cowel nodded and practically dragged Mason through the open door. "How do people like that ever manage to get married?"

Mason said that Fira must have a lot more of her father in her. Or her grandmother. Or her aunt. Anyone but the woman who actually gave birth to her. He just couldn't see a connection beyond the hair. And the temper.

Famadore appeared at the door with four bags tucked into the crooks of his arms. One was for Mason and Cowel and held some cheese, a few plums, two loaves of bread, and their refilled flasks of water. The other three he called workmen's compensation. "To tide me over until I get another job." They sat in silence on the Delacorte front step, each chewing on a hunk of the bread, until Fira appeared at the door, her eyes swollen, the pile of clothes she had insisted she didn't need in one hand and several sheets of folded parchment in the other. She asked to speak with Famadore alone. Mason watched a conversation full of embraces and then watched Famadore bow to them before disappearing down the street.

"Will he be okay?" Mason asked as Fira joined them. She answered with a nod. "What about you?"

"Oh, don't worry about me. This is the fifth time she's told me never to come back. What will happen is Frank will come home and she will tell him all about it. He will agree with her, of course. Then, a week from now, I'll get a knock on my door. It will be Frank, sent on behalf of my mother with an apology, begging me to come back home."

"Will you?"

"I don't know. It was only a two-vase fight. We've had worse . . . that is, back when she used to keep a bunch of them sitting out. But this did feel a little different. She didn't have to fire Famadore. I feel bad for him. And the letter. That's a lot to forgive."

Mason finally found his moment and was happy when Fira didn't flinch at his hand on her shoulder. "So the letter—was it, you know . . . I mean, was there anything important in it?"

"Actually, it's funny you should ask," Fira sniffed, looking directly at Mason. "There's a part in here about your father."

It was only a small part of a letter that spanned seven pages in small script. Most of it, Fira said, was personal, stuff her aunt wanted her to know about her mother and father—her real

father—and some words of encouragement, telling her to follow her dreams.

The reference to Edmond Quayle was near the beginning, in
a section where Moxy Firaxin described the journey of the ten
who left from Highsmith. She *was* with them, it turned out, at
least for a while. Though Mason wanted to read the entire letter, Fira kept pointing to the one paragraph where Edmond
Quayle's name appeared.

*We are supposed to be headed to the village of Galen's Cove, buried
about a third of the way up the mountains, but a few of us are starting to have doubts. The locals have heard of Snowbeard's treasure,
but none of them have ever seen a coin of it. There have been adventurers come this way before us, they say—hundreds—all asking the
same question. Less than half have passed back through. Still, it is not
courage that is lacking among the party, only conviction. I think we
are chasing after ghosts. Morlin has also voiced his concern, suggest-
ing we head east instead and hire ourselves out in Velmore or
Yorkville. But the Warrior Poet insists. He knows the stories. He reads
us passages from books. The treasure exists, he says, and it is buried
in the Windmourns, guarded by a dragon more fearsome than a
thousand orcs. We are not afraid of dragons. Only of becoming fools.
Strange that nine of the finest heroes to walk the Alley of Highsmith
should be following the footsteps of a man who scribbles in books all
day. In all the years we have known him, Edmond Quayle has never
steered us wrong. But this time, I'm afraid, the bard is chasing his
own imagination.*

"You see. There it is. Toward the bottom. That is your father,
right?"

Mason didn't speak. Just kept reading the paragraph

over and over again. He squinted at the words as if they were hieroglyphs. He could feel the world spinning around him.

. . . Nine of the finest heroes to walk the Alley of Highsmith . . . following the footsteps of a man who scribbles in books . . .

"Your father was leading the expedition," Fira said, her tone hopeful. She was smiling at first, but the look on Mason's face caused her to stop.

Mason shook his head, holding the letter out to Fira as if it were on fire. "This doesn't make any sense," he said. "He was one of the ten. One of them. My mother always told me . . ."

Fira looked back and forth between Mason and Cowel, confused. She went to grab the letter that was offered to her, but though he held it out, Mason refused to let go of it.

"I mean, that's not him, is it? A *bard?*" Mason turned to Cowel. He found eyes full of sympathy but not much surprise.

"Sorry, Mason. I didn't know or I would have told you."

"He's still your father," Fira said.

Mason tilted his head to one side and then the other, as if rolling something slowly from ear to ear. "But my mother always said . . . She told me stories."

"*His* stories," Cowel said, then added, "You're making too big a deal out of this. Your father was a good man. Read the letter."

Mason stared at the letter. Nine heroes. One bard. His father hadn't been one of the heroes.

"You don't know him any better than I do, any better than she does." Mason pointed to Fira. "I have no idea who he is," Mason said, "or was."

Cowel took a step forward and tried to put a hand on Mason's shoulder, but a sharp look warded him off.

"Don't touch me," Mason said.

"Well, at least your father didn't sit behind a desk making stuff up. He actually experienced it. He actually went out and did something worth writing about."

Mason took two steps backwards. "Sure, he did something. He abandoned my mother and led nine other people to their deaths."

"You don't know that."

"Read the letter. Her aunt knew. He was a fool."

"You shouldn't talk about your father that way," Fira interjected.

"At least you knew him," Cowel said, advancing toward Mason, who began to retreat. "Look at the two of us. I live with my drunk uncle in a shack in the backyard of what used to be my house. I don't even remember my father. *She* just got thrown out—again—by her own mother. She never even met her real father. And you stand there bitching because your father wasn't *exactly* who you thought he was and because you have a mother who loves you so much that she wanted you to admire him as much as she did. Just let it go."

Cowel stood right in front of him now. Mason wiped his mouth with the back of a clenched fist. He didn't say anything; he just shoved the letter at Cowel, who took it reluctantly. Then the son of a bard turned and walked away, certain of only two things: that he had to keep his back to them and that he couldn't stop his feet from moving.

In all the years we have known him, Edmond Quayle has never steered us wrong.

What few memories Mason had of his father involved stories in one form or another. His father would be away for days and would return with fairy tales. Songs of valor and daring fit for a boy of five or six—the kind of stories that would keep you up at night, your imagination juiced. They were grisly and elaborate, and they were always told in the first person plural: *we* traveled, *we* confronted, *we* saved. In the recountings, Edmond's name was never actually mentioned.

When he was six, Mason didn't notice. It didn't occur to him that his father never used the word *I*. He didn't consider that, unlike the other heroes who rode through the gates of Highsmith, Edmond Quayle rode without armor and always at the rear. None of it mattered to a six-year-old boy who flopped around the house in his father's oversize boots and swung tree branches at imaginary orcs.

Mason guessed it didn't matter to his mother, either, as long as his father came back.

She had to have known, of course. Perhaps to her, he *was* a hero. Or maybe when he left, she glorified him, giving Mason, and even herself, some reason to hope. After all, a hero would find a way to get home, but there's no telling what might happen to a bard. Maybe she told Mason what she thought he wanted to hear, what every boy of that age wants to believe: that his father is invincible.

But in giving Mason something to aspire to, someone to worship, she had also given him something always to fall short of.

Until one day an adventure falls in your lap. Then you actually start to believe. Even though you know better, you start to think you can be one of *them*. Because the sons of heroes have it made. It's in all the stories. The orphan farm boy who discovers his father was once the king becomes a prince. There's always a sword waiting to be pulled from a stone. In the songs, a boy's future is dictated by his father's past. Mason had started to believe that maybe he could do more with his life. That he could take his father's place. After all, the sons of heroes usually inherit their fathers' swords.

Mason inherited a book. Which is why he stared sullenly down the unfamiliar street. Deep inside, there had always been the hope that one day he would follow in his father's footsteps.

Quayle's Guide to Adventures for the Unadventurous.

As it turned out, Mason had been following his father all along.

Mason wandered past the opulent architecture of Heartwood's Upper East End, oblivious to the fluttering of people. The image of his father reciting bedtime stories—nose wedged between the pages of a book, peeking over the edge at Mason huddled in the sheets—loomed before him, and Mason followed it through the streets. After a while, the houses dropped from three stories to two, then to one.

Mason's feet eventually planted him outside a row of shops—most of them full of pewter and cheap threads. Lodged among them was a shack not too different from the one where he spent his own working days back in Darlington.

The sign—a piece of bark—said MADAME PERUGI'S HOUSE OF STARS in gaudy gold lettering with a misshapen star in each corner. The door simply stated ASTROLOGER. None of this enticed Mason. He knew of several such shanties in Darlington, all inhabited by thieves or quacks. Any other time, he would have walked past it without a second thought.

But then he saw a piece of parchment nailed next to the one closed window. Something about it spoke to him, and he approached to get a closer look. From the moment he read it, he knew that, scam or not, he needed to hear what Madame Perugi had to say.

Worried about your future?
Left without a sense of direction?
Feel like your world's turned upside down?
Madame Perugi can help you.
She'll tell you the truth, straight up,
with a shot of ale for a chaser.
Come inside and learn your future.
*Two silver pieces for standard reading.
Crystal ball extra. Ale not included.

Mason figured he had a couple coins to spare.

It *was* a scam. At least, part of it. The part about Madame Perugi actually being *Madame* Perugi, for one. In fact, Madame Perugi was actually a paunchy bald man, with pipe smoke coming out of his nostrils and hair coming out of his ears. This revelation, revealed when Mason pushed back the curtains and stepped into the hazy "reading chamber," caused him to falter.

"Before you even ask," Madame Perugi growled from a table, "my name is Joe Perugi, this is not an act, and I put that on the sign because no one believes that a fat, balding man can tell the future. But you put 'Madame' on the wall and they'll believe anything."

"Oh," Mason said.

"And before you waste any more of my time, why don't you set your two silver pieces in that bowl there."

"Oh," Mason said again, but while Madame Joe took three puffs on his pipe, Mason composed himself, fished in his pocket, and produced the coins, clinking them into the empty bowl. "Right," he said, sitting in the only other chair at the table.

"Welcome to Madame Perugi's, where we tell you only what you want to hear. As you can see on the board"—Joe Perugi used the end of his pipe to point to a sign posted behind him—"we are running a special today on readings. We can give you a card reading for the usual price of a palm job. That's when I throw some pretty pictures onto the table and tell you what they mean."

"Okay."

"All right, but first let's just get some basics down. How old are you?"

"Don't you know?"

"Believe me," Joe said, smoking away, "I could figure it out, but it would use up too much of the psychic energy, see? It's just a whole lot easier if you tell me. So, how old?"

"Fifteen."

"Name?"

"Mason Quayle."

"Profession?"

"Bard."

"Sorry about that."

"It's all right."

"Any girlfriends?"

"What?"

"You got a girlfriend? A personal life-quest partner? Anything?"

Mason thought of Fira Firaxin but shook his head. Then, he thought about Cowel and shook it harder. "Isn't that one of the things you're supposed to tell me?"

"Listen, kid, don't tell me how to do my job. I'm only protecting you. You have a fragile psyche."

"I do?"

"Or else you wouldn't be in here talking to me. Now, let's say you're bothered by some cutie back in the neighborhood and you think the two of you are going to get hitched or some such—you're, like, madly in love, right? And you come here and I look in your future and see that you are actually destined to be with some dame from across the sea. That's just the kind of thing I'm *not* going to tell you, because then, you'll just go break up with your girl because you know you aren't meant to be together and miss out on what could be a really fun time."

"But wouldn't I just break up with her anyway?"

"I'm not going to map out every second of your life, kid."

"So you're saying there are things you won't tell me."

"If you want to hear it, I'll tell it. I'm just trying to be nice."

Mason nodded and then sat nervously in his chair as Joe pulled a deck of bent and beaten cards from the shelf behind him, shuffled them once, and then started to flip them over.

"All right, let's see what we got. Giant peacock. Crossed staves. The hornless unicorn, some guy with a sword through his head—that's never good."

"What does it mean?"

"Means he probably just cut his brains in half."

"No, what does it mean for me?"

"Don't know yet. We have to take these things in order. Tells a story, see. This is just the beginning. All right. Let's see here. Okay. Huh. That's interesting. Tomorrow you are going to wake up as a fifty-year-old woman with chronic hemorrhoids."

"What?"

"Oops. Got this card turned the wrong way. There we go. That's better. All right, the cards say you are on a journey."

"Yes."

"You're looking for something."

"Yes."

"But you haven't found it yet."

"Yes."

"Good. It's settled, then." Joe looked up from the table. "Is there anything else you want to know?" He leaned back in his chair, taking another contented puff on his pipe.

"Yes, there's more I want to know! All this stuff is obvious. What kind of predictor are you?"

Joe put his hands up and Mason noticed how muscular the Madame was. "Fine. You don't have to get pissy. Just ask me and I'll tell you."

"How about this, for starters: am I going to find a hero to save the stupid town?"

"Oh, *that*. You want to know the answer to *that*. Silly me. I mean, I thought you *knew* that one already. It's sitting right in front of you. Yeah, I saw that one easy. It's in this poor bunny chewing off its own leg here."

Mason looked at the card. Sure enough, it was a picture of a rabbit that had been caught in a trap and had chewed its own leg down to the bone. It was all the more horrifying because somebody had painted it in too-vivid colors.

"So I guess that's a no."

"Not necessarily."

"I'm not necessarily going to find a hero, or it's not necessarily a no?"

"Is finding a hero necessary?" Joe squinted through the smoke.

"I'd say so."

"Then it's not necessarily a no."

"But what's the answer? Am I going to find one or not?"

"Sure."

"Sure?"

"More or less."

"What does that mean?"

"It means kind of, but not really."

"How not really?"

"It's all a matter of perspective."

"Could you just tell me yes or no?"

"Normally," Joe said, leaning back, "I'd say yes, but there are other forces at work."

"Other forces?"

"They are hindering your journey."

"Like the trap the bunny is caught in?"

"This isn't about the bunny anymore. Get off the bunny."

"What do you mean, then? Other forces, like pixies or something?"

"You've had problems with pixies?"

"I don't know—have I?"

Joe caught something in Mason's eyes, or maybe just the welts on his neck and chin. "According to the cards, you've already gotten past the pixies. No, there's other stuff. Malevolent stuff."

"Like what?"

"Well, let's see." Joe flipped over another card. It was a picture of a ship tossing on a stormy sea. "Oh, that. You'll want to forget about that."

"Forget about what?"

"It's not relevant. It's a glitch card."

"Glitch card?"

"It doesn't pertain to the current situation. It just kind of slips in. Glitch in the system."

"But what does it say?"

"It's about your first time kissing a girl."

"What about my first time kissing a girl?"

"You don't want to know."

"Why don't I want to know?"

"It's a ship tossing on a stormy sea. There are lightning bolts shooting down from the sky. There's a tidal wave about to engulf the ship. Do I have to draw you a diagram?"

"So it's not good?"

"Just forget about it. Let's see what the next card . . . oh, jeez! Oh, lords, no! Stop! Oh, man!"

Sitting on the table was a picture of a skull set in a smile. The skull was yellowing from age, and there was a dark, billowing cloud hovering over it. A raven was settled beside it, plucking out the last pieces of flesh from one of its eye sockets. The moment he turned the card over, Joe's face scrunched with pain, and he had started banging on the table with one hand as if the card itself was ripping his heart out.

"What? What is it?"

"Aw, crapping bastard!" Joe said, the grimace starting to fade.

"What? What is it? Am I going to die?" Mason turned around quickly, half expecting an executioner to already be standing behind him. Joe's eyes were tightly closed. "Just tell me, *am I going to die?*"

Finally, Joe sighed. "Of course you're going to die—what kind of stupid question is that?" he said, still wincing slightly.

"Then what? What is it?"

Joe hissed and took a couple of deep breaths. "You know how when your leg falls asleep and then you move it suddenly, you get that kind of burning sensation?" Joe reached underneath the table to massage his calf. "I hate that."

Mason mustered the smile of someone who would rather say nasty things. "So the card isn't about my death?"

"You mean this grinning skull of black death?"

Mason nodded.

"No."

"Really?"

"Really. It's just a metaphor. Everyone says it's really not a bad card—some change in your future. In your case, I think it's an ironic commentary."

"Ironic commentary?"

"That's why it's grinning. It knows something funny about you."

"What? What does it know?"

"It's not saying."

"Well, read the card. Just tell me," Mason said, exasperated.

Joe snapped back, "I told you, don't tell me how to do my job. You want to go find out your future for yourself, be my guest. I don't need any crap from you."

"Sorry."

"It's all right," Joe sighed. "Let's just turn over the last card and tie this all together, shall we?" Joe turned the bottom card face up. It showed a rather large man sitting at a table in a cramped room. He had two faces on opposite sides of his head. One face frowned while the other grinned mischievously.

"Right."

"Right what? What is it?"

After one last puff, Joe dumped what remained in the pipe onto the floor beside him. "It's the two-faced lying bastard."

"What does it mean?"

"It means that in the very near future you will be duped out of some money by someone who is much bigger and stronger than you."

"The *very* near future?" Mason asked.

"So close you can almost taste it. In fact, if I had to guess . . . and . . . yes, there . . . there it goes. You see, it did come true.

Thank you so much for coming. I hope all of your questions have been answered."

Mason stood up. "Wait a minute, *none* of my questions have been answered!"

"On the path of life, the mysteries make the adventure," Joe said matter-of-factly.

"But I don't want any more mysteries. I want answers. Or I at least want my money back."

"I foresaw you were going to say that," Joe said.

Mason reached toward the bowl, but Madame Perugi put one very large hand over the top. "Touch it and I will accurately predict the exact time each of your fingers breaks."

Part of Mason wanted to fight, even though he knew he would lose, and he'd be out the rest of his coins and sporting bruises. He wanted to draw his sword and stand up for himself. But that wasn't who he was. There were no heroes in these cards—just bunnies chewing off their own legs.

"Fine," Mason said, and he turned and parted the curtains.

"Hey, kid," Joe said, his voice losing its threatening edge. "One other thing. You got to forget all that crap about your dad."

"What?" Mason stopped and peered back through the opening in the curtains.

"Your father. The ghost you're chasing. You're getting it all mixed up. It's not about inheritance or destiny or any of that. You have to make your own adventures."

"How did you . . . ? I didn't say anything about . . . I mean, did you see that in the cards?"

"The cards are crap. I just use them because if people sit here for only thirty seconds, they feel like they aren't getting their money's worth. The thing about your dad I knew the moment you sat down. I saw it in your eyes." Joe Perugi smiled.

"He wasn't exactly who I thought he was."

"Right. Who is? We see what we want to see. Eventually—not now, because you are too close and you have to push on—but eventually, you are going to have to learn to let go. But not until . . ." Joe's voice trailed off into a whisper.

"Not until what?"

"Not until you meet him again," Joe said with a wink.

"Meet him? What do you mean? You mean my father?"

"More or less." And before Mason could speak again, Joe raised his hand. "I can't tell you any more because I don't see any more. Now, get out of here and let me smoke in peace."

And with that, Mason found himself back outside, in front of the door to Madame Perugi's House of Stars.

Feel like your world's turned upside down? the sign asked him.

Mason looked down the long path he had taken to get there. There was nothing to do but start walking.

When he finally made it back to Fira Firaxin's former porch, ready to offer an apology to her and Cowel, Mason found his longtime companion stretched out in the grass, barefoot, with Steed grazing beside him. The witch was nowhere to be seen. The fact that Fira had disappeared made Mason's heart sink down to his ankles. He had really thought she would still be there, waiting for him at least to say he was sorry.

Cowel didn't look at all surprised to see him. Without a word, Mason fell beside him. The sky suggested that evening was almost upon them. Mason didn't say anything about where he'd been, only that he was exhausted. He nodded toward the house questioningly.

"She left. Back to the woods. Said there was some stuff in that letter, stuff she needed to talk to her grandmother about. She wanted me to tell you she was sorry."

Mason said he had come to say the same thing, that he had acted like a jerk. He didn't say anything about the psychic. Cowel would probably want to go himself, and Mason could feel the day closing in. Cowel agreed, somewhat, with the jerk thing.

"We could talk about it, if you want. We don't talk about these things."

"We're not married," Mason said.

Cowel sat up and looked at Mason. "You know, the way they talk about him, your father really was good at what he did. *The* Warrior Poet of Highsmith, no longer anonymous. And that book of his is really pretty good."

"I know. Did she say anything else about the letter—the rest of it?"

"Only that at the time she wrote it, Fira's aunt was considering leaving the other heroes to seek her fortune north. There were other parts—last wishes, some regrets. Mostly she just told Fira to be herself."

"Did she—Fira—say anything else? You know, anything about me?"

"Only that it didn't matter who your father was."

Funny, Mason thought. *Coming from Joe, it sounded like prophesy. Coming from Fira, it sounds like sympathy.*

"Did she say if she was coming back, at least?"

"I didn't ask."

"You should have."

"I know. She really was something."

"Yeah."

"Yeah."

Mason savored the image of her standing at the foot of the stairs, eyes brighter than her flaming hair, upper lip curled between her teeth, cheeks plump and pink with rage. Judging by his smile, Cowel was enjoying a similar vision.

"I don't know. You think a witch and a plume salesman . . . you know?"

"I don't think so."

"You're probably right," Cowel said with a sigh. "She gave me the address of her stepfather's business. She's almost certain he can help us."

"I don't suppose we have any other choice."

"It's almost day three, Mason. I hate to say it, but we are running out of time. We'll have to get back, heroes or not. I don't trust the duke."

Mason had already come to the same conclusion. "Do you think Fira's stepfather is still there? I don't want to have to come back to this house again."

"You've met Mrs. Delacorte. How late do you think *you'd* stay at work every night?"

Frank Delacorte's Hooves for Less was centrally located in the business district of Heartwood, just two blocks south of Heartwood Cured Meats, which many of the town's residents found suspicious. The lot consisted of a huge fenced field with at least thirty horses, a few of them—the showcase models and the year-end clearances—tied to posts out front. A sign above the office claimed that you got all the horse here without all the manure, and another advertised low, low prices on all thoroughbreds from now until winter.

Mason and Cowel had barely reached the farthest corner of the lot before the boisterous voice of Frank Delacorte assaulted them.

"Why, hello," he said, smiling so large it looked as though

he would break his own jaw. "That's quite a beast you have there." He shook both of their hands the moment they dismounted, throwing his arms around their shoulders as if they were old friends. He was *exactly* the way Mason expected him to be, which was a first for the past few days. "Welcome to Frank Delacorte's, where the jokes are always lamer than the horses. What can we do for you?"

Looking at the man, you could tell why Mina Firaxin had married him. He was everything she ever wanted in a man, which is to say rich. Aside from that, he was as wide as he was tall and featured hair-sprouting moles on his chin. His coal black hair was slicked back and polished on top, and he wore clothes dyed so many colors that it looked as though a rainbow had sneezed on him.

"Interested in a trade-in? Move up to a better model—a horse more suited as a two-seater?"

"No, sir. We were actually hoping you might help us find someone."

Frank Delacorte spoke like a man running out of breath, filling each one with as many words as possible. "That's a shame, see, because this here horse isn't going to last much longer. You can see it in his eyes." Frank Delacorte snapped his fingers right in front of one of Steed's eyes. "See? No reaction. Brain dead. I mean, the legs are good, but he's lost his drive."

"Stick your finger in his ear and watch what happens," Cowel suggested.

"Actually, Mr. Delacorte, your stepdaughter suggested we come see you."

Frank frowned. "What has she done this time? She didn't kill her mother, did she?"

"No. Nothing like that. Though there *were* some vase issues."

"Pity," Mr. Delacorte said, though whether he was referring to the vases or his wife was unclear.

"She thought you might be able to help us find a hero."

"A hero, huh? You do know I sell horses, don't you? I mean, you can kind of tell by the piles of crap on the ground." Frank Delacorte laughed.

"Listen, Mr. Delacorte," Mason began.

"Call me Frank."

"Okay . . . Frank," Mason said, glad they weren't in the Hive anymore, "we are *desperate*. All of the heroes we know are either retired, asleep, or faking it. If we don't find someone to help us soon, our village will be overrun. So please, if you've ever sold a horse to a single hero in your entire life, please just tell us."

"We'll pay you," Cowel added, saying the magic words that made Frank Delacorte's eyes light up.

"In that case, I think I know of one fella who might do in a pinch."

The Hive was especially rank and rambunctious that evening, a pack of drunken sailors having accidentally set their own sails aflame. Smoke from the fire hung heavily over the docks, and that, combined with the smell of two barrels of pickled shrimp that had tipped off a wagon and spilled on the road just outside his door, was enough to make Sal Beerbalm shut all the windows and keep a rag dipped in whiskey pressed to his nose. He had given up drinking just that afternoon, but he found the fumes calming, especially when he sucked on a corner of the rag.

Otherwise, evening was upon them and the Hive was vibrating. The streets were crowded. No doubt, all of his buckets would be full again come morning.

A knock on the door promised one customer already.

Sal Beerbalm adjusted the rag under his nose, opened the door, and beckoned the stranger in.

A man entered the inn, nearly seven feet tall, and dressed in a cloak with a leather belt. He was fully bearded, with another six or seven beards worth of hair peeking out from his chest. He looked lean but muscular, and Sal noticed his yellow eyes before he noticed he wasn't wearing any shoes. The man seemed unarmed, though his appearance suggested to Sal that it didn't matter.

"Welcome to the Spiraling Albatross. What can I do for you this evening? Bed, booze, or both?"

"Neither," the cloaked figure rumbled, his voice a husky purr that probably would have been a growl if only he spoke louder. "I'm looking for someone."

"Aren't we all, buddy?"

"A young man. A scout. He was looking for someone as well."

Sal Beerbalm pretended to get interested in a blank page of his ledger. "Sorry. Sailors, brawlers, and drunks I can do. But no scouts. Now, do you need a room or not?"

"His name is Mason Quayle. From Darlington. I understand he was headed this way."

Sal squinted at the stranger. He had been around long enough to know when something wasn't his business, and this clearly qualified. Yet Sal also knew that things that weren't his business could *help* his business. The question was how much.

"Actually, two gentlemen from Darlington passed by not long ago. I might even be able to remember where it was they were headed." Sal Beerbalm held out his hand.

"Tell me where he is" was the gruff reply, but Sal just kept his hand out, rubbing two fingers and his thumb together. After a shrug, the stranger reached into a pocket concealed inside his cloak and pulled out a bottle.

Inside was the most beautiful thing Sal had ever seen. A kind of dancing light suspended in a dark blue liquid, bright enough to spill out through the glass and bathe both him and his visitor in its glow. You could tell just by looking at it that it was extraordinary, maybe magical, and worth far more than the copper pieces Sal would have accepted. He couldn't believe that the whereabouts of two foolish boys who had passed through only a day ago was worth such a thing.

"What is it?" Sal couldn't help staring as the man twisted the bottle in his hand. It looked as if someone had caught a falling star and then somehow kept it burning, and Sal said as much.

"It's the moon, actually—or the light of it, at least. One beam encased in this glass prison," the man purred. "A most extraordinary feat."

"From the moon, you say?" Sal Beerbalm continued to stare, transfixed.

"A full moon, to be specific." The cloaked man clutched the vial firmly in his fist and pressed his thumb onto the top. "And before you make me go through all the trouble of taking a drink, I'm going to ask you one more time . . ."

—7—

How the Dead Speak
to the Living

It didn't take a genius to figure out that something was wrong—the crumbling walls, vines bursting through brick, one window broken. All the lights were out and no one answered the door, even after four knocks.

"I don't think anyone's home. I guess we just leave, then," he said, but she had already pushed open the unlocked door and stepped inside. Perlin Salendor grunted, wondering why more people didn't bother to lock their doors. He had been sober for an entire day and it was making him irritable. Yet here he was, tagging along, partly out of a sense of duty but mostly out of curiosity. They were carrying Cowel's note blaming the duke for some impending catastrophe, and Dierdra Quayle wanted specifics.

Inside Darlinger's estate, there was hardly any furniture to be found. The walls were bare, the floors filmed with dirt. Dierdra suggested that the duke's servants had robbed him blind, but Perlin could tell by the sound of her voice that she didn't really believe what she was saying.

It was at the top of the stairs that they heard whimpering coming from a nearby room. Instinctively, Perlin sheltered

Dierdra with his body and then reached for the nearest thing he could find that looked like a weapon. Thus, armed with a three-branched candelabrum, Perlin inched open the bedroom door, Dierdra pressed close behind him. "Be careful," she whispered as the door swung open the rest of the way, revealing a sight that caused her to clutch Perlin's arm even tighter.

They stared at the sword sticking—like a ship's mast—out of the mattress of a four-post bed. There was no blood on the sheets, but a piece of parchment was pinned there.

On it was scrawled a very short message.

3 Days Left

"Don't touch it," Dierdra hissed. But knowing a sword was much preferable to a candelabrum, Perlin made the exchange anyway, tearing the note in half. And then they heard the whimpering again, coming from the bedroom closet. Perlin raised the sword with his right hand and reached out with his left. He threw open the closet door and Dierdra screamed.

Huddled in the darkness was the town's savior, knees to chest, head on knees, and one arm wrapped around himself like a sash. He was staring at Perlin's feet, mumbling a tumble of syllables—Perlin could make out only the stuttered word "goblin." The duke's clothes were filthy, and he had streaks of dried blood on his face. His hair was clumped and knotted, and he smelled as if he had missed his chamber pot at least once.

"What happened?" Dierdra asked in a whisper of disbelief, but neither of them could imagine a scenario that could have reduced their only hero to this.

"Stay here. I'm going to check out the rest of the house."

"Shouldn't we get somebody?"

"Who? He *is* the somebody. Just stay here and slap him around a little bit—see if he won't come to."

"But what if he doesn't?" Dierdra asked.

"Slap him anyway."

Perlin left Dierdra, his head throbbing even harder now, the sword clutched tightly with two hands. In all his years as a blacksmith, he had held thousands of swords, but he had never once had to use one.

Heading into an upstairs study, Perlin Salendor found a shelf holding a few bottles of fine liquor. A couple of empty ones were perched on the floor nearby, one with a hand still wrapped around its neck.

A hand connected to an arm connected to the rest of a goblin, who had passed out on the floor. A goblin with a sock on his face.

Perlin Salendor shook his head, then reached for one of the still-full bottles on the shelf.

Like his father before him, Mason Quayle was mountain bound.

He and Cowel had spent the rest of the evening gathering a few more supplies, then found shelter at an inn called the Three Seasons (CLOSED FOR WINTER, explained the sign). It had looked promising enough but had no rooms, much like the other two inns they had checked. This one *did* have a place to sleep, though, with room for Steed, and the keeper of the Three Seasons promised to charge them only what it was worth—a mere three coppers.

The stables where they found themselves came furnished with six other horses and a drunk who kept stealing the one blanket Mason and Cowel shared.

All night long, with Cowel snoring on one side of him and

the stranger grabbing the covers on the other, hay jabbing him in the neck and sores on his butt from riding, Mason struggled to fall asleep. He lay there, reluctantly wide-eyed, staring at the leaking roof and making a catalog of everything he knew about mountains in general and the Windmourns in particular.

Short of the fact that they were awfully beautiful—you could see that from right outside the stable—what Mason knew about mountains in general made him shiver. They were treacherous. They contained caves. Those caves contained nasty stuff like spiders, worms, and snakes, which wouldn't be so bad except that all of them were *giant.* Something about mountains made things that you could normally squash with your boot heel the size of horses—the minerals in the water, perhaps. There were a hundred different places to break your leg and a hundred different creatures that would chew it off for you when they found you.

About the Windmourns in particular Mason knew only two things. They had swallowed eight of the greatest heroes of Highsmith and one bard. And there was a man who lived in them known only as Hunter. That's what Frank the used-horse salesman had called him. Not *the* Hunter. Just Hunter.

Fira's stepfather had never actually gotten a real name, which seemed odd, given what else he knew about the man: He lived in a village called Galen's Cove less than halfway up the mountains' north peak. He had two children and was fairly successful—he had purchased the most expensive horse Frank had to offer. He had scars lining both arms and part of his neck. Then there was the bit about the sword. It had been the real selling point for Cowel, who still had only his kitchen knife stuck in his pants.

"You don't see too many fur traders carrying swords," Frank

Delacorte had said. "You hunt wolves with a bow or with traps. You don't need a sword. And you certainly don't need the kind of sword *he* carries." Mason had to admit this Hunter sounded just like what they had been looking for.

The problem was finding him. It would take most of the day to get there, Frank said, using the switchback path that the trappers used when they descended to Heartwood for trading. He had never been himself, but he understood the path to be dangerous in spots.

"The Windmourns aren't just any mountains. There are stories."

"Like Snowbeard's treasure?" Cowel prodded.

"Sure. And a lot about dragons. Two-headed bears. A giant man-eating toad." Figures, Mason thought. A regular size toad he could handle. "But stuff even stranger than that. Stones and trees that come to life. Monsters made of mud. Whatisits," Frank said with a shiver.

"What is what?" Mason asked.

"What?"

"You said, 'What is it.'"

"Right."

"What is it?"

"Lots of them," Frank said, nodding.

"Lots of what?"

"Whatisits. You have to watch out for them."

"But what is it?" Cowel asked.

"Exactly."

"No. What *are* they?"

"Oh. I don't know what they are. I've never seen one myself, but I hear they're everything terrible all wrapped up together—some warlock's experiment gone awry."

Mason told him that was more than enough information,

thank you. Anything else and they simply wouldn't find the courage to go.

It had all given him a lot to think about and had helped him muster only three hours of sleep, which could partly explain why Cowel's voice seemed so irritating in the morning.

Steed's ears were pinned back as he scrambled up the winding mountain path. The base sloped gradually, but before long the rock erupted, making jagged, jeering faces. They could no longer see Heartwood below them, though they could still make out the forest. True to the mountains' name, Mason could already hear the wind's plaintive moan as it wound through the hollows.

Cowel was jabbering on about Fira Firaxin, something about how maybe he might like her a little—that is, if Mason didn't . . . you know . . . whatever. Mason wasn't really paying attention, and he wasn't dreaming about Fira (though he had had some trouble keeping her out of his head). He kept thinking about how easily people believe what they want to believe. How his mother would still be waiting by the door. How the people of Darlington swallowed tales of the duke's improbable victories against overwhelming odds. How the finest heroes of Highsmith saw a storyteller's dream as their ticket to winning back their town. And yet, somehow, between Cowel's mumbling, his own thoughts of home, the howl of the mountains, the plod of Steed, and the grumble in his stomach that wouldn't go away, Mason thought he heard the sound of loose stones skittering down from the slopes ahead.

"Did you hear something?" he asked, interrupting Cowel's commentary about how it was definitely the orange hair.

"No. Did you?"

"No."

"Then why did you ask?"

"I thought—I don't know. It seemed like there was something."

"Well, was there?" Cowel turned to look behind them but saw only the stone-scrabbled trail they had been crawling along for hours.

"I guess not."

"Then don't scare me like that." This at least caused Cowel to be silent for another fifty steps, occasionally looking behind them and suppressing a sneeze.

That's when they saw it, just off the path, its head buried between two rocks and its tail tucked between its legs. Steed was walking right past it, and Mason, looking up at the mountain's outline and wondering just where this stupid village was, didn't even notice—not until Cowel tapped him on the back and pointed to the tuft of fur squirming its way between the rocks.

"I think its head is stuck," Cowel said as Mason shifted Steed from mosey to full stop. From behind, Mason heard a "poor little thing." Cowel had always had a soft spot for anything fuzzy. He had tried to take in several stray dogs over the years, but his uncle always refused on the grounds that it would be easier for the mutts to find food just about anywhere *other* than the Salendors'.

"I don't think that's a good idea," Mason said as Cowel slid off Steed's back. And took cautious steps toward the small animal, which was twisting its body back and forth, half obscured by the stones, its fur rippling.

"I'm just going to move one rock. I'm not going to adopt it or anything."

"I don't know, Cowel. I mean, we don't even know what *it* is."

But as soon as Mason said it, he knew. At that same instant,

Cowel bent over and put out his hand. And as soon as he did *that*, the tail that had been tucked between the creature's legs suddenly jumped to life, revealing a twisting appendage that started as fur but quickly changed to scales, finishing with what looked like a scorpion's stinger at the tip. Cowel found his sneeze as the creature pulled its head free, revealing a face that no one—not even Dierdra Quayle—could love.

Frank Delacorte was right; it was everything horrible and terrifying somehow bundled into one small package. One look at it caused Cowel to topple over.

"What *is* it?" he screamed as the thing showed its whole self—three sharp horns, jaws wet with snot-thick saliva, front claws clicking against stone. It had the snout of a wolf but the thick, leathery skin of a lizard, and its cheeks sprouted whiskers that looked more like quills. It sported a mane of coarse black hair.

Then there were the teeth. Row after row of serrated razors. Two tusklike fangs protruded upward from each side. And that was inside only the *mouth*. There were more teeth actually set inside the creature's *nostrils*. The thing could eat you with its nose.

The whatisit settled on its haunches, its scorpion's tail curled for a strike, then sprang from its rock, horns and claws first, nose and jaw gnashing. In a move that seemed much more nimble than Mason would have ever given him credit for, Cowel rolled to his right, banging his elbow into a rock but at least avoiding the creature's claws. Mason leapt down from the horse, drawing Dirk's sword. For once, the blade felt good in his hand, as if it belonged there.

The whatisit went to defend itself, turning toward Mason and shaking its tail. It let out a hiss and took two calculated steps backwards, feigning retreat. Then it jumped again.

Mason could see the snout and the wide nostrils with their tiny teeth snapping open and shut. He could see his own arms moving, Darlinger's sword dancing in front of him. He wasn't entirely sure what was happening, only that he stepped sideways and swung and the beast rolled over twice, leaving the end of its snout on the ground behind it.

Mason watched the wounded creature and then stared at the sword, impressed, as if *it* had done all the work. The nostril-less whatisit looked at Mason with dolorous eyes, its bloody stump oozing and its prickly whiskers folded back. Mason watched it slink away, whipping its hideous head back and forth. Then he heard Cowel scramble to his feet and turned to see him with his knife in one hand, pointing with the other.

It was an ambush.

The snout-less whatisit was actually part of a whatarethey.

Mason's sense of accomplishment instantly withered as four more creatures revealed themselves from behind the rocks, circling around. Mason and Cowel were nearly surrounded by ugly.

"We have a serious problem," Mason said as he backed into Cowel.

The injured whatisit had rewedged itself between two rocks, content to let its siblings do the work. Mason turned one way and then another, not sure which of them to face.

"If we have to fight, you have to take three of them," Cowel whispered.

"What? Why three?"

"You have the sword. I have a kitchen knife," Cowel said as the whatisits inched closer. Mason noticed that two of them didn't have horns, though anything that could bite you with its nose was dangerous enough.

"That's not fair. Two of us, four of them. Fifty-fifty."

"Sword takes the majority. New rule."

"Fine, you take the sword," Mason said, though he didn't bother to hand it over.

He knew he couldn't defend himself against more than one of these beasts at a time. But he refused to believe that *this* was how it would end: him and Cowel dying in complete obscurity, a quarter of the way up a mountain, at the nose teeth of a creature so hideous nobody knew what to call it.

The innkeeper said they must have left early. He had gone out to offer them breakfast only to find they had already disappeared. The drunk in the stable said he knew where they were going because the short one kept mumbling in his sleep.

The drunk was a little reluctant to talk at first, but there were ways to persuade anyone.

"Where is Mason Quayle?" The stranger pulled out a bag of coins.

These two had better be worth it. After all, she wasn't thrilled about doing this favor to begin with.

She wrapped her cloak around her, pulled herself back onto her horse, and rode on. Tracking these two had been a chore, to say the least. She had picked up the trail in the Hive with little trouble, but she lost them in the Winding Woods—that is, until she stopped at a witch's cottage to ask for directions. From the Hive to Heartwood to here—the whole journey had taken her more than a day, and for some reason, she was angry. At her mother for being so controlling, at her father for trying so hard to make up for his past, at herself for being so selfish. There was, after all, a town's livelihood at stake. Granted, she had heard her mother say only terrible things about it, but that was no reason to just let the people there abandon their homes—or worse.

But she hated mountains. Too many places to hide. Moreover, she didn't understand why her father didn't just ask her to go to the town directly. Why this stupid escort service? Surely, these two could take care of themselves. They knew what they were getting into.

That's what she was thinking when she heard it—the sound of a wounded animal echoing from a bend in the path. The sound that told her to stop making assumptions and hurry up.

This was it. That same slow-motion sensation he had had in the Rusty Nail with a bulging dress looming over him. The sense that something fantastic and dreadful was about to happen to him. But there were no sleeping swordsmen beside him this time, just Cowel with his pitiful knife reaching out for Mason as the first whatisit charged.

Its snout would have found Mason's throat, but Cowel spun the creature around, pushing him into Steed, who snorted at having to be involved. The beast skidded among the rocks and then turned to renew its attack just as two more leapt from above. The fourth just circled around behind them.

Cowel slashed but missed. The creature slammed into him, knocking them both to the ground, where Cowel managed to give the beast a swift kick in the head. Mason was not so lucky; another whatisit aimed for his legs and managed to rip three gashes in his thigh with its tusks. Mason reached for Steed's saddle with his left hand to stay upright, but the horse took a few timid steps backwards and then finally bucked twice, sending the already off-balance Mason flat on his back, the sword wrenched from his hand. Mason saw the fourth beast lower its head and gambol toward him, ready to burrow its snout into his chest.

Then it careened sideways, its legs giving out beneath it and its body skidding on the ground.

Mason didn't have time to appreciate what had just happened as the tail of another one drove its spike into his shoulder. He felt it catch fire immediately and instinctively turned and grabbed at it, at that very moment hearing the whistle of air being split.

Mason stared dumbfounded at the arrow's shaft sticking out of the beast's neck, which caused it to gasp once before slumping to the ground. Arrows apparently were falling out of the sky. At exactly the right trajectories. At just the right moments.

And then, before he could make any sense of it, it was over. All five beasts were dead, including the one whose snout had come much too close to Dirk Darlinger's sword.

A stranger stood over Mason, blocking the sunlight but radiant herself, like the cover of a book. Mason knew at once that she was a divine being.

"Are you two *completely* stupid?" the being asked.

Mason blinked at her. He wouldn't have guessed divine creatures talked like that. He didn't bother to croak a word—he just stared at the mysterious woman bathed in light. Then Cowel knelt beside him and prodded his leg with a finger. Suddenly, the rest of Mason's senses sparked and he screamed.

The angel moved forward, the light shifted, and Mason saw that it was only a woman perhaps four or five years older than him. She wore a studded leather tunic that fell just to her hips, a belt with two long daggers as brackets, and pants tucked into worn boots that looked a lot like his own. Over her shoulder were slung a bow and quiver, with only a few arrows left. Her muddy blond hair was pulled into a tightly braided tail.

She propped Mason against a boulder, carefully cut the shredded strips of his pants, and peeled them from the wet wound as Cowel pulled water and a spare shirt from the saddlebag. No one had bothered to answer her question yet. As she worked, Mason noted her features: ruddy cheeks, a hawkish nose, a fullness in her lips, and a stiff chin. She was no Fira Firaxin. But Fira Firaxin hadn't saved his life. The woman looked into his eyes, and Mason was almost certain he had seen her somewhere before.

Cowel inspected a spot of blood on his own shoulder.

"Are you hurt?" she asked him.

"A scratch."

It was the most stoic Mason had ever seen Cowel in all the years he had known him. He wasn't even sneezing. For a moment, Mason resented him for it.

"The cuts in the leg are deep, but the shoulder's not bad," she said, taking the spare shirt from Cowel and wrapping it so tightly around Mason's leg that he screamed again, then bit his lip—he certainly wasn't going to let Cowel out-macho him. "What kind of idiots get off their horse while traveling through the Windmourns?" she asked. Mason looked at Cowel, the one who had wanted to *help* the poor defenseless-looking three-horned, stinger-tailed, blood-lusting monstrosity that tried to kill them, but Cowel didn't say a word.

"Don't you two have any idea where you are?"

"We're new at this," Mason said.

"We aren't very well armed," Cowel added, holding up his knife.

Mason looked at the sword by his hand and then studied this woman—the outfit, the weapons, the condescending attitude—realizing that they had just happened upon exactly what they were looking for. Anyone who could fell five whatisits in the space of three breaths could surely hold her own against orcs. Mason looked at Cowel to see if he was thinking the same thing, but Cowel only stared at Mason's leg with a look of concern.

"I'm—" Mason started to introduce himself, but she beat him to it.

"Mason, I know. Or Cowel. Which is which?"

Both of them sat there stunned. How did she know their names? Had she been following them? For nearly three days they had been hunting for someone like her, when all along someone like her was hunting for them?

"I nearly caught up to you in Heartwood. You two do leave an impression."

A wince from Mason interrupted her, his shoulders jerking backwards. Sweat beaded on his forehead and his cheeks burned.

"Is he okay?"

Mason smiled at Cowel to reassure him, but the flush of his cheeks suggested otherwise.

"On my saddle, there's a sack—inside is a bottle. Get it."

The woman pointed to her own horse, which neither of them had noticed before, standing by a rock thirty feet off. Much more excited than Steed, it started turning and kicking as Cowel approached until the woman hissed the name "Fury," which seemed to pacify it instantly.

"It's a good name for a horse," Mason said. "A good name for a hero's horse. I've read enough to know."

"I'm no hero," she said, inspecting the small hole in Mason's shoulder. "My father gave me that horse. He named it. Here, drink this, just one swallow." The woman pulled the cork from the bottle Cowel handed her and gave it to Mason, then took it back to soak Mason's shoulder and the bandage on his leg. It burned at first, but then Mason felt his skin grow cold, the pain dulled.

"Thank you."

"It won't last long, and it will hurt worse later, but I don't want you coming down with anything. After all, my father would be a little disappointed if I just let you die."

"Die?" said Mason.

"Your father?" said Cowel.

"He's the one who sent me after you. Made a point to come all the way out to see me for just that reason. Said by the looks of you, he knew you were destined for trouble."

"Who—" Cowel began, but the woman—this woman who rode a hero's horse and had a hero's sharp eyes, who talked and dressed and killed like a hero, but who wasn't a hero—kept up her habit of answering questions before they were finished.

"When she's in one of her moods, my mother just calls him the good-for-nothing Bastard. His real name is Lorn, but you probably know him by a different name.

"And my name is Isabella," she said. "Isabella Owltree."

Sometimes, though not often, because it gets complicated, heroes fall in love with each other.

Most of the time it's easier not to. Most of the time you don't want to see the man or woman you love in harm's way. Besides, such relationships are often too competitive in nature. Yet there had been a popular rumor around Highsmith well over twenty years earlier, in the pre-Darlington days. The kind of rumor on which bards feast and about which local newspapers speculate. After all, very few of the heroes on the Alley had ever gotten involved with each other and even fewer ever married, so it had been no surprise that the more Brendlor Bowbreaker and Arlena Owltree had been seen together, the faster the rumor spread. The speculation persisted, even when

Brendlor began dating Myra Hern, a mason's daughter from Highsmith's East Side—right up until the moment that Arlena Owltree left town, not coincidentally on the very day Brendlor Bowbreaker and Myra Hern were to be married. Everyone guessed Lena's leaving had something to do with Brendlor and their love affair, but nothing could be proved for sure.

What they didn't guess, because Arlena Owltree refused to say and Brendlor Bowbreaker felt no need to share, was that she was carrying his child. It was a matter of unfortunate timing for all involved. Lena and Brendlor were finished, their love smothered almost as fast as it had ignited, but the promise of a child changed it all.

Or it would have, had Lena let it. Brendlor had done the honorable thing, of course, vowing to cancel his wedding and leave town with Arlena, promising to marry *her* and raise their child together. But Arlena Owltree was a proud woman and interpreted Brendlor's proposal as an act of charity, turning down everything he offered, claiming—rightly—that she could take care of the child herself, and promising—falsely—that she would bear him no hard feelings.

Arlena Owltree had cursed him every day since while raising her only daughter to be strong, independent, willful, and, with any luck, a total man-hater. But Isabella didn't entirely catch on. She was fascinated by her father, by his past, by the story of his and her mother's passionate involvement. She saw herself as the product of deeply romantic forces. For a long time, she pictured herself as the shunned and haunted child in a tragic poem, the living symbol of an illicit love.

Until one day, when she was eight years old, and a man had showed up at her doorstep with a new pair of boots. The day she met her father, Isabella called him a bastard as she had been instructed to do but couldn't help hugging him as she said it. He had come to spend a day with her at least twice a year ever since, telling his wife he was going to some semi-annual boot-makers' conference.

His most recent visit had been less than two days ago. He had brought news that caused her mother to flare up bright red with anger, news about the town in which they had both grown up. That's when Brendlor had made his request, describing for Isabella the two young men she was looking for and the short time she had to find them. Said that they were innocent, fresh faced, and naive.

Clearly, he had been putting it nicely.

Cowel and Mason exchanged looks. She didn't tell them the whole story, only that her father had insisted she come escort them for the remainder of their quest, and that her mother had protested at first but allowed her to go.

"But wait a minute," Cowel said. "Why send you after *us* when he could have just sent you to Darlington? They're the ones who need you. We're fine."

Cowel realized how stupid the last part sounded only after he said it.

"He thought you could use my help finding more heroes. You *have* found heroes, haven't you?" Isabella added when she noticed the blank look on both of their faces.

Mason's nod said, *Of course we've found heroes—what do you think we've been doing all this time, silly woman?* But Cowel undermined it with a "Yeah. One."

"*One? One* hero?" Isabella looked at Mason, who nodded less emphatically this time. "Well, who is it? It better be somebody good. I mean, I better have heard of him."

Mason and Cowel just stared at Isabella Owltree. Cowel kind of shrugged.

"You *have* to be kidding me," she said, shaking her head. "You've been on the road almost three days, you've been through at least three different towns, and *I'm* the best thing you've found?"

"You *could* take it as a compliment," Cowel suggested, but Isabella turned and glared at him.

"Do you know how many arrows it takes to bring a rampaging orc down?"

"A whole bunch?" Cowel guessed safely.

"*One* hero cannot defend an entire town—I don't care who it is. You need three or four, *at least,* and even then, the chances are good they aren't all coming back."

"But we just saw you take out five of *those* things," Mason said, pointing to one of the whatisit carcasses.

"That doesn't mean anything," Isabella Owltree protested. "Whatisits have tiny brains," she said, squeezing two fingers together. "There isn't room in their heads with all of the other crap sticking out of them. They sting themselves with their own tails. Orcs are different. They're organized. They're methodical. They have *weapons.*"

Mason figured this wasn't a good time to point out that the particular orc threatening the town had the assistance of goblins, trolls, and ogres as well. No sense adding to her irritation.

Isabella leaned back onto her hands with an exasperated gasp. "My mother said this would happen. She said it wouldn't do any good and Brendlor should just let you die on the road."

Mason thought Arlena Owltree sounded like a charming woman.

"There is another," Cowel mumbled from where he sat, sort of scrunched up into a ball. "Hero, I mean. That's why we're in the mountains."

"He's a hunter," Mason added. "With a huge reputation."

"Huge," Cowel confirmed. "Like, this big." He pulled his hands as far apart as they would go, then adjusted them inward a little.

"What's his name?"

They looked at each other.

"Um . . . Hunter."

"*Hunter?* Hunter the hunter?"

"We don't really know his name."

"But we know where he's from." Then Mason repeated what Frank had told them.

Isabella Owltree bowed her head. "How much gold do you have left?"

"About a hundred."

"Or less."

"You're certain there is no one back in Darlingville or whatever it is who can help?"

Mason thought of his mother the dreamer, of old man Frinkmeyer, of the hemophobic Dirk Darlinger. Cowel pictured overweight bartenders and spoiled teenagers, lazy shoe cobblers and drunk uncles.

Both of them said it was doubtful.

After all, most of the town didn't even know what was coming.

They were about to find out.

Darlington Square was usually deserted, but today people leaned out of windows, squeezed under and over wagons, and sat on shoulders to get a better view of the woman standing in front of the largest of the eight Darlinger statues. Dierdra was surprised that this many people still lived in the town. Maybe it would have been better to do what Cowel had done and leave a note. Instead, she stood on the stone bench overlooking the square and found that her legs barely supported her.

The past few hours had been full of revelations: the warning on the bed, the passed-out goblin in the study, the blubbering duke in his closet. It was through the goblin, and not the duke, that Dierdra and Perlin discovered the full weight of their predicament. Rudely awakened by a pail of cold water and threatened with the business end of a sword, Sockface the goblin wasn't much for keeping secrets.

Soon after, the Darlington Volunteer Street Patrol and the Darlington Volunteer Fire Brigade were summoned and given the quick version. All of them demanded to see Darlinger before they were convinced. A hero's reputation, after all, was hard to kill. Yet Dierdra met even more people who had been growing suspicious over the past several years.

To help spread the word, Perlin had scrawled notices and posted two dozen signs:

Darlinger a Fraud
Orc Invasion Immanent
Meeting This Afternoon
Come or Die

Which could explain the large turnout.

Dierdra Quayle stood in the center of the bench with Perlin behind her, his hand on her shoulder to make sure she didn't fall or faint. To the right and left sat Exhibits A and B, respectively. Exhibit A, a hung-over goblin in a cage. Exhibit B, a slumped-over duke, who had been awake for nearly two days, who hadn't eaten in three, and who had mumbled only apologies. Unfortunately, no matter what Dierdra said or how loud she screamed to be heard, the crowd's attention was focused entirely on Exhibit B and what they might do with him.

"Flog him!"

"Leave him to the wolves!"

"Put him in the cage with the goblin and let them duke it out!"

Eight years of taxes. The building-up of the town's reputation. The "Darlington Anthem." All a scam, designed to sap the town of its coin. All they could think of was how best to make Dirk Darlinger pay them back for everything he had taken. Dierdra could feel the swell of the masses as they pushed against each other, threatening to overwhelm the too-short line of volunteers who stood between them and the duke. It wasn't until Perlin, cupping his hands around his mouth and practically choking up his own lungs, yelled, "Shut up, already!" that the call for Darlinger's blood dwindled to a murmur.

"We have more pressing concerns."

And Dierdra explained the situation, including the possibility—however remote—that someone might already be on the way to help them. But because they were so ill prepared—with no weapons or soldiers, with a gate more decorative than functional and walls that hadn't been repaired in years, with only a handful of hunters with any real skill and no heroes to speak of, and with so little time to get ready—should any of them stay?

"What chance is there—*really*—that someone is coming to help us?"

Dierdra Quayle looked at Perlin, who just shrugged. He loved his nephew and, deep down, hoped only the best for him. But Perlin knew Cowel was no adventurer.

"I don't think it's something we can count on," he said.

The people of Darlington erupted in a discordant symphony of shouts. Dierdra watched the crowd ripple with doubts and ultimatums as people searched for courageous words to mask their fear. Dierdra knew that the town would not be able to come to a consensus. Most people would leave, but some would stay in the blind hope that their faith would see them through. She no longer bothered to make herself heard above the crowd. She could make the decision only for herself, and for her, it was simple.

She knew he would come back.

With all of this excitement, with a mass exodus on the way, and with the still-seething undercurrent of whispers calling for the duke's head—amidst all this commotion, it was no surprise that no one noticed the man who had fallen asleep while leaning against a signpost, having paid a merchant to tie him up and bring him there, or the two armed figures who were riding through Darlington's unmanned gates.

It had been more than an hour since they had managed to pull Mason up into a saddle, his leg still asleep from Isabella's potion. An uneventful hour, save for the periodic "conversations" that passed between Isabella and Cowel, all of them starting with, "You're certain you can't make that horse go any faster?"

Isabella Owltree had Mason in front of her on her own horse, trailing behind Cowel. They plodded along, Mason occasionally looking down at the muscular arm Isabella had wrapped around his waist. Riding this strange horse in these strange mountains with a stranger's arm coiled around him, he just couldn't stand the silence anymore. "Pretty up here."

Actually, the view was clouded over, they were nearly surrounded by rocks, and sometimes they'd pass the remains of something already gobbled down to the bone.

"I guess," Isabella said. There was a pause as Mason waited for her to say something stupid back so they could both feel silly about all their pretenses and start a real conversation.

Nothing.

"I wanted to thank you, you know, for what you did back there."

"Got it."

"I mean, if you hadn't come along, we would have been—well . . . I don't know. Do you think they would have eaten us?"

"I don't know."

"I mean, what does a whatisit eat?"

"I don't know."

"Well . . . anyways . . . thanks."

"Okay."

The silence settled between them again. Mason tried to interest himself in Steed's tail swishing back and forth. He started humming a song but got only a few bars in before interpreting the sigh from behind him as a hint. He thought about his father's book, but it was tucked away in one of Steed's saddlebags, impossible to reach.

"This is a nice horse."

"Yep."

"I bet it goes pretty fast."

"Sure."

"So. You're the daughter of two heroes, huh?"

"Yep."

"And that doesn't . . . you know . . . automatically make you a hero?"

"Nope."

"Oh. Okay." Mason sucked on his lower lip, then added, "It's just—I always kind of thought that you sort of, you know, grow up to be like your parents."

"I hope not," Isabella said. The tone in her voice suggested that Mason should just enjoy the peace and quiet, but in three days, he had learned not to give up so easily.

"Do you go on adventures like this a lot?"

"Only when my mother lets me," she said with another sigh of exasperation.

"Your mom's a little controlling?"

"You might say that."

"Brendlor . . . Lorn . . . What did you say you called him, again?"

"My mother usually calls him Pisshead. Or Scumwad, if she's around children."

"Oh."

"But I've pretty much taken to calling him Dad."

"Right. He never said anything about you—to us, I mean. We didn't know you'd be looking for us."

"That's the problem with illegitimate children—we don't often get to be the topic of conversation."

"Oh. Right." Mason snorted a laugh.

"What?"

"Nothing." Mason stared straight ahead. "It's just that we have a lot in common. My father left when I was six."

"Was he a bastard, too?"

"No. Just a dreamer."

"Sorry. That was a rude question. My father told me. I know the story."

Which version? Mason thought to himself, but he didn't ask. "Kind of funny, isn't it. I mean, that both of us grew up without our fathers."

"I suppose so."

"I don't mean ha-ha funny. Just odd. Everywhere you look, there's a messed-up family. Cowel's got only his uncle."

"That explains some things, at least," she said.

Mason turned around in the saddle to look at her, but the movement caused his leg to hurt again and he turned back. "Like what?"

"Like how he dotes on you, for starters."

"He doesn't *dote* on me."

"Whatever."

Mason looked ahead at Cowel, who occasionally turned around to make sure he hadn't been abandoned. "It's okay," Isabella said to Mason. "We don't get a lot of doting in my house."

"You should spend the night with us sometime. My mother invented doting."

"My father tries. But when you're around only a few days out of the year, it's hard."

Mason thought about the boot salesman from Riscine. Lorn Breckenridge was probably a great father to the children everyone knew about, but that didn't necessarily mean anything.

"He says I'm the smartest kid he's ever had," Isabella continued. "Mother says that's because he wasn't around to get in the way."

"That's what you get being raised by a hero."

"You have no idea what it's like," Isabella said, suddenly irritable, though it only caused her to hold on to Mason tighter. She was right, of course, though Mason didn't know it until yesterday. "She's demanding and, like you said, controlling . . . and *so* high maintenance. Oh, and combative. The other day, she threatened to kill this guy who just *whistled* at me. In seconds, her sword was drawn and she was huffing and puffing her way across the road."

"Sounds tough."

"She is. And did I say she was a slave driver? She makes me study six hours a day. History, geography, languages, an hour of archery every day, and at least an hour of meditation. It's supposed to put me *at peace with nature*"—Isabella made quotation marks in the air with her free hand—"but I don't think she's at peace with anything. And she never lets me go anywhere unless she tags along. I was absolutely shocked when she agreed to let me do this. It's how I know she's up to something." But Isabella didn't say what she thought her mother was up to.

"But you learn a lot, I guess."

She ignored the comment. "My mother considers it some kind of badge of honor that she raised me by herself. She has this whole stoic-woman thing going for her."

"My mother is out of her mind," Mason said.

"Aren't they all?"

"No, really," Mason said. "She lives in some make-believe world. Sometimes I kind of get sucked in."

"There are worse things."

"I guess."

"I just wish, sometimes, that I could be normal, you know?" Mason could tell that Isabella didn't expect an answer because she just kept talking. "Just average. Have a normal family. A normal life. Average expectations. To not have to do great things or be some phenomenal person. To just live my damn life and be happy. Just normal and happy."

"I don't think there's too much normal out there anymore. Though there's still plenty of average to go around."

Isabella didn't say anything else. Mason caught another

glance from Cowel—a look of concern that could possibly be construed as doting.

"It's kind of an ugly world," Mason said finally, thinking of bullies and frauds and whatisits. He turned to get acknowledgment from the daughter of two heroes, and she surprised him by smiling for the first time.

"I wouldn't give up hope," she said. "You never know when something good is going to come along."

It came soon after, in the form of a young man standing along the path clearing a trap. He and Isabella kept their bows leveled at each other until introductions were made. The trapper was on his way back to Galen's Cove. It wasn't smart to stay out in the mountains past dark, he said. Cowel thanked him for stating the obvious.

"We are looking for a hunter," Isabella said.

"Our village is full of them. We aren't far. My father is the mayor. He can help you, provided he doesn't kick you out."

The young man threw his catch and his traps over his shoulder and started climbing back up the stones that led to his village, moving quick enough on foot to keep up easily with Steed. Less than an hour later, they rounded a boulder and descended a steep slope to find themselves in a village that used the mountains as walls, needing only a gate manned by one guard for protection. The trapper nodded to the guard.

Entering the town, Mason could tell that Galen's Cove had suffered a large fire at one time, the memory still etched on scorched stones. What few people they passed eyed them with furtive, slingshot glances.

The mayor's house sat among the first cluster of three by the gate. The mayor, a man called Flayden Fobbs, was no less sus-picious than the townsfolk, pulling his pants up over his gut as a sign of authority the moment they stepped inside. His wife, a wisp of a woman by comparison, peered at them through bug-eyed spectacles.

"Who are these people?" the mayor asked as his son set his traps outside the door.

"I found them on the trail. They say they are from Darling-ton."

The husband and wife exchanged concerned looks.

"We were attacked on the way here. My companion is wounded," Isabella added. Mason wondered why the band-aged leg didn't give it away.

"I'm afraid we don't have much to offer you," the mayor said, sucking out any remaining heat from the room. Isabella Owltree explained why they were there, whom they were looking for, and that they had no intentions of staying long. Once they found this person, they would leave, she said.

"He carries a fancy sword and has scars along his neck and arms," Mason added. Again the mayor and his wife traded glances. Mason could tell by the way her chin was set that she would have a lot to say after they left.

"What business do you have with him?"

"It's a personal matter," Isabella said. "He's a friend of a friend."

Mason looked to Cowel to see if he was about to sneeze, but his friend just looked exhausted. "You say you're from Dar-lington, huh?" The mayor spoke as if determined to catch them in a lie.

"Formerly Highsmith," Cowel added, trying to be helpful but earning a disapproving stare.

"We know what it was," the wife said reproachfully. Mason thought of the letter from Fira's aunt. His father and the others must have stopped here, and they would have said where they were from and where they were headed.

"You'll have to leave your weapons here," the man said. "We don't like strangers, and we don't permit them to go armed."

"That's fine," Mason said, though this earned him a stare from Isabella, who probably took baths with her belt full of daggers still strapped around her waist. She hesitantly laid her blades and bow on the table next to Mason's borrowed sword and Cowel's knife.

"Darren here will escort you." The mayor of Galen's Cove then turned to his son and, without even bothering to whisper, said, "If they do anything out of the ordinary, don't hesitate to sound your horn, and if you have to defend yourself, kill the woman first."

Mason could tell by her expression that Isabella Owltree was not flattered.

As they passed through the town, Darren leading the way with his hand on the hilt of his dagger, Mason noticed still more evidence of a tragedy. Several of the buildings looked newer, and one was still just a burned-out shell. Townspeople stopped and watched them cautiously. They soon walked by a cemetery, where they heard the moan of wooden chimes. Mason asked why there were chimes and Darren said it was just the town's custom, but he said it in such a way that Mason knew his one question had been used up.

Their walk seemed to take them clear across town, to a place that looked as if it had been tucked into the corner in order to keep it out of sight. Fira's stepfather had said the man was wealthy, but the stone cottage they stood before couldn't have held more than four rooms. In the sky above them, the moon was only a sliver.

After only one knock, a young boy answered. Mason noticed he had bright blue eyes. The boy looked at them strangely, as if he had never seen so many people at his door before, and the mayor's son gave him a smile.

"Edmond, is your father home? He has some guests."

They were ushered inside as Darren bid them goodbye, and the little boy led them to a rug by the fireplace and asked them to sit down. There weren't enough chairs to go around, but the nervous boy didn't even offer the two that were there. Mason could hear someone fussing with a baby in another room, a soft voice begging it to eat, as the little boy disappeared through the only other door. Cowel whispered something about the lack of trophies hanging on the wall. If this guy was a skilled hunter, he wasn't a proud one.

The boy reappeared with a man rugged and worn in the face. He wore plain clothes and was unarmed—no fancy sword to be seen. But even with the hair that had already grown silver and the thick cords of scar tissue running up along his neck, Mason recognized him. He had seen him in sketches from his father's books.

"I'm Brax. Brax Balen. Welcome to my home."

Isabella stepped forward to take his hand when Mason sputtered something, not even meaning to say it out loud.

"Balenfoe."

"What?" whispered Cowel.

"Balenfoe," Mason said louder this time, looking up at the scarred hunter.

"I know that name," Isabella said, taking another glance at the man. Cowel simply looked confused. Obviously, he didn't pay much attention every time he and Mason took their short-cut through the Alley back in Darlington.

Brax smiled, though his eyes were distant. "I shortened it to Balen. And you are?" he asked, addressing Mason specifically.

"I'm Mason. Mason Quayle." Mason expected something—a look of surprise, perhaps—but Brax's face was fixed. "This is Cowel Salendor. From Darlingto—I mean, Highsmith. This is Isabella Owltree."

"Owltree?" This *did* seem to surprise him. "I knew an Arlena Owltree once."

"My mother."

Suddenly, as if on cue, the woman who could be heard in the other room appeared in the archway, a baby girl dozing contentedly on her shoulder.

"It's all right," Brax said to her. "Just friends of old friends. I'd like to introduce you all to my wife, Lilah, and my sleepy daughter, Syble. And this," he said, taking the boy by the shoulders and pulling him, squirming, to the front, "this is my son. Edmond Quayle Balen."

Mason blinked twice. Madame Perugi had been right, after all.

"I knew I was going to meet you," Mason said, holding his hand out for Edmond to shake.

"I always wondered if you'd get the chance," Brax said. Then he turned to Isabella. "Your mother was an excellent hunter and a courageous woman. Judging by your dress, I'm guessing it rubbed off." Isabella nodded. "And you're Perlin Salendor's boy."

"Nephew," Cowel corrected, still lost as to who this man was.

"Right, right. It's just that he always spoke of you as his son. At least, that's what I remember, but it was some time ago. You look like you've had a hard journey," he said, taking in Mason's bandages and the blood on his shoulder, Cowel's torn clothes and the welts on his face. "We'll get you something to drink and find some warm clothes." Then, he stared directly at Mason, and it was as if everyone else in the room just disappeared.

"You act almost like you were expecting me," Mason said.

Brax smiled. "As a matter of fact, yes."

The steamed chocolate, Cowel said with his salesman's grin, was the best he'd ever tasted, causing Lilah Balen to smile for the first time since their arrival. Brax let them warm themselves before he spoke again, and Mason reluctantly let Isabella inspect his wounds and borrow fresh bandages before asking the question that mattered most.

"Your father," Brax began.

But Mason knew before Brax said it.

He had kept up his fantasies, of course—that his father had run away and found a new life, that he was being kept prisoner—but these were cold comforts. As long as Mason didn't know for certain, he could believe anything he wanted.

But he knew. Even before Brax put his hands on Mason's shoulders as he had done to his own son only moments before. He knew when he had read the letter from Fira's aunt. He knew because of the way his mother kept looking out of windows. Because it was the only explanation she refused to accept.

And still, it hit him the way the morning cold does, creeping up from the space between the covers you try so hard to keep wrapped around yourself till you wake up shivering. It washed over and through him and drove its hooks deep into his skin and anchored itself there—the unmistakable truth that's always passed in an apology, in a "so sorry for your loss," the way the living speak of the dead. This, Mason realized, was where the journey ended.

"You know what happened?" Mason asked after he had been given enough time, after he bore everyone's glances long enough, after he offered a nod that gave everyone permission to speak.

"In the fire. A building collapsed. By the time we found him, he was almost gone."

Mason thought of the black streaks on the stones of the buildings they had passed and pictured his father, nothing but a shadow, staring through the flames.

"Thirty-four people died that night."

"What happened? What started it?" Cowel asked.

Brax looked to his wife, who seemed to want to pour herself into the cup on her lap, as if getting permission for what he was about to say.

"We did."

There was a long silence.

"Most of it is in your father's journal," Brax continued, ignoring the look on Mason's face. "Everything but the very end. Most of our time was spent on horseback getting from place to place. It always gave him plenty of time to write.

"Our last adventure was no different. We made it here on the fourth day. It wouldn't have taken so long had we not stopped to be heroes all the time; we were all so idealistic. This town was a lot friendlier then. They had seen their share of adventurers, all of them heading further up into the Wind-mourns, half of them looking for the same thing as we were. But we had your father, and nobody had studied the fables surrounding that treasure more than he had. If anyone could find it, we could. Enough money to pay off the duke, rebuild our reputations, or build a town of our own.

"Of course there were only eight of us by that point. Gaeus Gandor had gotten sick on the third day and had stayed in Heartwood to rest. I never heard what happened to him. That's also where we lost Moxy Firaxin. She never really believed in the treasure—she was a smart one. She split and headed north, I think. She pretended she was visiting relatives and would catch up, but we never heard from her again."

Mason thought of Fira's letter and wondered if Cowel was going to say something about it, but neither of them spoke. They just stared at the man whose eyes were somewhere else.

"On the fifth day, the eight of us started up the mountain with all of the blessings of a town that couldn't imagine what we would end up bringing back with us.

"It's a remarkable town, actually. For three hundred years, it has withstood everything the Windmourns could throw at it, and the Windmourns have a lot to throw. In the nearly two days it took for us to reach the north mountain's peak we encountered orcs and avalanches. We lost two horses and Cassius Coldhammer lost a hand, though he refused to go back. After all it took to get to the top of this mountain, we weren't surprised that no one had found Snowbeard's treasure. I doubt any one hero could make it there by himself. There were *eight* of us, seven of the finest heroes Highsmith had to offer plus your father, and we struggled. But we did make it. To the exact place your father predicted the treasure would be.

"Of course," Brax said, resting a hand on the back of his neck, "of course, you can't believe everything you hear. Bards—even the best ones—are prone to elaboration. *Especially* the best ones. The fables have it that Snowbeard had a huge palace built at the peak of the Windmourns, with emerald-laden towers and a moat of molten silver. All we found was a giant cave. And some treasure."

"So there *was* treasure?" Cowel asked.

"Yes, but it wasn't Snowbeard's—or if it was, he wasn't the pirate the legends claimed. It was a modest sum—I don't remember how much. Good enough for a week's work split eight ways, I suppose—just worth the effort we put into it, but certainly not equal to our dreams. It was a myth, see. Snowbeard, the towers, the never-ending chests of gold. Words that men chase after."

"All a lie," Mason said.

"No, not all of it," Brax said with a cough. "The part about the dragon . . . that was real. And it somewhat explained what treasure there was. But we didn't count on there being two of them. A mother and her child. We killed the child without knowing, and then, we suffered the mother's wrath. She met us just as we were leaving the cave, the gold packed onto our saddles and the smaller dragon's teeth distributed among us as souvenirs. Devon had cut out the heart and burned it as part of a ritual, and then each of the seven heroes took a drink of the dragon's blood. We didn't know that there was another one, of course, though we learned soon enough when we heard its scream. If you've never heard a dragon scream before, you can't imagine it. It'll stop your heart.

"All of the stories about *her* were true—that her claws were the size of my arms, that her chest was stenciled with the strikes of swords. She smelled the death of her young and it drove her into a rage.

"Roland drew his blade and we all followed suit. Cassius told your father to stay out of the way—commanded him, in fact, or else he probably would have joined. He wasn't really a fighter, your father, but he knew that the odds were against us." Mason tried to picture his father drawing a sword against a dragon, but all he could see was a man sitting beside his bed reading him fairy tales.

"Still, we fought like dragons ourselves, the blood of the young one inside of us. There was a chance, had we been at full strength and had we not just bested the young one, that we might have slain her. I like to think that if we had, we would have all given up being heroes then and there.

"But she was too much for us, and though we injured her, we knew her fury would outlast ours. We had no choice but to retreat, gathering our wounded and galloping back down the mountain, fearful that she would follow. There were only five of us left, counting Roland, who was doubled over, broken, and barely breathing on your father's horse. We left the bodies of three heroes on top of that mountain. Falgony, Telor Dane, and Morlin Xalador. We hoped that their deaths would be enough to satisfy her. We were wrong.

"The townsfolk were cautious, surprised to see us. Apparently, few ever made it back, and none with any treasure to speak of. But something about our wounds set them on edge—the black streaks along our armor, the burns on our skin. Still, they tended to us as best they could. Devon and I took up a patrol at the front gate, and Cassius stayed with Roland. Your father retreated into a corner of an inn and started rifling through the few books he had brought. At the time, I didn't know what he was doing, but later—afterward . . ." Brax's voice trailed off. No one said anything. After a couple of deep breaths, he squeezed his son's shoulders and continued.

"It was well into the night, nearly dawn. We were all exhausted. It had become increasingly clear that Roland was passing on, but I thought the rest of us were free. That's when I heard it. It was low and muffled, but there was no mistaking the sound of those giant wings. We barely had time to sound the alarm before she was upon us.

"If only we had stayed there, at the cave. If we had just let

her finish us off. But we didn't. We ran. We tried to save ourselves and brought her vengeance to an entire town. She didn't
discriminate—just destroyed everything she saw. The town's
hunters were used to wolves and goblins. None of them had
even seen a dragon before, though they had long ago guessed
that they shared a mountain with one. Realizing our responsi-
bility, Cassius, Devon, and I drew her into the town square,
hoping to either kill her or, by our own deaths, quell the rage
in her heart. It was in that second battle that Cassius fell and I
was burned. I lay on the ground, helpless, as the dragon's
flames blazed across the town. And that's when I saw him.
Your father, standing in the middle of the burning village.

"We would have all died if it hadn't been for him. I'm still
not sure how he did it. Your father read constantly. He knew
all kinds of songs. He could speak a dozen languages, even the
ancient ones."

"He spoke to it?" Cowel asked in disbelief.

"He sang to it, actually. Of all the memories, Mason, it is the
image of your father kneeling in the middle of the town that I
remember most vividly. The buildings around him on fire,
streets echoing with screams, and he just fell to his knees there
in the middle of the chaos and started to sing. As loud as he
could, eyes closed, though few of us could hear it above the
shouting.

"But the dragon heard. Don't ask me how. Devon, who was
the last of the heroes still standing, said he recognized the
sound, like a dirge—a funeral song in honor of the dragon's
loss. It was an elegy. And it was atonement.

"Whether the dragon understood the words of the song is
beyond my comprehension. I personally think it was something else, something in the sound of your father's voice. But
he sang, your father, and somehow, the dragon heard him and

headed straight for him. My sword lost and the arm that would have wielded it badly burned, the best I could do was yell for him to run. Still, he kept singing.

"Then there was a moment, I swear to you, when he opened his eyes and he and the dragon looked at each other.

"Then it just flew away."

Brax shrugged. It seemed a strange gesture, out of place— one several years in the making. No one said anything. Cowel rubbed his eyes, trying to focus. Mason found it a tremendous effort just to swallow.

"The dragon saw something in your father's eyes, heard something in his song, something they shared. Just a look and it disappeared. We all watched as the beast launched itself into the ashen air, breaking through the clouds of smoke it had created. We were paralyzed. We didn't know if it was circling around for another strike. Your father was the only one who seemed to understand. He pushed us, as he always did, to keep going, to save who we could.

"All total, fifteen buildings burned down that night. Your father was trapped in one of them. He and Devon heard screams coming from inside. The whole thing collapsed on top of them. I was the only one left." He coughed and then worked to find the voice he had swallowed. "We buried them here. I can go with you in the morning."

"Why did you stay?" Mason had to ask the question twice because it didn't come out the first time.

"I should have returned to Highsmith. I know that. I should have found some way to tell you, but I was ashamed. I felt responsible for what had happened. I was the only one left. I vowed to make up for it somehow. I gave all the gold we found to the village, but I knew that wasn't enough.

"So, for almost ten years, I have lived here, helping to repair the damage we caused, to heal some wounds. I've made a family. I'm sorry I never sent word. I suppose . . . I guess I always thought you might come to find out for yourself."

Mason wanted to say it was all right, to comfort this man the way his own son did, little Edmond holding his father's hand and staring up so high into a face with scars that hadn't faded yet. But he couldn't find the energy to speak. Brax Balen stroked those white ribboned memories and then turned to a shelf behind him, taking out several sheets of curled parchment bound with a strap of leather.

"Your father's," he said, holding them out. "All material he was hoping to add to his book. I'm sorry to say I've read them—a hundred times over. I can only assume he'd want you to have them."

Mason took the papers and couldn't believe how dry they felt, as if they would crumble at his touch.

"He talked about you often, Mason. He said you were the only thing he'd ever created that was worthwhile."

Mason stood. He feared that if he spoke, he would spit sand. It took some time to gather enough saliva worth swallowing. "I think," he finally said, speaking first to Brax and then turning to Cowel, who had already stood up with him, "I think I need to be alone for a little bit."

"Certainly, dear." It was the first thing Lilah Balen had said, and she ushered Mason toward the back door. "There's a light outside and some chairs."

"We'll be here," Cowel said. It was a stupid thing to say—as if they had anywhere else to go. But Mason knew what he meant.

The villagers of Galen's Cove hang wooden chimes for one year, on the gravestones of all those the mountain takes. The dead have one year to tell their stories, and then the chimes are removed and the voices are allowed to pass into the stone. In the distance, Mason could hear the chimes speaking.

He rubbed the parchment between his fingers. How many of his father's songs had he heard? How many of his stories were true?

More than anything, he wanted his mother to be here. To understand. But he wasn't quite here himself. He tried to shake himself free of the dreamy haze blanketing him in the same way clouds swallowed stars. He peered down at the letters scrawled in his father's hurried hand, struggling to make them out in the meager light of one lantern hanging beside the back door.

They were mostly notes. Lines of poetry and rhyming couplets—snippets of future works, captured like fireflies in a glass jar. Then, suddenly, the scattered bits and pieces stopped, replaced by marching lines. The journal of Edmond Quayle comprised the last few pages of parchment—starting from the moment they left Highsmith, an entry kept mercifully short.

Day 1: Unable to write much. Cannot bear to picture her there, standing at the door. She is too understanding. The heroes' spirits are higher than I've seen them in months. For them, this is a chance to prove themselves to themselves—they have no one else that needs it. For me, it is the realization of a dream. I can feel it out there, though I know it's still worth less than what I've left behind.

Day 2: Distractions all around. Roland cannot bear to see a quest go by. Today, we passed an altercation between a lord and a beggar. To his credit, Roland handled the situation without violence, but the lord was offended and didn't know exactly whom he was dealing with. Now, we must delay our journey for a duel that will take place in the morning. No doubt, it will not take long and will make for a nice short piece to add to Roland's legend, but it seems hardly worth the trouble. Cassius mumbles that there's no reason to wait till morning, that Roland should just go knock on the man's door and gut him on the porch. I enjoy riding alongside Cassius.

Day 3: The duel lasted only seven seconds—doesn't give me much to write about—and we were on our way till something even more pressing held us back. Gaeus has fallen sick. Morlin said it's serious but not deadly and that what he needs is at least a week in bed. Gaeus, of course, denied it and fought us to get back onto his horse, but he was dizzy and could barely stand. We've set him up at a nice inn in Heartwood. The heroes are sad to leave one of their numbers behind, and Moxy claims that it is a bad omen and that we are destined for more trouble. To be honest, I am not sure she believes. She has relatives in Heartwood to visit and told us that if she isn't back by midafternoon, we should leave without her and she will catch up.

(Later) It is drawing near evening and Moxy Firaxin has yet to show. Roland insists she will meet us farther on in the mountains, but I have my doubts. The ten are down to eight and we are not even to the mountains yet.

Day 4: Orcs. The duke's reputation does not extend this far. We were ambushed near the base of the Windmourns in the twilight hours of morning. There were twenty, at least, to our seven—I do not count myself. Still, even with those odds, we left fourteen of them face down in the rocks and sent the rest scurrying back to their caves. Only Cassius was seriously injured, losing his left hand, which makes it hard for him to swing his hammer. He insists on continuing, though. I will try to write a poem about this battle tonight in Galen's Cove, where we are to spend the night, though I do not feel I have it in me. I'm starting to have doubts, though I don't wish to share them with the others.

Day 5: We left at dawn, mostly hopeful, and have already arrived at Windfall, the mountains' northern peak. Though there is no fortress, there is a cavern, and by the smell of it, at least one part of the fable is true—whatever treasure lies within is undoubtedly guarded by a dragon. Whether it is the dragon of legend seems irrelevant to these seven heroes—though any dragon makes a formidable opponent. I keep telling them to be careful, but they laugh. Seven heroes and the Warrior Poet of Highsmith against one dragon hardly seems fair, they say. They are prepping themselves for the confrontation, nonetheless.

Then, Mason noticed, the manner of the writing changed, growing unsteady and erratic. The ink on the last pages was smeared. He wondered how many times Brax had read them, living through another's eyes the moments he couldn't bear to see again through his own. Mason squinted in the light, tracing his finger along the pages and following his father's sentences to their end.

The dragon is dead, but so are we—at least in spirit. For years, I have followed this fable—to find that it was just that.

The cave did contain treasure, but the chests the dragon guarded were mostly empty and broken. We found three thousand gold, a few trinkets, some precious stones, three shields, six swords, and a rusted suit of armor, all scattered among the bones of what looked to be at least thirty men. If any of this belonged to Snowbeard, we cannot know. All told, there can't be more than five thousand here. Certainly not worth the trouble we went through to get it or the injuries suffered by Cassius and Morlin. Certainly not enough to bribe the duke or save our town. Snowbeard's treasure doesn't exist.

Falgony is nervous. She insists that something isn't right— something about the bones. The dragon they killed, she says, was entirely too small to have fed so much and so often. She insists it was just a pup, though Morlin claims that no pup could have basted his arm the way this one did. Still, she suggests that we leave immediately, and I trust her instincts. Brax and Devon are packing up the treasure—what little of it there is.

It is a shame to have come this far. It is a shame to have left in the first place.

With any luck, I will be back in Highsmith in two days.

We have returned to the village of Galen's Cove with half of our number.

Falgony was right. The dragon we killed was only a youngling. Its mother heard its death cries and met us at the mouth of the cave. With her wings spread, she seemed the size of the mountain itself. The heroes fought bravely and at first looked as if they might be victorious, but she was only sizing us up. Falgony and Telor were the first to fall, followed by Morlin, burned alive. It wasn't long before we were scrabbling down the mountain, practically falling off it, praying that she would not follow. She did not.

Roland is growing ghostly by the minute. He was smashed against the rocks, and most of his bones are broken. I'm afraid he will not make it. During the course of our retreat I could still hear the dragon's scream in my head. Its loss echoes down from the mountains and is carried to us by the wind. I think of the

*bodies we left behind and mourn for them. They were brave. I
cannot help but cry for joy that I am not one of them, that I will
see my son again, and this shames me.*

*The town is shuttered in, the people closing themselves off in
fear. Though they tend our wounds, some whisper that were
are bringing a curse upon them. I do not blame them, but we
cannot leave Roland here. He is not fit to ride. I am unhurt but
also torn to pieces. I should leave now, slip out into the shadows
and ride home, go back to where I belong. I know none of them
would think worse of me for it. But what would I think? I only
know that I am afraid—afraid of pain, afraid of death,
afraid of loss. I'm afraid my son never got a chance to know
me.*

*I cannot get the image of Dierdra out of my head. I see her
holding Mason as we walk down the streets of Highsmith. I can
see the sunlight in the windows. When I come back empty-handed,
I hope she will forgive me. If, for some reason, I can't get back, I
hope she finds strength in Mason. I hope he doesn't grow up to be
the fool his father is. The work of all my days is summed up
there. I miss him terribly. I miss them both.*

There is a bell ringing.

I think the dragon has found us.

*We must do only and always what we can to realize the debts
we owe to those who love us and pay as we are able.*

I can hear the beat of its wings in the night.

Mason read those last two pages twice. He would have read
them once more, but for now all he could do was sit and wait
for his blood to move again.

He lost all sense of time passing. He pictured his father, eyes
closed, singing his song of the dead. He pictured his own lyre

buried in dust on the shelf, one string seemingly irrevocably broken. And for once he knew what he wanted to be and where he belonged, and he felt strangely whole.

He was pulled back into the world through the back door. Cowel was standing there.

"Did you find what you were looking for?"

Mason stared out at the mountains. "More or less."

"He's not coming back with us," Cowel said.

But Mason knew that already. He said he understood and that there was nothing they could do about it. It didn't seem to be what Cowel wanted to hear.

They were joined by Isabella, who had the sense to close the door as Cowel's voice rose, for fear that he might say something to offend their host.

"But how do you *know?*"

"I just know."

"And all I'm saying is that you need to *talk* to him. He doesn't owe *me* anything. But you, your father. You have a history. He'll listen to you."

"He won't come."

"Then beg him. He won't have a choice."

"He won't come," Mason insisted. He didn't bother to add that it was precisely because of Mason's father that Brax Balen wouldn't budge. He couldn't risk that Edmond, that six-year-old boy, would have to grow up without a father.

Cowel put his hands up in protest. "So what now, then? No one else in this town is going to help us. Balen says they don't trust outsiders, and they think your father was some kind of wizard or something, that maybe he was even the one who summoned the dragon in the first place."

"What do you want me to do?"

"I don't know. But we can't just let it go. Not now. Not when we're so close."

"We're not close."

"What are you talking about?" Cowel glared at his best friend.

"Even if we could persuade him to come with us, it wouldn't be enough. It was never going to happen," Mason said.

"There are other villages. Scattered throughout the mountains. We could try one more," Cowel suggested.

"It takes at least a full day's ride to get to Darlington from here, maybe more. And that's on a horse who knows how to gallop. It would be cutting it close," Isabella said.

"Fine. Then let's just do it ourselves." Cowel was getting angry. Mason thought of the seven heroes at the top of the mountain, sitting around broken chests and rusted armor. Like them, Cowel had gotten his hopes up. Mason knew how he felt. "I mean, we've got her, right?" Cowel said, pointing to Isabella. "And we can handle ourselves. I mean, before this, I would've laughed at the suggestion, but now I feel different. I don't know. I mean, if I had to." Cowel's cheeks were burning.

Isabella was more realistic. "If we leave tonight—ride through the night—we could make it to Darlington by tomorrow evening. Just to make sure. Even if nobody has told them, everyone could still make it out in time."

"You said only an idiot whose brains had been pulled from his nose would ride through the mountains at night," Cowel said to her, almost instantly forgetting the courage he had summoned only moments before.

"Someone needs to tell them. And if your mother and uncle have already left, who does that leave? That is, assuming you don't trust this duke or his assistant."

The more he thought about it, the more certain Mason was

that Percy and Darlinger had left town already, taking everything they could carry and leaving the rest to burn.

"A day to get there?" Mason asked.

"Maybe less. We could get there quicker with fresh horses, perhaps."

"There is a place we can get a good deal on those," Mason said.

Then Cowel got angry again. "Wait. Wait. What are we saying here? That we're done? We go back and tell everyone to give up? To get out? Dammit, Mason, we could have just stayed in town and done that!"

"What do you want to do?" Mason's voice was calm, which only infuriated Cowel more.

"I don't know. Fight back. Have something to show for it. It's easier for you. You got something out of this. Don't you care that you failed? We *failed*, Mason. We aren't heroes. We're just two pathetic guys on a lame horse in the middle of the damn mountains yelling at each other!"

"I'm not yelling," Mason pointed out.

"How can this not piss you off?"

Mason just looked down at the journal.

"Mason's right," Isabella said, putting an arm out as if ready to drop Cowel to the ground if he got too worked up. "The best thing we can do is get back as soon as possible. If they don't know, then your telling them will save their lives."

"And if they do know?"

"Then you are welcome to stay and defend the empty town by yourself," Isabella said.

Cowel stood between them, fists clenched with nothing to swing at. Finally, he looked at Mason. "This can't be it," he said. "It can't just be over like this. It just can't end like this."

But Mason didn't say anything. Nothing he could do would change the ending now.

★ ★ ★

If her mother knew that she had agreed to escort these two back down the Windmourns in the middle of the night, she would have thrown two or three fits, interrupted only by a deep-enough breath to keep throwing. Isabella was thankful, more than anything, that she hadn't been with them for their entire journey. She would have had to kill one of them just to get the other one to shut up.

The three of them agreed to leave as soon as possible. The town wasn't too happy to have them, anyway.

The farewell between Mason and Brax was short and solemn. Brax didn't bother to apologize for not coming along. Mason didn't ask him to reconsider. Mason shook the hero's hand, bowed to his wife, and winked at his son and said, "Nice to meet you, Edmond." Isabella made a point to smile sweetly at everyone before she left, which was hard for her.

Mason still had one more stop to make, and Cowel decided to go with him. Isabella volunteered to procure the few provisions they would need to get back to Darlington. Mason, after all, still had some gold left—they had never found anyone to spend it on, especially since Isabella refused to take any payment for her services. After collecting their weapons from the mayor's—presenting him with a note (Isabella called it a permission slip) from Brax saying it was all right—she agreed to meet them at the cemetery after her errand.

The nearest tavern was called the Snoring Giant, named after its owner, who was seven feet four and incurably lazy. Isabella asked for her few items, including a sword for Cowel. The tavern owner apologized for not having any spare weapons and then asked where she was from. She said she was with the party from Darlington, figuring the word had already spread that there were outsiders in town.

"Darlington, you said?"

"Not me personally, but my companions. Why?"

"No real reason. It's just that there was someone else who stopped in here not a few moments ago looking for some folks from Darlington. Woke me up from my nap and didn't even bother to buy a drink before he left."

"You didn't know him?"

"Never seen him before in my life. Kind of a hairy fella— and not too polite. Judging by the looks of him, I'd guess he was in a hurry to find you."

Isabella Owltree thanked the bartender and left him a gold piece for his trouble.

By the time she was out the door, her bow was already off her shoulder.

The graves of the four heroes sat in their own corner, fenced off from those of the rest of the town. Edmond Quayle's was in the very back. The stones of the other heroes of Highsmith were all marked with their common names. Roland Warbringer had become Roland Wallendorf. Cassius Coldhammer was simply Cassius Kettle. Devon Bladedancer was Devon Miller. Here, they weren't heroes, just men who no longer had make-believe names they had to live up to.

Edmond Quayle

Mason had never asked his mother about his father's name, why he was always just plain Edmond Quayle. Now, he wondered why he had hidden his name from the world, why he was always just the Anonymous Warrior Poet of Highsmith. He wondered what he had been hiding from and whether he ever wanted to be found.

EDMOND QUAYLE

DEVOTED HUSBAND AND FATHER

That's all that had been set in stone. That was his father's permanent legacy, long after all of the books had turned to dust.

"I'm sorry, Mason." Cowel was kneeling beside him, exhausted. "I guess I've been waiting to say that for a long time. You know, about this in particular."

Mason nodded.

"I can only imagine how you must feel." Cowel looked at Mason, and Mason smiled back.

"I'm glad we came. I mean, I really wasn't looking for him. At least, I didn't think I was."

"I guess that's how it happens."

"I guess."

"It *was* a hell of an adventure—I mean, for a complete and total failure and all."

"Yeah. It was."

"I know this is a really clichéd thing to say, but he'd probably be proud of you."

"He'd probably be pissed at me for leaving."

"Well, that, too."

"But I think I've got something I can write about now."

Cowel gave that some thought, then offered up a title. "'The Adventures of Cowel the Heart-Stoppingly Gorgeous.'"

"I was actually hoping I wouldn't have to make stuff up this time."

"Just plain old gorgeous, then."

Mason reached over and put his arm around Cowel's shoulder. "I'll see what I can do."

"Mason Quayle?"

The third voice came from behind them. At first, irrationally, Mason thought it was the voice of his father. He and Cowel turned and peered through the darkness to see a figure wrapped in a cloak with a hood, which he peeled back to reveal deep yellow eyes. The man wore a bushy beard that nearly covered his ears and exploded down into the V of his cloak. Mason noticed he wasn't wearing any shoes.

"Are you Mason Quayle?"

Mason nodded. The man reached into his cloak. Cowel put one arm protectively across Mason's chest and stepped in front of him, one hand on his kitchen knife as if expecting to see a weapon in this stranger's hand.

But all the man pulled out was a small flask containing a shimmering liquid, a kind of pearled blue that he held up to the sliver of moonlight and shook.

Cowel took his hand off his knife. "Sorry," he said as the man with the flask smiled and winked. Mason stared at the bottle, which seemed to have captured all of the light that remained in the world.

"Not a problem at all," the man said as he popped the cork and took a swallow.

That was when they heard Isabella screaming Mason's name.

The change was almost instant.

The man dropped the flask and threw off his coat, and by the time it fell in a heap on the ground, he was no longer a man. He had grown a foot taller and was now completely covered in thick brown hair. His nose was a snout, his pupils were slits, and the snarl of his lips revealed teeth turning to fangs.

Before they knew what was happening, the werewolf lunged.

The first strike caught Cowel across the head as he followed through on his instinct to shield Mason, the force of the blow driving him downward and knocking the knife from his hand. The second strike came just as the werewolf's claws had finished forming. They tore a gash in Mason's right arm to match the three on his leg. Mason stepped backwards and twisted to avoid tripping over his father's headstone. Losing his balance, Mason heard a yowl from the creature as an arrow struck it in the back.

The werewolf turned and growled at Isabella, who notched another arrow even as she ran toward them. Mason drew his sword and lunged, but the werewolf dodged the strike and leapt on top of him. Mason dropped the sword and lashed out with his arms, striking the beast across the snout, kicking it as hard as he could in the ribs, and then rolling free. The creature would have been right back on top of him again, Mason's throat in its teeth, had Isabella's second arrow not caught it in the leg. She was then upon it herself, her bow abandoned and her daggers drawn, aiming for the creature's neck.

But the werewolf was too quick for her, lunging swiftly from a crouch and catching her off balance. Mad with pain from the wounds Isabella had inflicted, the werewolf howled and rushed her. She rolled left and slashed at its chest, but she missed as it snapped its head and sank its jaws into her arm, then tossed her to the ground before turning to Mason, who was struggling to get up.

Finding the sword beside his father's grave, Mason managed to get into a crouch as the creature limped toward him. He held the sword in his left hand, his right arm useless and his head ringing. He could taste copper in his mouth from biting his own tongue. He thought of his father in the middle of the town, singing his song of the dead.

The werewolf gnashed its teeth and hunched over, coiling itself. It was wounded, perhaps fatally, but still had plenty left to finish the job it had been sent to do.

And then Mason saw the blood-lust drain suddenly from its eyes. Saw its shoulders droop, the sneer of its snout slacken. Its legs quivered for a moment, and then it collapsed with a whimper.

On its back was Cowel, his kitchen knife driven as far as he could push it and his face pressed into the creature's furry hide.

Mason blinked at him twice, then looked one last time at his father's stone before slipping into a welcoming darkness.

— 8 —

Darlington's End

Mason awoke to see Edmond Quayle standing over him, bathed in light.

He blinked and Edmond smiled. Mason stuck out his tongue, though he found that little bit of movement hurt. Giggling, Edmond ran out of the room.

Mason tried to get up to see where he was, but it hurt too much to move. He could hear voices in the adjoining room. The shuffle of feet. With an effort that felt far greater than the reward, he managed to prop himself onto his elbows just as Cowel appeared in the doorway. He was holding a glass of something that smelled revolting, bringing back memories of the swallowed pixie.

Cowel didn't look good. His left arm was in a bandage and a swollen purple bruise covered half of his face, making his head even bigger than it already was. His bottom lip was cracked down the center.

"You're awake."

Mason raised an eyebrow.

"I guess that's obvious, though. Broke my arm," he added, following Mason's stare, "but I guess that's obvious, too." Cowel came into the room and stood by the bed. "Lilah says you should drink this as soon as you wake up. For the pain."

"Lilah?" Mason asked, taking the glass and finally realizing what that meant. "So we're still in Galen's Cove?"

"Yes. We're still here."

"What time is it?"

The look on his face suggested Cowel wasn't eager to say or didn't feel he had to.

"Cowel."

"It's the last day. It's already dawn. It's over, Mason." Cowel pointed to the sun breaking through the mountains.

Mason spit out words, forgetting momentarily that every muscle hurt, even in his jaw. "But what about . . . ? I mean, we lost an entire day?"

"You were out cold. You took a beating. We both did."

"But what about the town? What if they didn't know? What if nobody told them?"

Mason strained to get up, nearly dumping the contents of his glass as he thrust it back at Cowel. He managed to get his feet onto the floor before the pain returned in full. He grabbed hold of Cowel's shoulder for support, then settled back down onto the bed.

"Shut up for a second and drink this."

Mason shook his head—clearing space, not disagreeing. But then he thought of his mother and pushed Cowel's hand away.

"Listen to me for a second," said Cowel. "There's nothing you can do. Isabella left yesterday morning. She took all of the gold we had left. She said she would take it to Heartwood and buy the fastest horse Frank Delacorte had to offer, and then she would ride as hard as she could to Darlington and warn them. She promised she would get there in time."

"She did that?"

"She said she would get there a lot faster without us slowing her down," Cowel added, smiling.

Mason felt his shoulders sink, grateful. It would be all right—though what would his mother think if she hadn't left yet, if she was there, waiting for him? "We still have to go," Mason insisted, as if saying it out loud would convince his body that it was up to the task. "We have to make sure."

"I know. I told Brax that we were leaving the moment you woke up. He said he didn't think it was a good idea but he understood. Steed is ready and we've got supplies, but I'm not going to let you even sit on the stupid horse until you can stand up without falling down."

It took a while, about six or seven tries, but eventually, with a full glass of Lilah Balen's elixir juicing through him, Mason made it from the bedroom to the front door, stopping by every piece of furniture tall enough to lean on. They said goodbye all over again. Mason thanked them for everything, tried to convince Lilah Balen—in as few words as his swollen tongue could manage—that he was fit to ride, and then let Cowel apologize for all the trouble. Edmond Quayle Balen watched them in wonder.

Steed was waiting unanxiously for them out front, intently studying a patch of grass. Cowel checked to make sure they had everything and then pulled Darlinger's blade from the saddlebag.

"Here," he said, offering it to Mason.

"Do you want it?"

"No. You take it."

"I don't really want it."

"What's wrong with it? This thing saved your life. Well, this sword, and Isabella, and me, and that sleeping guy back at the Hive, and probably a few other things."

"It's been a busy week," Mason agreed.

"So why don't you want the sword?"

"You said it yourself—whoever has the sword does the most work. Besides, my arm." Mason pointed to the bandages covering where the werewolf had snagged him.

In response, Cowel pointed to his left arm squirreled away in its sling. Mason didn't bother to remind Cowel that he was right-handed. He took the sword, knowing neither of them was in any real shape to do anything more with it, anyway.

The mayor met them at the village gate. Behind him, on horseback, were four of the town's hunters, well armed and quite used to journeying through the mountains. "You're leaving?" Flayden Fobbs said, though it was intended more as a declaration than a question.

"We thought so," Cowel said, suddenly unsure, staring at the four men and their long faces and long swords.

"Oh, you're definitely leaving. But we are concerned," the mayor said, "that you might cause even more trouble on your way out."

"You're sure you don't want the sword?" Mason whispered to Cowel.

"We won't cause any more trouble," Cowel said, though he knew he wasn't convincing. They had said as much two days ago—and then brought a werewolf into town.

"I'm making sure of it," said Mr. Fobbs. "These men will escort you until you are out of the mountains. Just to be safe. And I'm sure Brax told you already, Mr. Quayle, but if you or any other member of your family chooses to visit here again, we will have to speedily try and convict you for witchcraft and burn you alive."

Mason nodded.

"We hope you enjoyed your visit to Galen's Cove," the mayor said, without even trying to fake a smile. "Have a nice day."

With four hunters acting as bookends, the Windmourn Mountains were much less intimidating, though the hunters themselves made up for it, riding silently, the ones in front occasionally looking behind them to make sure Mason and Cowel knew how little they cared for being escorts. They weren't too happy to find that Steed wasn't in a hurry to get anywhere, either. Still, the six of them made it to the rolling curve of the south mountain's foot without trouble, neither Mason nor Cowel having whispered more than five words to each other the entire trip, for fear of being seen as conspiring. Then, the four hunters watched the two wanderers from Darlington head off in the direction of Heartwood. For all Mason knew, they were still standing there when the sun set, making sure he and Cowel didn't come back.

A stop by Hooves for Less confirmed that a woman named Isabella *had* come by yesterday and offered seventy gold pieces and a trade in for Frank Delacorte's fastest horse. Frank promised that if she brought his back in one piece, he'd refund half of her money and give her own horse back to her. He also said that he had not seen his stepdaughter in three days and that his wife refused to speak to him because he had taken Fira's side in their argument. Altogether, it hadn't been a terrible week, Frank said, but he would appreciate it if Mason and Cowel, and anyone they were associated with, would stop bothering him.

"Making friends everywhere we go," Cowel said.

Mason guessed that the road from Heartwood to Riscine would take them most of the day, given that they had agreed to go around the forest, but Cowel just shook his head and pulled a gold and brown feather from the sling around his arm.

"What's that?"

"It's the feather from my cap. What does it look like?"

"Yes, but what's it *for?*"

In response, Cowel just told Mason to hold on as tightly as he could, then leaned over and stuck the feather into Steed's ear.

Breckenridge's Boot Outlet and Apparel had a closed sign on the door when Mason and Cowel arrived, though it was only late afternoon. The feather had done the trick, and some of the lines that had been written by Darlinger's former bards actually seemed plausible as Steed had thundered across the landscape. Mason had winced in pain with the fall of each hoof until, finally, he had grown numb to it. He felt it mostly in his head, where the pounding drowned out all but the most intense thoughts, foremost among them the prayer that they would find the town of Riscine brimming over with refugees from Darlington.

At the very least, Mason had thought selfishly, *let there be one.*

But the town didn't brim. It looked the same as when they had left four days before: a few people lined the streets, and the sense of tranquility was still palpable. The last building they had encountered headed east now had become their first stop.

Imelda Breckenridge met them at the door. Seeing Cowel and Mason, one with a face like an eggplant and the other with thick bandages around an arm and leg, she guessed immediately who they were and flashed a look of sympathy, which almost instantly turned to hysteria.

"Have you seen my husband?" she asked before the two of them could even get a first word out. Though, admittedly, they were about to ask her the same thing.

"Um," Mason started, when Imelda launched into a tirade— something about Lorn having stopped by there two days ago, and she just knew that hussy had been with him, and boy, if he *ever* decided to come home, he was going to have to explain *everything* before she even let him back into the house.

"You said you saw him two days ago?" Cowel managed to interrupt.

"Why, do you know something? Is he dead? I told him not to go," Imelda Breckenridge said, then immediately launched into another fit. "If he's gone and gotten himself killed, I am *not* going to be happy."

Cowel was about to ask another question, but Mason was already limping back toward Steed, having heard enough. Cowel put a hand on Imelda's flailing arms and said, "We'll find him," then turned to catch up to Mason.

"You know what happened," Mason said.

"You don't think he . . . don't really think they . . . the whole town . . ." But Mason cut Cowel's words off with quick nods. "We should check one more place, just to be sure," Cowel said.

They ended up going to one of the town's inns, located on the square—which Mason noticed, with a deepening of the hole in his insides, was nearly empty. No one had seen Mason's mother or anyone from Darlington. Cowel thanked the innkeeper and chased after Mason, who was again already out the door.

"There's no one here," Mason said as they remounted, neither of them elaborating on what that meant.

Instead, Cowel handed Mason the feather and they begged Steed to go faster still.

They saw the smoke first. Mason could not put a name to the shapes it took. The black cloud curled around itself, billowing from the pyre burning outside the city's gates.

They were more than too late. Whatever had happened had been over for a while.

For reasons Mason couldn't begin to imagine, it appeared

that the town of Darlington had chosen to make a stand. It must have been a heroic gesture. And a futile one. The walls of the city were intact; there hadn't even been a siege.

Mason felt dizzy and let go of the reins. He would have fallen off had Cowel not held him up. The whole town had stayed. They had lost everything.

Cowel nudged Mason, who nudged Steed. There was no sign of movement anywhere. They passed the carnage of the battlefield, keeping their distance from the pyre, the stench already stifling. They could barely make out the shapes of bodies in the fire as they passed by fallen shields and axes, rusty swords and broken spears. What weapons the foolish first-time soldiers had had would have been ten years old; there wouldn't have been time to forge new ones. Steed snorted at the sight of a horse on the ground, flies already buzzing around its eyes.

The twin ivory statues of the duke were on the ground. One had been smashed like a Delacorte vase, the other simply toppled, broken in two. Mason expected to see the duke's own head, already sunken at the eyes, staring at them from a pike above the walls. But whatever fate had befallen Dirk Darlinger had not been displayed.

Cowel didn't say anything as they rode beneath the arch, but Mason could hear him stop breathing and then suddenly gulp in air as if he were drowning. The buildings had all been abandoned—either that, or the people who had been hiding in them had been ferreted out. The orcs hadn't burned the town, as Isabella had said they would. From the entrance you could still see the top of Darlinger Manor. Mason thought, with a glimmer of hope, that some of the townspeople might still be in hiding, locked away in cellars or attics or maybe all huddled in Darlinger's mansion. More likely, they had been captured. There were no bodies to be found, save for the ones in the pyre outside the city walls. Or maybe the homes themselves were filled with the dead. If either Mason or Cowel wanted to get down and check, neither spoke of it. They simply let Steed carry them down the street, headed in the direction of Mason's house.

Mason pulled on the reins and whispered for Steed to stop.

"I can't do it." Mason buried his face in the horse's mane and held his breath.

"Hush," Cowel said.

"No. I'm serious. I don't want to go any farther."

"Shut up!" Cowel hissed.

"Cowel," Mason snapped, his anger finally erupting. He twisted around in the saddle, only to find Cowel's good hand suddenly clamped over his mouth.

"Listen."

Mason whipped his head back, crazed, half hoping they were about to be surrounded. Even with one good arm, he swore he would find some little revenge. He reached for his sword.

"It's music," Cowel said, and pointed toward the center of town.

Mason pulled Cowel's hand from his mouth and listened. He could just pick out a strange sound, punctuated occasionally by a collective scream. His first thought was torture.

And then he recognized the tune.

He had played it before, back when his string wasn't broken. It was a quick little piece made popular because the lyrics were easy to remember. It had been written by the Anonymous Warrior Poet of Highsmith.

It was a song of celebration.

A block away they saw him.

In a cage, dangling from the second story of his own house by a makeshift beam jutting out of a window. It was hard to recognize him at first, as he was covered in mud. Fastened to his cage was a long piece of bark with the word HERO painted on it in sloppy white letters. Behind the bars, Dirk Darlinger held a bottle of ale, a gift from one of his own townsmen, perhaps, who had found just enough pity for the duke not to leave him out entirely. Mason didn't bother to keep himself from crying at the sight of the man he swore he never wanted to see again.

Below the cage, people danced, twirling to the tunes of three fiddlers who rocked back and forth on their heels. Cowel's eyes settled on the first familiar face he could find—Gwyn Broadmore. She was the most beautiful thing he could imagine—at least, until the next familiar face came into view.

Mason and Cowel slipped off Steed and stood there in the shadows of the evening, breathing it in: the spinning dresses, the dancing torch light, the impossibility. Darlinger's unkempt front garden was lined with tables, the tables lined with barrels. Between every blink of Mason's eyes was a revelation. Faces that only moments ago had been lost in a fire now blazed before him. Then his weak right leg gave in. With Cowel too paralyzed to try to catch him, Mason collapsed to his knees.

At one end of a long wooden table sat a man, near comatose and slumped in his chair, mouth open and drooling. Someone had put a pillow beneath his head, and he somehow still held a mug in his non-sword-bearing hand, though its contents had long since spilled on his pants. Two empty chairs down, Mason saw Perlin. Tugging on Cowel's pant leg, he pointed toward the table where Cowel's uncle sat next to a boot-maker from Riscine and his one-time lover.

Their daughter was sitting beside them. She must have heard Cowel screaming his uncle's name. Mason saw her stand and whisper something into her father's ear, and her father subsequently jumped out of his seat and pointed at them.

Mason managed to stand, and the two of them hobbled toward the others. Perlin whispered something to Isabella, who disappeared in the opposite direction, and then he, Lorn, and the woman Mason could recognize only by her resemblance to her daughter met them in the middle of the garden. Trailing behind, Mason watched Cowel embrace his uncle and then shake hands with Lorn and Arlena. Cowel's uncle reached forward and put his arm around Mason, squeezing him much too tightly.

"My mother?"

Perlin Salendor smiled, then pointed to the front steps of Darlinger Manor.

There was Dierdra Quayle, her dress smudged with blood and dirt, standing with Isabella Owltree on one side and a red-headed witch on the other.

It was only after an eternity of fumbling embraces, breathless sentences, and questions with answers much too complicated that the smell of roast pork finally reached Mason, and he begged for someone to find him something to eat.

They all sat at a table, Dierdra and Fira both fussing over Mason's wounds. They had turned Darlinger's house into a makeshift infirmary, and Fira had been working there most of the day, *these* townsfolk happy to have a witch in their midst. The women insisted that both Mason and Cowel should be inside as well—and would be, by morning—but so long as they stayed awake, they could sit at the table and drink it all in.

It was Perlin who told most of the tale, though occasionally, Dierdra would interrupt to correct a detail or note an embellishment. Cowel's uncle had had a good deal to drink already, so some of his particulars about the events of the past three days were fuzzy. He started with the note Cowel had left him, and Dierdra's visit, and Sockface the goblin, and the meeting where it had looked as if the whole town was going to collapse into chaos until a couple of ghosts showed up and took charge. They weren't much to look at, but in the absence of the great Dirk Darlinger, Brendlor Bowbreaker and Arlena Owltree were the best any town could hope for. Those two and a swordsman with droopy eyelids convinced the crowd that they could defend their homes and that more help was on the way, though Brendlor later admitted he was making that part up. Fira showed up on the afternoon of the fourth day at the suggestion of her grandmother, who said it was just the kind of thing that would piss her mother off and make her aunt Moxy proud.

Then Perlin spoke with a gleeful glint of getting his fires roaring again. He and a few young boys had worked straight through the fourth day repairing swords and armor dug up from old chests and underneath beds, finding an edge to every blade. By the time they were done and everyone was gathered, they had a force of two hundred men and women, armed with everything from butcher knives to sharpened broom handles, all led by two semiretired heroes from the Alley, a witch, and a sleep-fighting swordsman.

And at dawn this morning, the raiding party of Bennie the Orc, only a hundred and fifty strong, had been shocked to find a legion of Darlington's finest waiting for them.

"It was a glorious sight," Perlin said. They even let Darlinger watch from his cage beside the statues that the townsfolk had busted the night before. There had been talk of turning him over before the battle took place, as a compromise, but Dierdra somehow convinced them otherwise.

In the end, Perlin said, it was a slaughter. Though several

were injured, the number of deaths for the town could be totaled on one hand. By last count, there were forty orcs, twenty-three goblins, seven trolls, and an ogre in the pyre outside the city. All the others had fled.

The stories kept coming. If he had parchment and a quill—and if he could write with his left hand—Mason couldn't have copied them down fast enough.

How Brendlor nearly cried when Perlin offered to sharpen his ax.

How Fira Firaxin whipped up a potion to keep Corner the swordsman awake and another to put him to sleep at just the right moment, and how the entire town was instructed to give him lots of room on the battlefield. How the swordsman skewered seven orcs, four goblins, and the one ogre during his morning nap.

How Isabella Owltree showed up just as the battle began and promptly joined in the fray, adding four orcs to the five whatisits that started her week.

And the hundreds of other tales, told by a town now full of heroes.

And despite these acts of valor, the one underlying and ironic truth was that they had Dirk Darlinger to thank. Without him, Brendlor said, the city would have fallen for certain. Mason said he didn't understand.

"Back when the Alley was full, the orcs were tough. Battle hardened. Fit. But these—" and here Brendlor snorted "—these orcs hadn't been in a battle in years. They were fat and lazy. They couldn't remember how to swing their own swords. Half of them ran at the first sign of a fight, realizing they no longer had it in them. They had grown such bellies feasting on the fruits of Darlinger's gold that they couldn't even fit into their armor."

A toast went round the table. "To Dirk Darlinger's fat and

lazy orcs." It was a toast they would repeat for the next three months.

And as the stories unfolded, gushing from every villager who came by to thank them for bringing the heroes back to Highsmith, Cowel leaned over to his friend.

"This town is in sore need of a good bard," he said.

By dawn of the next day, Darlinger's gardens were filled with people too tired to walk back to their homes, but the sun brought a more sobering reality. There were injuries to be treated and four townspeople to be buried. Brendlor insisted that the orcs might regroup and attack again and promptly set about organizing the town's defenses, but only after sending a messenger to his wife with a note explaining the situation and imploring her to come join him.

The Owltrees accepted the town's offer to take up temporary residence and watched as the town's builders set to work restoring Arlena's old house on the Alley, where Isabella would eventually become the most famous second-generation hero of Highsmith.

Corner the swordsman agreed this place was much preferable to the Hive and bought Roland Warbringer's old house from the man who owned it—a Mister Dirk Darlinger—for the ultracheap price of the three coins he had found wrapped in a note four days earlier. That it was Darlinger's own gold that paid for it was never mentioned.

As for the town hero, his punishment at the hands of the new council of Highsmith was much less severe than what he would have suffered at the claws of the orcs. With his house appropriated, his other properties sold, his title stripped from him, and only three coins to his name, he was seen leaving town the next day. One of the most famous heroes in the five lands simply disappeared and was never heard from again, except in bards' songs—and most of those were satires.

The sun rose that morning to find Dierdra Quayle standing beside her son. Cowel slept stone-heavily in the next bed over.

"How is my sweet boy?" All of a sudden, Mason was six years old again, as if his father had just walked out the door.

He didn't mind. The best part of any adventure was coming home. They talked about what was happening within the city walls. Dierdra said the town had been renamed—or, at least, *un*-renamed—and how, speaking of names, she had heard Mason's whispered at least twice this morning in the streets.

It took a while for her to find the courage to ask. "Your father," she began, but apparently, she was waiting for something—perhaps for Mason to finish the sentence for her.

And he wanted to. He wanted to tell her everything—about the treasure that didn't exist, and the dragon that did, and all the stories that were told by the Warrior Poet of Highsmith—but he knew it wouldn't matter. It was just another version of the story she had already told herself a hundred times over.

So he told her the truth. He told her what she already knew.

He told her that his father was a hero.

Every Tale Needs an Ending

Half of the houses are still empty, their roofs still threatening to cave, but the Alley is returning to its former reputation. Most of the newly printed signs hanging over the eaves bear names unfamiliar to those who grew up here—Vordan Vilefoe and Mina Misthunter—names that start to sound generic, even a little ridiculous. Three weeks ago, some hotshot calling himself Alden Allslayer, hearing that Darlinger was no more, migrated all the way from Magladon to try to win the town's respect, and people wondered if they didn't have another duke on their hands. But he wasn't that much better than the rest and turned out to be a nice enough guy for all of his bravado.

As one walks a little farther down the Alley, the names become more recognizable. The home of the Owltrees, restored to all of its glory, sits next to Perlin Salendor's new smithy. He and Cowel are still living in the old one, but the new business is up and running and Perlin figures he'll be able to buy back his former house in a year or so. It is no secret to anyone that in the past month Cowel's uncle has fallen for

Mason's mother. But as Cowel keeps reminding him, it is a fool's quest. Sure, she might flatter and flirt, blush when Perlin compliments her, and take baskets of bread to his shop, but she can't love two men at once. Not everything turns out HEA.

Next to Perlin's is Breckenridge's Boots, which only recently moved from Riscine to Highsmith. Somehow, Brendlor Bow-breaker convinced Imelda that the move had nothing to do with his old flame, despite the fact that his hair is dyed red again. His taste for adventure rekindled, the hero-cum-boot-maker-cum-hero is often out orc hunting, leaving most of his business affairs in the hands of the town's most profitable plume salesman.

And so it is Cowel who can most often be found behind the counter at Breckenridge's, offering a free plume with every pair of boots. He and Brendlor recently released the Air Bow-breaker series. Lined with fine wolf pelts imported from the Windmourn Mountains and featuring a weatherproofed deer-hide exterior, they come with steel-tipped toe guards and frog-skin ankle-support modules to insure a safe journey. Cowel is liberal with his employee discount, and nearly everyone owns a pair.

If you can't find Cowel selling boots, no doubt he is across the street at Firaxin's Potions Emporium. It wasn't long after the town's defense that Cowel admitted some unignorable feelings for the witch, and he usually spends at least an hour a day in front of a mirror, desperately trying to convince Grandma that his intentions are honorable.

At the edge of the Alley, right next to Corner's on the Corner, sits a box-shaped building, relatively modest in comparison to those around it. On the post outside sits a sign, though it doesn't say everything its owner once dreamt it would—not yet, anyway. On the sign, sometimes, sits a bird. It is a wholly unremarkable bird, brown and beige and missing a few feathers. It seems to have no real purpose in life. Mostly, it just squawks and ruffles its tail feathers.

Inside the building sits a bard. The two have some things in common. Both were blessed with keen eyes and cursed with big noses. Neither is a consistent bather. But the bird has a tendency to only peck at its food, whereas the bard eats every meal to the last crumb. The bird is wary of strangers, but the bard knows that that's how all friendships begin. People passing by the bird wonder why it doesn't just fly away, but they also usually make a point to stop and say hello to the young man inside.

Mason Quayle rubbed the feathered end of his quill against his chin. With any luck, he could get this done before the morning ended. It had taken him three months, more or less, to get it down. It was too long, he knew, and any audience would be eager for the last lines—just so they could get on with their lives. He looked down at the sheets of parchment spread across his desk. It was all in there: friendship, treachery, bloodshed, sarcasm, even a little romance. He probably hit the family thing a little heavily, and he knew he described the sun too much, but overall, he was satisfied. All it needed now was an ending.

Mason read again the last lines he had written. He was stuck and rapped his head with his knuckles. What he really needed was a moral, but nothing too cheesy or dramatic—he hated that stuff. Finally, he hit on it and began scribbling down the lines as they came.

When you've faced a whatisit and encountered a witch,
When you've sneezed yourself stupid and slept in a ditch,
When you've swallowed a pixie and then vomited it free,
Been attacked by a psycho in a size twenty-three,
Been stalked by a werewolf with the moon in a jar,
You start to remember how lucky you are
To not do such things every day of your life,
To have to visit old lovers and piss off your wife,
To fight giants in dresses or fat orcish clans,
Carry brooms through the forests or blades in your hands,
To wear sores on your butt cheeks and your arm in a sling,
Ride for days with a poet who can't even sing.

Because being a hero's not as grand as they say.
There's not enough glory and not enough pay.
There are too many monsters and not enough lords.
There are too many dragons and not enough swords.
There are too many damsels in too many towers.
Too much to do and just not enough hours.
So, leave most of the work to those naturally bred,
Born with blades in their hands and a helm on their head.
For the time will soon come when you, too, are called forth
To summon your courage—establish your worth.
And no doubt you will triumph, the day will be won,
But when it's all over, be glad that you're done.
Because most of us aren't really heroes, per se,
We're just everyday people having heroic days.

Mason brushed the sheet, making certain the ink had dried, and then gathered all of the parchment together. The title page gleamed in gold letters.

The Ballad of Cowel the Heart-Stoppingly Gorgeous
by Mason Quayle

Scribe of "The Queen Bee's Defeat," "Darlinger's Demise,"
and the award-winning "The Heroes Return to Highsmith"

He looked again at the title, wondering just how far poetic license extended, and then searched in his desk for a nice ribbon to tie it up. Probably a satin blue would be best; Cowel would call it prissy, but outside of shoes, plumes, and witches, he really had no taste.

There was a hurried knock as Mason screwed the lid back onto his inkwell. The door to the Bardery was flung open by a woman dressed in bronze armor with a bow slung across one shoulder and a spear resting on the other. She looked just as beautiful as the day she saved his life.

"Several trolls just attacked a caravan in the western pass. They're starting to become a nuisance."

"Trolls, huh?"

"I'm going with Corner and Alden . . . and *Mother*, of course." She rolled her eyes at the word. Mason looked at Isabella Owltree and then up at the lyre sitting on his shelf, which was now full of books, some of them his own.

"So how about it? Are you coming? Steed's already saddled and ready to go."

Mason Quayle smiled and pulled a satchel from underneath his desk. There wasn't much inside—a flask of water, some parchment and quills, and a copy of his current best seller—a long-awaited collaboration between the Warrior Poet of Highsmith and his son. On the way out the door, he grabbed his sword from its normal resting place in the corner.

With *Quayle's Guide to Adventures for the Unadventurous* under one arm and a blade that used to belong to the greatest pretend hero in the land tucked under the other, Mason Quayle emerged.

* ACKNOWLEDGMENTS *

*I would like to thank Jennifer Greene, Jim Armstrong,
Susan Buckheit, and all the fine people at Clarion Books for
giving a new bard a chance and helping him sing.*

*I would also like to thank my parents, Wes and Sheila,
for their encouragement. My children, Nick and Ella,
for their laughter. And finally my wife,
Alithea, for all her love.*

ABOUT THE AUTHOR

John David Anderson lives in Indianapolis, Indiana, with his wife and young twins. This is his first book.